DREADFUL THINGS

MICHAEL LAIMO

Contents

The Chicken Man... 1

The Layover... 16

Halloween Three 24

Through the Eyes of the Victim...................................... 31

Room 412 38

Err 48

Anxiety 66

The Alley Man 84

The Potato... 90

11:11 100

The Juggling Jester's Final Appearance.............................. 106

Slugfest.. 116

The Radio.. 130

Banalica.. 139

Heirloom 158

Gila Way 171

Upside Down.. 190

Sleep Tight, My Love.. 197

One Last Breath 204

1-800-S-U-I-C-I-D-E 219

Becoming One with the Great Old Ones............................. 224

The Chicken Man

Inside the holding pen, hell reigned.

One-hundred-degree heat and clouds of ammonia and fecal matter beat down upon Dave Richardson as he grabbed a chicken making a valiant bid for escape. For the millionth time he wondered if the chickens knew their fates had already been written. *Shit*, he thought. *If it weren't for Delmar, these chickens wouldn't even exist in the first place.*

Delmar created. Delmar laid down the law. And Delmar slaughtered.

He chased the chicken in a rambling circle, slipping in a thick patch of manure as he grabbed the thing around its genetically altered bulk. This one was as plump as they got! The chicken clucked up a frenzy, pecked furiously at Dave's hands and drew blood, adding to the fifteen years of battle wounds he'd accumulated. No pain registered. He'd lost all feeling in his hands years ago.

A pair of handlers followed close behind and retrieved the escapee. The man on the left, like his handler associate, did not speak English and forced a smile as the chicken attempted another escape, feathers flying everywhere.

It was here that Dave reminded himself how lucky he was to have a job. Didn't matter that the place was rife with disease, filth, and rot. The damn immigrants were showing up by the truckloads and were willing to work for half the pay and barely any benefits, and that was all that mattered. They also wore industrial gloves and surgical masks, a commonsensical precaution not even considered fifteen years ago when Dave started working at the Delmar plant.

The Government had turned a blind eye long ago to these "contract growers", as the corporation made certain that Uncle Sam's palm was well-greased (and not just with chicken and turkey fat). Apparently the growling stomachs of the American consumer were paramount to the aches, pains, and diseases of a few thousand illegals.

But what about me? he thought, wiping filthy sweat from his brow.

Dave was one of the unlucky ones who'd started working the slaughterhouse assembly line years ago. He began as a handler, gathering the chickens by the thousands (one at a clucking, scratching, poking, pissing, shitting time) and stuffing them into containers where they would be driven to the plant for processing. He would handle approximately eight-thousand chickens a day, and had the scars to prove it, not just from the scratches and the biting, but also the disfiguring diseases he'd obtained from the feces and urine that'd seeped into his wounds. His hands had become a purple knot of scars, and as far as he was concerned weren't worth protecting with a pair of gloves. *It slows down production,* he'd once argued to plant supervisor Edwin Stroebecker, that good-for-nothing chicken-ass, who'd insisted that all new workers wear protective gear. *It lowers our insurance rates* was chicken-ass's reply, and he'd sent Dave on his merry way, brandishing that hideous gap-toothed grin of his, spitting tobacco juice in Dave's path.

After two years on the job, Dave was promoted to the position of "hanger". For an additional eighty bucks a week, he'd spend two four-hour shifts fastening the feet of thirty birds a minute into metal shackles on a rolling conveyer. Bucking and thrashing, the chickens would travel twenty feet into another room where they were dipped into electrified water and consequently stunned.

Farther along, their dangling heads were efficiently lopped off by a razor-sharp metal wire, but only if the bird was properly shocked. Sometimes the charge in the water wasn't turned up enough and the chickens came out of the water quite alive and conscious. The "lopper" would then miss a lot of these chickens and slice across their breasts instead. Bleeding to death, these chickens were considered waste, and subsequently dumped.

In one eight-hour shift, Delmar turned 150,000 live chickens into packages of ready-to-eat meat.

It was in his position of "hanger" that Dave collected some additional injuries: two torn rotator cuffs from the repetitive movement of hanging chickens (one every two seconds, eight hours a day). More cuts on his hands and arms; eye infections from feather dust and spraying urine; respiratory ailments that resulted in a daily routine of coughing up blood and brown hunks of lung.

After five years of hanging, Dave was promoted to foreman—the position with Delmar he held today. Not only was Dave earning more than twice the salary as those starting out as handlers or pen cleaners, but he was also in charge of those working the eight hour shift he was on.

"Don't let any more of 'em git away," he told the handler, who smiled idiotically and nodded as he shoved the chicken into a container already holding three birds. The handler pressed against the caged door with his hip and squeezed it shut, crushing the head of the chicken he'd just captured.

As long as they were alive and properly stunned when they hit the lopper, then that's all that mattered.

The containers were carried from the truck into the slaughterhouse. The workers there joked amongst themselves in Spanish and many of the cages were tossed back and forth. Some of them were dropped. The chickens in them clucked in frantic protest.

"Dave! Git your sorry ass over here." Stroebecker. The supervisor marched across the killing floor, a half-eaten turkey leg clutched in his hand, grease coating his chapped lips and nicotine-stained moustache. His blood-stained t-shirt, all too tight, divulged three inches of midsection that bulged over the hidden waistline of his jeans. Purple stretch marks zig-zagged their way around his enormous belly-button. Dave wondered if Stroebecker might be able to lay an egg from that cavernous opening in his gut.

Dave stepped through the sea of blood, feathers, and dust on the floor toward his boss. Stroebecker grabbed Dave by his thinning ponytail and led him toward the dropped cages.

"See that? That there's a dropped cage. Got three chickens in there that ain't gonna end up on anyone's dinner table. Damn things are *broken*."

One of the handlers moved to grab the cage. Stroebecker released Dave's hair and handed his turkey leg to the handler, who used two gloved fingers to clutch Stroebecker's lunch. The blood and dust on the handler's glove didn't seem to faze anyone, Stroebecker included.

Dave pinched a brow and fixed his supervisor's blank gaze. The man, known to be a bit loose in the gears, had a crazed look about him today, not uncommon but disconcerting all the same. It was cyclical thing, this madness, a once-a-month uproar that usually kept the workers in line. Dave wasn't sure if there was a method to the super's madness, or if he had a loose gear upstairs spinning out of control.

You had to be a bit mad to work in this neck of the industry anyway, and Stroebecker fit the mold flawlessly.

Stroebecker leaned down, opened the dropped cage and pulled a chicken out by the leg. The bird flapped its wings frantically, sending up a cloud of brown dust. Urine and feces dripped down his forearm. "Well what do ya know. That there's a *good* one. Ain't nothing wrong with it far as I can see. You just got lucky Richardson."

As always, Stroebecker's once-a-month routine held up production, the point he presumably aimed to prove in no way worth the time wasted. The fat man carried the flapping chicken to the first of the hangar lines and hooked it up by the legs. In this position the chicken remained oddly still, as though rumors of its fate had somehow seeped into its little brain. It clucked once and disappeared into the stunning room.

Beyond the empty shackles, three more hanging lines remained in production, and the workers there watched the supervisor's mad performance without pausing in the hanging of their load of chickens. Damn efficient immigrants could do the job with their eyes closed if they had to.

Despite having been promoted to plant foreman, the raise in pay Dave had earned over the years couldn't keep up with the cost of living, and he was unable to escape the two-room trailer he'd lived in by himself since he turned eighteen. He'd earned just enough to pay the rent and buy some canned goods at Piggly-Wiggly to go along with the "broken" chickens he'd lifted from the killing floor. Some of these chickens, along with the soon-to-be-dead egg-layers, were sent off to a separate processing plant and used exclusively to manufacture nuggets and the like. The rest were swept up and either delivered to the local landfill or buried in the fields behind the plant. Dave had always thanked the good Lord above that he never had to do *that* job. Killing chickens was one thing. Burying the dead was another.

Stroebecker trudged back to the dropped cage, eyes fixed intensely on Dave. They'd never really gotten along, and Stroebecker made sure, at least once a week, to make Dave's life a bigger hell than it already was. Perhaps he'd been threatened by Dave in some oddly twisted way. Maybe he was simply out of his mind.

Stroebecker dug into the cage and yanked out another chicken. This one was unresponsive, limp in the supervisor's fat hand. Dave noticed some feathers stuck in the grease on his fingers.

"Now this one here's a dead chicken, Richardson." He held it up close to Dave's face. Its eyes were bulging from its head, ruptured and bleeding. A lump of a tongue, blue and jagged, swelled from its beak. "Know why it's dead? Cuz you haven't been keeping tabs on your handlers. I saw with my very own eyes ...*your fat, beady, chicken-ass eyes...*

those men who are under your supervision tossing the cages from the trucks with you just standing there watching like a goddamned wart on my ass. And you and I both know that you can't be dropping the cages cuz that'll kill the chickens. And a dead chicken ain't worth nothing to the man upstairs. Get my drift?"

Dave nodded and took into account that all this standing around bullshitting about what he'd done wrong was cutting into Delmar's productivity much more than a few dead chickens did.

Stroebecker grabbed Dave by the ponytail again, the dark look in his eyes now glistening with a sheen of madness. "You gotta pay the price, douchebag."

And it was here as Dave was tugged along the endless lines of inverted chickens that he realized just how far out of alignment Stroebecker's gears had shifted. The man had never gone this far, and the dark, empty look in his eyes made Dave realize how much trouble he was in.

There was a three-foot wide area between the wall and the fourth line of chickens where the workers would stand and make certain the birds were properly shackled. Stroebecker let go of Dave and shoved him against the wall. "Watch this," he said, wrapping a thick, meaty palm around a passing chicken's gut. He squeezed. The chicken clucked. He squeezed harder. The chicken clucked louder. Shaking his head and clearly not getting the results he wanted, Stroebecker fisted his other hand and shoved it inside the chicken. The bird made a noise that was part frenzied cluck, part scream of agony.

The super grinned crazily at Dave, and yanked out an egg.

Dave felt a tremor in his stomach. His heart pounded furiously, striking at his chest wall. What was the man up to? Three nearby workers, their shift now interrupted by their supervisor, stood close by, perhaps wondering the same thing. Stroebecker took a step back and again grabbed Dave's ponytail. This time Dave found the means to fight back, offering up a weak and wholly inefficient attempt to shove the fat man away. But Stroebecker had at least a hundred and fifty pounds on Dave, and leaned into him, pressing him against the wall. Dave wasn't going anywhere. And neither was Stroebecker.

Dave's breath escaped his lungs in a painful gasp. He twisted his head from side to side, but with no avail. Stroebecker's fat hand came over and down, right on top of Dave's head. The egg smashed with a muffled pop. Albumen and yolk oozed down into Dave's eyes. He shuttered his lids as Stroebecker ground the egg into his hair.

Dave cried, "Damn it, what the hell are you *doing*?" He heard Stroebecker shouting something and when he opened his eyes saw three workers with their hands buried wrist-deep into the conveying chickens. The loud clucks from the chickens echoed Dave's slamming heart.

Stroebecker shouted, "Bombs away!"

After a moment's hesitation, they pummeled Dave with the eggs. One hit him squarely in the face. Stroebecker guffawed and yelled, "Ten Points!" Another one hit Dave on the chest. The next one missed, hitting the wall behind him with a solid *crack*.

Stroebecker grabbed Dave's wrist and yanked it up the center of his back. Dave screamed out and shook his head back and forth, trying to blink the bits of cracked eggshell out of his eyes.

"More!" the fat super yelled. "He wants more! Dontchya Richardson?"

Dave squeezed his eyes shut, tried to move but was a prisoner to Stroebecker's weighty madness. The three workers, a sort of nutty glee shining in their eyes now, plucked eggs out of the passing chickens and hurled them at Dave. Stroebecker yelled at more workers and they immediately joined in on the frenzy. Eggs hit Dave in a seemingly never-ending succession, many in the face, some against his chest. In a few minutes he was completely sheered in raw egg and cracked shell.

All he could do was keep his eyes and mouth closed, and wait for the madness to stop.

Finally, the eggs stopped coming. Dave used his free hand to wipe the gooey mess from his face, and opened his eyes. Stroebecker was leaning in close, horrible turkey-leg breath hot against Dave's wet cheeks.

"I've got a job for you Richardson. Come with me."

Stroebecker released Dave's wrist and grabbed him by the front of his wet shirt. All the dripping raw egg on him seemed not to phase the crazed supervisor. Not in the least.

And what Stroebecker did next made Dave wonder if he would survive the ordeal.

After the super screamed at the men to get back to work, he led Dave out into a storage room abutting the slaughterhouse. He shut the door behind him and shoved Dave against the wall, pressing his fat, sweating, stinking bulk against Dave's heaving chest. Dave gasped for air, the weight of the man's body too heavy to combat. Dave was smothered.

Stroebecker leaned close in to Dave, grinning through his yellow, greasy moustache, revealing the dark gaps between his yellow teeth.

"I love eggs, Richardson. How about you?"

And with that, Stroebecker began licking the raw egg off of Dave's face.

In all of Dave's life and everything he'd ever seen in his years here at Delmar—the slaughters, the blood, the huge buckets of chicken heads, the dumpster full of rotting male chicks discarded because only the females were good for egg-laying—nothing could compare to having the hideously obese, horrible smelling monster named Edwin Stroebecker licking raw egg off his face. He made every effort to shove the man away, but it was useless. Despite being nearly crushed, the oppressive heat in the building had sucked the strength and breath from him, virtually incapacitating him.

The man's tongue felt like sandpaper, each lick like a stab from a knife in his heart, first his neck, his cheeks, his nose…and then ever so slowly moving up, all over his ears, licking…licking…licking all that raw egg from every inch of his face, moaning as he did so, and damn it to all hell if Dave didn't feel something rigid rising out through the layers of fat on Stroebecker's body, something pressing up against his own leg as the fat super flicked his tongue out against Dave's lips, making certain to replace all the raw egg on his face with his horrible, warm saliva.

Dave wanted to scream, dear *god* how he wanted to scream, but was too scared to open his mouth should—heaven help us—the man decide to slip his tongue between Dave's parting lips. So Dave screamed as best as he could with his lips sealed, and it would have been considered pretty loud if not for all the working machinery and the clucking chickens on the other side of the wall.

Stroebecker shoved his oppressive girth against Dave. Dave grunted painfully. So did Stroebecker. Tears filled Dave's eyes and ran down his cheeks as Stroebecker grabbed him, again, by the ponytail.

"C'mon Richardson…"

Winded, all Dave could do was follow the man's lead as he was led outside into the fields behind the factory.

The killing fields.

This was where the pipes in the slaughterhouse floors led. In addition to those chickens that died on the way to the slaughterhouse, millions of gallons of water were used at the end of the day to flush out the remains of a half million birds: over 1500 tons of guts, chicken heads, fat globules, feathers, and blood. All hosed down the huge drain at the east end of the slaughterhouse.

Dave had always wondered what happened to all the guts and feathers once they settled into the earth. Was it all absorbed into the ground? Did animals and bugs eat it all up?

He was about to find out.

Apparently all those chicken remains weren't as biodegradable as one might think. Or if it was, it was simply too much for the earth's stomach to hold, and it saw no choice but to regurgitate it all back up for the world to see.

Their feet squelched in the soft muddy ground as they walked farther into the fields of weeds. The stench grew unbearable, assaulting Dave's nose and urging his gorge to rise. Flies by the thousands began to buzz about Dave, the sticky egg on his skin an unburied treasure for them to investigate. He shook his head, tried to pull away from Stroebecker's iron grip, but the big man grunted and plowed forward like a goddamned bulldozer, parting the waist-high weeds as he moved deeper into the killing fields.

The farther they moved in, the softer the ground became. Dave's feet sunk in to the ankles. The stench grew unbearable and he vomited down the front of his shirt.

Stroebecker laughed. "Got a bit of a cleanup for you to take care of, Richardson." The weeds thinned, and they came upon a chain-link fence.

Dave lurched forward, the swollen fingers of his free hand clutching the fence for support. He stared ahead…and nearly dropped dead from the sight.

Here was the landfill. The place where the pipes from the slaughterhouse led. But there seemed to be a problem. It was overflowing with biological waste. All those years of hosing down the floors, flushing out the chicken heads and the guts and the feathers, the feces and urine. It was all here, a sea of it rotting for years in the center of a huge field instead of soaking into the earth, baking beneath the summer sun, a terrible secret kept a hundred miles away from the closest community.

Stroebecker grabbed Dave and yanked him along the length of the fence. Weakened, Dave could barely fight back, much less keep up with the fat man. His legs tangled up as Stroebecker pulled up a torn section of fencing.

"Let's go Richardson." With his strong, meaty hand, Stroebecker shoved Dave through the opening. Dave clawed at the slimy ground, but to no good use.

He began slipping down.

His shirt got snagged onto the fence and tore down the back. He managed to get two fingers latched around the fencing, but Stroebecker, a hideous glee shining in his eyes, kicked Dave's fingers, then shoved the fence forward and watched as Dave Richardson slid down into the pool of chicken viscera and waste. Dave looked up, saw the swath his body left in the thick coating on the wall of the fill before he plopped through the coagulating surface of the pool.

He fought against it, screaming, crying, reaching his arms up but feeling himself being pulled away toward the center of the pool, as though there was an undertow in its depths…or a shark, or some other horrible monster latching onto him, embracing him like bait. He tried to swim, but the sludge was too thick. Feathers adhered to his body; skeletal chicken heads with their eyes gouged out staring up at him; beaks and claws poking at him as though they possessed lives of their own…as if somewhere deep beneath the pool of blood and guts there existed a power, a being, a sentient *thing* guiding the pool and its parts about Dave as though it was all an extension of its unnamable self.

Finding himself at the center of the pool, the fencing now twenty feet away on all sides, Dave stared back at Stroebecker, his outline plump in the sun's shadow, his girth bouncing up and down as he pointed and laughed at his nemesis, Dave Richardson, foreman for the Delmar Poultry factory. And as Dave eyed Stroebecker back with hatred, that fat chicken-ass *murderer*, he felt the power beneath him pulling him down...down...down, and saw the souls of a *billion* chickens surrounding him as the pool of viscera gurgled up over his head...

At five o'clock, the bell rang and the workers left their posts. Stroebecker saw through the window in his office one of the immigrants making off with a live one lucky not to have met its fate with the lopper. Stroebecker had it in his mind to give the worker a piece of what he'd given that good-for-nothing Richardson, but for now let it slide. Richardson *had* to go, sooner than later. They guy was putting up some serious numbers, and the man upstairs was more than impressed with him at their interview last week. That meant Stroebecker's job was on the line—Delmar was making cuts by the dozens, and Dave had probably offered to do Stroebecker's job for less pay.

Sooner or later, Stroebecker would be toast.

But with Richardson now gone, Edwin Stroebecker's job was safe. For now. Until another foreman was called into headquarters. Then he'd have to keep very close tabs on the man.

He stayed late and caught up on the paperwork he fell behind on— *damn that Richardson!*—then went out on the killing floor to make certain the evening cleaners had properly flushed the floor.

There was an explosion out in the factory.

The walls shook. Stroebecker lunged forward, his bulk jiggling as he made his way along the rows of shackles. He went into the boiler room, then past the dozen loppers, still bloodied from the day's work. A group of men plunged out of the room where all the innards were sprayed, where all the waste was sent into the killing fields. They were covered in muck. Black, bloody, filthy, stinking, lumpy muck.

"The pipe!" one of them screamed in broken English. "Boom!"

The men, six of them, staggered past Stroebecker and didn't turn around to see the wave of thick waste tiding out of the room. It hit Stroebecker in the legs and surged up to his swollen gut, splashing him in the face as he fell back against the wall.

"Holy shit!" he screamed. "Somebody help me!"

The wave surged again, spilling out of the room, splattering against the walls, then towing back only to surge forward again, bringing with it more remains from the backed-up system. Another explosion shook the room. The tiles in the walls cracked. Dust rained down. The waste splashed up into Stroebecker's face, harder this time, seeping into his nose, his mouth, his eyes. He coughed and gagged, wiping his face furiously with trembling hands. The wave surged back, and as it did he attempted to stand, but slipped back down, shoes unable to grab a firm hold on the flooded floor.

"Bossssss..." came a hideous voice from the waste room. Deep and gurgling. Invasive and determined in its dreadful tone.

Stroebecker gazed up...and through the dripping mask of filth on his face beheld a thing not born of this earth, a thing that stood manlike in the threshold of the room, but in its very existence was more...*chicken* than human. It was covered with filthy rotting feathers, only a small portion of them at its swollen breast retaining the white hue they once held. The rest were black and brown, withered and stained with blood and sewage. Its legs were tendon thin, devoid of anything resembling human flesh, the bones now bound with a multitude of chicken claws, thousands of them united in a bid for muscular balance and strength.

Stroebecker pressed back against the wall, staring now at the thing's face...a visage composed of rotting chicken heads gathered from the place from which it just came: beaks lined and piled in the place where human lips should have been, poking out six or more inches into a single moving bill that clucked a deeply hideous sound not born of human nor fowl; its eyes, now multifaceted orbs composed of the eviscerated eyes of a hundred or more chickens, each rolling as one; and the rest of its face, doused with decaying feathers and dark patches of grainy skin.

And yet, despite the horrible deformity and freakishness of the monster before him, it still held on to the human features that were once its own, that were once Dave Richardson's.

It opened its beak composed of beaks, and growled, "*Bosssss…*"

"Oh dear god, help me…" Stroebecker uttered, sliding along the length of the wall, through the pool of blood and waste on the floor.

The chicken man leapt forward, clucking in its horrible deep tone, its tongue, blue yet shockingly human, spilling from its mouth and dripping a thick runner of saliva. Stroebecker screamed as the thing sunk its newly formed talons into his thighs.

Peering down at him with its terrible chicken face—Stroebecker could see the gruesome detail of the chicken heads carpeting the top of its skull, as if they had somehow been sewn together—the chicken man spread its wings, showing amid its splay of rotting feathers two purple-knotted human hands at the very ends of its wings.

The chicken man clucked…and with alarming speed shoved a scarred hand deep into Stroebecker's exposed belly-button. Stroebecker's breath escaped him, replaced now with an all-consuming wave of agony as the chicken man's hand disappeared into his hefty flesh. It dug deep down, leaning forward with all its weight as its groping, tearing fingers prodded and searched.

Its beak open and from within gurgled out, "*Noooo eggggg heeere…*"

It pulled its hand out, trailing out a rope of intestine ringed about two if its knotted fingers. Using the intestine as a leash, it splashed through the pool of waste, pulling Stroebecker with it. The fat super flailed through the pool, the agony twisting through his body as he was dragged into the hanging room nearly stealing his consciousness.

"*No, dear Jesus, no!*"

And as he was dragged away by the chicken man, he could peer only at the swath of blood his body was leaving behind, first floating upon the surface of the waste, then on the damp floor as the pool thinned out.

Now, below the shackles, his blood gathered in a dark pool.

The chicken man yanked Stroebecker up with surprising strength and shackled him up by the toes. Stroebecker bucked and thrashed as much as he could, but his near-dead weight and gushing injury was too much for him to combat, and he fell nearly motionless with the top of his head pressed against the floor and his blood flowing across his torso, into his face.

The shackles began to move. Stroebecker could see the chicken man's clawed feet dart by as the shackles moved him into the boiler room. His head banged against the side of the electrified pot of water. The shackles pulled him forward, a severe pain now registering in his toes as the bones were dislocated. He flipped up and over the side of the pot into the electrified water. Volts darted through his body. But what was enough to stun a chicken merely tickled a man of nearly three-hundred pounds. He emerged choking, but still conscious, his line of sight following…

Oh my God…

The chicken man had never let go of his intestine. It had come out of the hole in his navel like string from a party favor, at least thirty feet of it trailing back into the last room.

Life was escaping Edwin Stroebecker, and finally he was finally stunned as the chickens were…or were supposed to be when the lopper took off their heads.

But, as he'd known, those that weren't proper stunned moved around too much, and the lopper would slice through someplace other that their necks, like their breasts.

Or if you were Edwin Stroebecker, just below the knees.

The last two things Edwin Stroebecker heard before he died were the sound of his legless body thumping to the floor, and the sound of the chicken man clucking with laughter.

The workers arrived the next morning to find quite a mess. Their supervisor hadn't arrived for work yet, and neither did their foreman. They looked around, unsure of what to do. There was a delivery scheduled in an hour, and the cleanup crew apparently hadn't done their job last night. There was blood everywhere, and a horrible smell coming from out back.

"Over here, guys."

The workers followed the voice into the hanging room. There was more blood on the floor here, and a whole pile of what appeared to be chicken guts beneath the lopper.

"Seems as though the drainage system backed up."

The workers turned and saw Dave Richardson standing in the doorway.

"What happened?" one of the workers asked.

Dave eyed the workers intensely. "Every now and then someone tries to hose a whole chicken down the drain. Seems like a real big one got caught."

Dave peered down at the pile of guts. Peeking out amid the viscera and feathers was a human eye. Dave used the toe of his boot—a boot that barely held the claw hiding it—to shove the guts over it. "I'm the new super here," Dave said. "Let's get this mess cleaned up before the truck gets here."

The men nodded and got right to work.

And Dave went to his new office, scratching the itch on his back—*damn feathers*—that wouldn't go away.

The Layover

US Air flight 1166 finally came to a stop at gate 18. Tony stood up as the FASTEN SEATBELT light went out, stretched out as best he could beneath the overhead storage bins, and let out a long sigh while awaiting those ahead of him to disembark.

He was pretty tired. The original flight was delayed, then canceled, and then following four hours of waiting at the Will Rogers International Airport in Oklahoma City, he was finally rerouted on the red-eye to Boston's Logan, via a short layover in Pittsburgh.

He yawned and rubbed a hand down the back of his neck as the twelve or so passengers began to file out. He had a pounder of a headache and another hour of waiting before his shuttle left for Logan. He looked at his watch. It was 1:30 AM.

Twenty-nine-year-old Tony Vintano had slept through most of the flight. At first he wasn't very sleepy because of the two large coffees he drank while holed up in OK City, but as the plane was taking off, napping became imperative due to undying circumstances: he had to take a shit, and the only way to avoid a visit to the claustrophobic confines of the "lavatory" was to sleep it off.

He had not successfully visited the bathroom (in sitting fashion) since the previous night at home in Boston following a bowl of his mother's spaghetti; she always cooked him a big meal before business trips. Twice since then he'd tried to go, once upon arrival at the hotel and again at the airport prior to boarding the plane. All intentions were good, but nothing had come. The urge to go didn't hit him until he was in the air, safely belted in. Predictable.

Once airborne, his diminishing comfort swiftly turned to agitation as the pressure in his posterior increased. He popped two nighttime aspirins in hope that sudden sleep would help hold in the four meals—big company expense ones—that he'd eaten over the past thirty-six hours. It worked; he slept until the plane landed in Pittsburgh.

Entering the waiting area of gate 14, he stopped momentarily at one of the blue seats there and checked his tickets for the departure time and gate of his connecting shuttle. Gate 16, 2:15 AM. Good. He was right where he needed to be and didn't have to haul ass across the airport like that guy in the rent-a-car ads. And the flight from OK City must have been a little late, so the layover was minimal now, just forty-five minutes.

Then, the inevitable happened. A sour grumble emanated from deep inside his gut, pointing out to Tony that he had unfinished business. Those four meals that had sought escape earlier were back, knocking at his back door. He rubbed his stubbled face, then placed his tickets into his briefcase. He checked his watch again. 1:41. Plenty time to squeeze it out. He shouldered his case and walked away from the gate to find a restroom, watching a few tired travelers pacing and lazing about with no direction in mind. Looking back over his six years of travel experience, he realized that he'd never been in an airport at this time of the night. It seemed uncomfortably barren, like a mall before closing or Fenway Park towards the end of another futile season. Most of the shops were closed as well.

Signs ahead to his right designated the restrooms. Tony advanced through the one labeled with the outline of a male.

Inside the empty men's room, there was only one color: gray. The ceramic tile walls, the metal stalls, the stainless-steel sinks and urinals, all similar dull shades. Overhead, a single lamp threw a pallid sheaf of light over the stalls, casting shadows across the walls and floor like black blankets. The small room had an institutional aroma, like pine disinfectant; it seemed that it had been cleaned just a short time prior.

Tony entered the last of the six stalls there, placed his bag down next to the toilet, dropped his drawers and took a seat. He always did most of his best thinking with his pants around his ankles. Tonight, however, he would have to make an effort just to keep awake; the drowsy effects of the aspirin still lingered. Some thirty seconds into his movement, Tony heard footsteps enter, that of dress shoes echoing across the tiles. They led directly into the stall next him, stopped, then turned to slam the door shut. Tony squirmed and rubbed his tired eyes, a bit aggravated, feeling a bit violated. Couldn't the guy sit a stall or two away?

Suddenly, like a shotgun blast, the man in the stall next to him belched loudly, and vomited.

The surge was a powerful one, a roar that echoed from somewhere deep inside his gut and possibly beyond. It connected with the toilet water full force, sounding as if it parted the porcelain-held sea straight down to the cesspool. In an instant, discomfort seized Tony and provoked him to clutch his shrinking crotch, which along with his colon involuntarily cut him off.

Then another roar came, this one louder than the first, followed immediately by another torrent of puke.

Tony sat still, quiet. He closed his eyes tight and prayed it away, wishing it all wasn't happening. He heard the trickling and spitting of saliva amidst pained random gasps and wheezes. He listened to the man's shoes scraping the tiles. Every nuance was there. And as the man heaved a third time, a stench exploded from the stall, sending Tony's nostrils to an unexplored territory that reeked of hard-boiled eggs and Romano cheese stuffed into sweaty sneakers.

Tony began to sweat profusely. Eyes closed, he pulled a strip of toilet paper and wiped his brow. Meanwhile, the vomiter showed no signs of letting up; he carried onward, puking a forth, and then a fifth and sixth time. Each bellow seemed to increase in force, each extruding forth a voluminous amount of vomit that slapped the water as if the innards from a school of gutted dolphins were being shoveled into the toilet. Tony had never heard anything like it. His stomach clenched, his teeth too, and he had to force himself to gag back the contents in his stomach.

He couldn't take it any longer. Shit or no shit, it was time to get out of there before he began puking too.

And it was only as Tony stood to pull up his trousers—he did so quietly as he wasn't sure if the vomiter was yet aware of his presence—that things really started to get out of hand.

The vomiter purged again, this time with a sound that was not present in any of the previous releases. It was a...gurgle, a low guttural moan strangely similar to the wail of a cat in mid-orgasm, only somewhat muffled. Also different was the sound of contact, for the water in the toilet was obviously mistargeted, and *splash!* was now *splat!* as the tiles were layered.

Freaking out, Tony cowered back against the opposite wall of the stall, his growing fear and disgust causing him to breathe in audible pants. At that moment the vomiter became very quiet, stopped spitting and gagging as if he became aware of Tony's presence.

Tony crouched down to pick up his bag, first twisting his head to peer into the shadows of the twelve-inch space at the bottom of the stall wall.

What happened then was something that he could not have foreseen.

An ebb of blood swelled from beyond the confines of the vomiter's stall. At first he did not know what was happening. It started slowly, filling in the cracks between the tiles on the floor. Watching curiously, he neglected to move his bag before the red puddle poured forth like spilled paint, covering the floor, his bag, his shoes, all in its path.

He pushed frantically against the door with a cry, trying to escape. It squeaked, but didn't budge. He turned back, groaning, facing the stream of blood.

Now much more than blood was making its way over. At first glance it looked like streaks of wavering threads within the blood, but as he bent over to contemplate it further, he could only stare in shock. Flowing amidst the blood in an almost sensual slowness were what appeared to be veins, dark blue and gray, slithering over like dead snakes floating upon the surface of a pond. Amidst the veins, small meaty chunks came through like insects riding the surface of a rain puddle.

Tony stepped back in horror and revulsion, fumbling at the door, feeling the warmth of the blood through his shoes. He finally pulled it in and escaped the confines of the stall, leaving his bag behind in exchange for his freedom.

He moved to an area of the floor by the urinals that had not been tainted by the ebb—about three feet opposite the vomiter's stall—and stopped there. Dropping to his knees he again peered under.

There weren't any feet.

He stood back up, confused, scared. Then he hesitantly called out: "H-hello?"

He waited, but no reply came. "You okay in there?" Absurd question. Slowly, he stepped to the stall and after a moment of pause, knocked. "Hey in there, speak up." No reply, however he could still hear breathing, a bit quieter than before. He looked to the restroom entrance, hoping someone, *anyone* would walk in, take over the responsibility of this frightening mess.

Then, a loud knock came from inside the stall.

Tony jumped back, startled. He leaned down again in search of feet, but still there were none. He pondered as to what his next move should be. Jesus, this was a health and safety issue now. The guy was obviously very ill, maybe about to pass out, maybe dying and in need of help. He could not leave him alone here. What if he did die? That was not an option. He couldn't live with himself if that happened.

With no alert to the occupant of the stall, he stood, took two big steps, and kicked in the door.

Shot with a bullet of terror, a staggering Tony struggled to bear the burden of his own weight as he attempted to assimilate the image before him.

Hunched atop the toilet seat was a man, a…pilot. His uniform-clad body was splattered with blood from head to toe, a virtual puddle of gore saturating the chest through to his skin, the remainder of his body streaked in crimson like a finger painting. His face was a bloated visage that strained like an overfilled balloon about to burst, the veins at the forehead purple with pressure, both nostrils running thin trickles of blood over paled skin. The eyes, blackened underneath like two ripened prunes, bulged with dilated pupils that wavered atop the swelled whites like congealed drops of blood floating in yellowing pools of pus.

A sudden agonizing screech came from the pilot, startling Tony like a wicked alarm in the middle of the night. He jumped back unblinking, his sweaty fingers groping for the stainless steel of the sink behind him. He failed in his quest for support and slipped down hard on his back end. At that point, all attempts to move seemed impossible. Every muscle straining, trying desperately to as much as twitch.

Then the airman's teeth, previously clenched vice tight, started to chatter as if mechanical; he looked like a ventriloquist's dummy possessed by some malevolent evil. Through this oral din, through all the blockage gurgling in the back of his throat, Tony heard the pilot growl one word. He wasn't sure he had heard him correctly, but he had to trust his ears for there would be no opportunity for the man to repeat himself.

Gremlins...

Shaking uncontrollably, Tony managed to get to his feet, trying desperately to break his astonished gaze from the gnarled pilot. He crossed his arms in front of him, holding in the memory of the word before it escaped him.

The teeth then stopped chattering as suddenly as they started, the mouth frozen in a wide-open position. A little more blood trickled out down his chin. He made a short snorting sound and Tony leaned back hard against the sinks, trying to yell but unable to do so for fear stole his voice.

Something began crawling from the pilot's mouth.

His jaws had locked open because something was holding them that way. Two little hands the size of dimes, each with four tiny fingers, prying the mouth open by the upper and lower jaws. A sucking noise sounded, similar to a dentist's mouth vacuum, and then a little...man, drenched with blood and bile, began forcing its way out. A tiny bald head emerged, as round and smooth as a cue ball. Looking out, its lidless eyes, each the color of dull pennies, bulged wildly like a deer's caught in the headlights of a speeding car. It looked like a mini-human with Progeria, like a six-inch mutant Uncle Fester.

Losing it, Tony lurched away as blood began bursting from the pores in the pilot's face. And upon finally exiting the bathroom, he repeated the word over and over and over…

Gremlins…

Tony was freaking, shaking in panic, his thoughts running amok as he took a first-class seat on the plane. He'd immediately run from the bathroom to the gate where his plane had begun boarding. He counted the seconds as if they were hours, in sweaty prayer for his safe arrival home, or at the very least, away from the airport. He would concern himself with any mental therapy once he locked himself away in his apartment with a bottle of Tequila or Absolut.

Gremlins. He remembered watching a program, on the Discovery Channel he thought, about WWII pilots' stories of little men that inflicted havoc by tearing apart the planes as they were in flight. Many had claimed to have seen them. But these were just stories, weren't they? Could gremlins be real, now attacking the pilots of the planes?

The passengers—fifteen in total, all of them back in coach—had finished boarding, and the doors to the plane were shut. With the plane in taxi, Tony grew tired, mentally and perhaps physically drained from his experience, and closed his eyes. His mind, a serious mess, jumbled thoughts like an ocean wave churning the fine sands of a beach, mixing all reality with imagination and fabrication. And before Tony realized that he still hadn't completely relieved himself, he fell asleep.

"Sir?"

Tony felt a hand lightly jarring him. He looked up. An attractive woman—a flight attendant—stood over him. She had blond hair, blue eyes, and a pleasant smile white with teeth.

"I'm very sorry to wake you sir. We're circling Logan and I need you to fasten your seat belt."

Tony looked down, bleary eyed, still half asleep. He fastened his belt. The flight attendant thanked him and walked through the curtains to check on the other passengers.

He looked to the lavatory door, and like a bell, the pounding returned. He still had to go.

Then, he remembered.

Gremlins.

It had to be a dream. He sat up in his seat, at once agitated. Think, think, was it a dream? It had to be...

He unbuckled and rose from his seat, prepared to give in and use the lavatory when the door to the cockpit opened and the Captain emerged. He was white as a ghost. He forced a smile in Tony's direction, and rushed into the bathroom ahead of Tony, shutting the door behind. A click of the latch inside was heard, and the OCCUPIED light illuminated.

Tony had not smiled back. He instead diverted his gaze to the floor, to his shoes.

His bloody shoes.

Sweat poured forth from his brow in panic, and as if a metal fork were being scraped across a chalky blackboard, he cringed as he heard the muffled sound of vomiting emanating from behind the sterile white of the lavatory door.

Halloween Three

Jake found just what he was looking for, his only real means of escape—the only solution to his problem.

"*We're having triplets,*" she'd uttered not thirty minutes earlier. He'd cringed and his heart dropped, a brick in the ocean sinking alongside the pinhead of sanity barely clinging to the crumbling walls inside his head. Just those three words...*we're having triplets*...tearing into his *crumbling* walls, dribs of insanity seeping through, one listless bead at a time...until it flowed more urgently as *the word* looped inside his head, a vicious circle, as the porous walls crumbled even more...

Triplets...

The *ding-dong* of the doorbell echoed through the trailer, an air raid siren riding the harvest wind to the spot where he kneeled inside the ramshackle shed, inflaming his ears before resounding chaotically in his head. Trick or treaters! His mind couldn't hold on to the fact that it was Halloween, doorbells and high-pitched voices reminding him how Samantha *that selfish bitch* had just tossed lollipops into the paper bags and pillowcases of a troop of...*children*, how she turned around as if looking at the clock, but looked at Jake instead and said, "*We're having triplets*". He'd braced his head with both arms and begged for lies that never came. The doorbell rang again. And again. Minutes passed, erasing painful memories in their wake, replacing them with something altogether *else*.

His stomach rolled back and he lifted his weighted head and ejected his sugarcoated dinner into a rusted bucket, the same one he spent two weeks peeing and shitting in before he could steal enough copper pipes to repair the trailer's plumbing.

The doorbell rang. *Trick or Treat!*

He shuddered, fleeting rational thoughts picturing the scene: Samantha trudging like a zombie to the door, three young masqueraders there, witness to twin dilated eyes, haphazard track marks, and an insincere grin fit for the junkie she was.

"Jake? Where the fuck are you?" she slurred. "You should be doing this. Did you forget that I'm carrying three of your children?"

Three.

Jake's skin crawled as it always did when she opened her mouth, but more than usual this time. *Painfully,* as if her words had claws. He understood. He knew what was happening. *I've finally succumbed.* He felt markedly different, a *changed* man now. No, not a man, but a monster. Uncaged, running on instinct. He tossed again, this time down his chest, then sniffed the air and grinned. He felt *possessed* with a newfound awareness that demanded he counterattack the abrupt, overwhelming fear obliterating his future like acid on anything. In no uncertain terms could he trade in what little life he still felt inside for...for who? Three strange unfamiliar *vampires* that would suck Samantha's heroin-encrusted nipples—and his measly pathetic life— bone dry, only to provide nothing in return?

He put an ear up against one of the rotting beams of the shed and heard the doorbell chime again. High-pitched wails ensued, coursing from the throats of *three* vampires, quickly followed by the soft slaps of sugar-weighted treats against the packaged surprises at the bottom of their feed bags.

One-two-three. *Thunk, thunk, thunk.*

He shuddered and dry-heaved a few times, soiled sweat and stench rising from him in near-visible waves. He could *feel it,* was surrounded by it, maybe even protected by it.

"Jake?"

Her voice. It scraped against his spine, the drag of a straight razor across a chalky blackboard. Still clutching dearly what he'd come for, he climbed to his feet and dragged his unsteady near-deadweight to the threshold of the shed. His shirt was tattered and stained, pants soiled, beard glistening with sputum. Blood trickled from the gouges in his upper arms, ripped skin wadded beneath his yellow fingernails. He shoved off from the shed, arms outstretched for balance in a struggle to achieve *unity* with the burgeoning monstrosity inside, reeling across frost-hardened soil and weeds toward the front of the trailer. Halfway there, his body came to an abrupt stop, during which time he allowed the walls to crumble even further, now in larger chunks, giving the thing he was terrified of free rein to expose its vile form, its hideous intent. Miraculously though, the shattered walls held back the grim entity that tormented him with possible escape.

But for how long?

The setting sun extended its orange rays across the roofs of the trailers in the park, painting elongated shadows upon the weathered face of the squalid trailer he called home. He pressed on and circled the dilapidated structure, watching as three children wearing masks—a skull, witch, and pumpkin—took turns ringing the trailer doorbell.

Ding-dong!

"Happy-happy Halloween!"

Samantha appeared, flaunting her graveyard smile. "You have to say Trick or Treat!" she announced in a voice that could've been a man's. They responded jubilantly and accepted some of the same spoils Jake had for dinner. As they turned, the child wearing the skull mask noticed Jake, and after hesitating, tentatively said, "Cool costume mister..."

Jake wiped the snot dripping from his nose, the vomit from his chest, and took a step closer, tightening his grip.

The kids jumped down from the top step and beelined for the trailer across the dirt path-street-road named Shamrock Place, at the same time Samantha slammed the rusted (and torn) storm door shut.

Triplets...

Jake muttered out loud, "Happy-happy Halloween," and with his free hand, pressed the doorbell.

Samantha saw him, stopped, then backed away.

The rusted storm door creaked as he stepped inside and shut it behind him, closing out the approach of another band of vampires. He gazed blankly to his right, toward the dying, sheetless mattress in the corner of the room, around it filthy clothes strewn every which way as if protecting the area like some kind of lame moat. He contemplated the barrenness of the room—one half of his cookie-box home—and tried to imagine *three* little vampires sharing it with him. With them.

The doorbell rang. He winced. It was *loud* in his head.

From behind the bathroom door: "Get the door, Jake!"

He took a calculated step forward, eyeing the bathroom door and the dried boot print still there from last week's dispute.

The doorbell rang again. "Jake, I…I heard you come in…lollipops are on the table." The tremor in her voice was as real as the monster now crawling out from behind the fallen walls in his head.

He approached the bathroom door in harsh silence, save for his abrasive breathing, and waited for her to emerge. The doorbell rang a third time.

"God-damn it, Jake!" The door flung open, and before she had time to raise her hands in defense, he slashed out with the spade he took from the shed, puncturing the muscles and tendons on the side of her neck. The cold, dirty steel scraped audibly against her spine. He could *feel* it as he forcefully excavated her narrow flesh until only the protuberance of the mud-caked handle was visible.

He only noticed the scissors in her hand, for likely use in her defense, as they clanged against the cracked tile on the bathroom floor. Blood oozed from her nose and mouth. Finally he let go, and she collapsed to the floor with a decisive thud.

Ding-dong…

Nighttime's granite blanket fell quickly over the trailer park, and in its moonlit cover, Jake spent an hour inside the shed, shaking and babbling and sometimes chuckling to himself as the freed monster in his head provided him with the strength he needed to bury Samantha's tri-impregnated body in a shallow grave.

Ding-dong, the witch is dead! What a happy-happy-fucking-Halloween it is!

Triplets…

The doorbell rang infrequently, and by the time he threw the last patch of dirt over her distended belly, it stopped altogether. He snuck back inside and sat on the stained mattress, praying that the vampires would stay far away, no more sugar-fuel for their fires. He remained there for hours, or so it seemed, rocking back and forth like an ocean buoy on a windy day, sucking one lollipop after another, stopping only to wipe the sticky drool from his face with his dirt-coated forearms.

Midnight soon gave way to the dark morning hours. A bold silver moon splayed its beams through the holes in the curtains, and he savored the tranquility it brought with the wind, softly blowing the dried leaves outside, the courting of the crickets and frogs in the distant barrens.

Then, after hours of basking in silence, in beautiful agony, the doorbell sliced menacingly into his personal utopia.

Ding-dong…

"Go away, vampires; go away, vampires; go away, vampires," he stuttered, the monster inside unexpectedly unnerved, cherry tongue lapped swollen.

The doorbell chimed again, and then again and again until chaos was back in his world and he could do nothing but recoil and hold his ears in an effort to block the incessant *ding-dongs* that continued on and on. Each ring taunted his monster, forcing it to veer off course and make him feel as if he were going to break down.

He let out an angry scream: "SHUT UP!", but like water torture on his ears, the ringing banged on and on with no stops in between chimes. He staggered to his feet and grabbed a knife from the kitchen drawer—the only way for the ringing to stop was to kill the vampires doing this to him! He stumbled to the door and grabbed the rusted knob. The sooner he offed the little bastards, the more quickly he could go back to making peace with himself.

Knife raised, he jerked open the door with his free hand, and…

…*three children at the door*…

…it dropped from his hand.

Triplets…

Writhing on his porch, they weren't really children at all. Yet. The nude bodies were small, eighteen inches tall if they'd been standing, bald with bloated milky-white skin. The grape-sized hands of each were knotted into paws and curled into their torsos. On one, the brain was exposed through a translucent skull, and on all, the eyes were lidless. Another had no bottom jaw and all were missing ears. And they were filthy, mud-encrusted amid the blood that oozed from the exposed veins that traversed their filmy see-through skin.

At once the air darkened around them and Jake felt a frost-like chill permeate his body. As he stared in frozen silence, the three bewitched preemies crawled toward him, high-pitched bawls of anguish and grotesqueness escaping their tiny scowling mouths. He broke his paralysis and staggered back, unable to tear his tormented gaze away. For what they were, they crawled—no, *wriggled*—remarkably fast into the trailer, droplets of underdeveloped flesh shedding away from their bodies as they squirmed across the threshold. As Jake finally backpedaled into the kitchen, one of the fallen cherubs climbed to its toeless feet and began to stagger to him, mangled arms outstretched, toothless mouth gaping, baby feet squelching against the cracked tiles.

Through the biological glaze on its face, it gargled, "Trick or treat, Dad-dy."

Groaning, gasping for air, Jake frantically clambered along the wall of the trailer, tripping over a lamp in the process, slamming himself to the floor. On his back, the premature infants climbed up and attached their puckering mouths onto his exposed arms and chest. He struggled to summon the monster within, but even *it* wanted nothing to do with what was happening. He kicked and flailed, then managed to dislodge the vampires—his *children*—before climbing to his feet and staggering out the door.

Silhouetted by the full moon, a human-like figure stood at the bottom of the steps, a dirty garden spade jutting from its neck.

Jake staggered back, off balance, arms flailing, then tripped over one of his children and crash-landed on his back atop the mattress where he and Samantha had conceived the triplets—*triplets!*—now crawling back toward him.

"*Jake...*" the thing on the porch belched out. The mother of his children trudged into the trailer leaving muddy tracks behind, looming over him, earthworms and grubs falling from its eviscerated belly. "*Children...are...hungry...*" Her voice, once simply annoying, then mentally grating, now bore into his mind and sucked at the blackness there until all remaining rational thought disintegrated.

He twisted his neck away from the thing once called Samantha and beheld one of the malicious infants up close and personal. In an unformed hand it held a lollipop, tendrils of blue veins and soft flesh threading away from its face as it shoved it—with remarkable strength—into Jake's mouth, lidless eyes staring into his soul, lipless mouth whispering over a bed of gravel, "Trick or treat, Daddy..."

Samantha dropped to her knees on the mattress, straddling Jake, dirt-filled mouth open, puckering as if to kiss him.

At some point Jake started crying, the monster within defeated, rebuilding the walls inside his mind. "W-what do you want from me...?"

Samantha's black tongue slid from her mouth. Mud and skittering things fell out and onto his face. Before Jake managed a blood-curdling scream, which would be heard throughout the trailer park, the mother of his children ripped open his pants and, with the same remarkable strength as its newborns, latched onto his crotch. "*Happy...Halloween...*" she gurgled before making sure he never again killed any more babies.

Through the Eyes of the Victim

Sarah Ballard walked across the Rialto Bridge from S. Polo into S. Marco, admiring the vendors exulting their current trade to those within earshot, be it masks, jewelry, or other festival-related souvenirs. Despite objectionable glances from old Venetians—all the tourists, really, through no real effort seemed to earn the locals' distaste—in adjacent streets and cafés, she greatly admired the glamorous colors and adornments festooning the carnival environs, a puppet show at the foot of the bridge drawing gleeful shouts from children, magic tricks performed by charlatans alongside juggling acrobats in San Marco Square. What a spectacle of tradition and magnificence, a truly perfect way to spend her final days in Europe.

She'd timed her trip perfectly, backpacking from London to Paris and ultimately landing herself in Venice on the 24th of February, on the eve of Martedì Grasso, the climax of the Venetian Carnival. She'd purposely left a bit of space in her backpack to collect a variety of souvenirs while in Venice—charming mementos to help preserve memories a disposable camera couldn't. Threading her way through the crowds and glimpsing all the vendors with ear-to-ear smiles and tuneful pitches of their wares, she wondered if purchasing another backpack should be her first order of business here. There were so many items that fascinated her—so many she wanted to call her own.

She passed a throng of people in the square, noting only now that many, if not all of those around her—excluding the old locals glaring at her—were wearing masks. There were a grand variety of styles, some covering the entire face, most only half. Some had long noses, others came adorned with wrinkles and eyebrows, all of them designed to allow the wearer to eat or drink. This triggered her desire to own one, as the aroma of espresso and pastry from the sidewalk cafés tantalized the growl in her stomach.

It would make the perfect souvenir to bring back home.

She meandered through the square, taking in the sights, the sounds, watching a multitude of masked faces passing by, the dark eyes within rolling toward her, alien-like in their obscurity. Was everyone watching her? Surely she wasn't the only unmasked person here. But she stuck out painfully, an obvious tourist, blonde hair and blue eyes all her life an asset, now making her feel self-conscious.

She shuddered as she wove in and out the flowing crowd, unable to shake the sudden *need* to hide her face. Looking around, she moved quickly across Calle del Mandola to a storefront whose cracked and taped window displayed a variety of masks. Beneath each one, a small placard identified them: Arlecchino, Pulcinella, Pantalone, Brighella. She'd seen similar masks before, somewhere, perhaps on the wall of the small theater she once visited in Greenwich Village, New York City. Their downcast grins and simplistic yet slightly harrowing furrows unnerved her, both then and now.

Beneath a Moorish stone arch in the storefront stood a heavy wooden door. Without hesitation, she pushed through it; a tiny bell above signaled her entrance.

Sarah looked around curiously. The walls of the small, narrow shop were almost completely covered with masks, some in various states of carving. A smell of sawdust and glue hung in the air, leading her to believe the masks were in fact made here, by hand. The faces of the masks, unlike those in the window, although traditional in their manufacture, seemed all too unique from one another, too *real* to her, as though they had been modeled after the faces of actual people. It was *creepy*, unnerving her so much she had to look away.

A dark shadow materialized from a thin door in the back: a tall, bent man in a leather apron with a scruffy goatee and mussed gray hair jutting at various angles. His eyes were dark and hollow, much like the numerous eyes peering out at her from the mask-wearers in the square.

"Yes, ma'am? In need of a mask for the Carnival, I see…" His voice rumbled, deep and hoarse.

Sarah nodded. "A *lot* of people are wearing them."

"It's a tradition that breathes life into Venice. You, my dear, shall soon see."

Breathes life…

Sarah smiled, her gaze once again drawn toward the many masks surrounding her, at their smiles, their scowls, their expressive eyeholes glaring down at her. "How much are they?"

"New masks are quite expensive, considering they are unique. And as you can see, I make them myself. But…I have a few used ones I can offer you, for say, forty euros?"

Sarah wondered if she looked that forlorn, so desperate that she couldn't afford much more than that. The truth of the matter was that the shopkeeper had guessed correctly, that in fact she was running low on funds, and while she had enough money for a few days' worth of food and fun in Venice, her days her in Europe were coming to an end.

"This…" the man said, "should suit you fine."

The man produced a mask from a shelf in the shop, completely black with very slight wear around the edges. Its features were angular, yet non-descript, showing little emotion at all. The mask's countenance was neither happy, nor sad. It simply *was*.

She loved it.

She exited the shop holding the mask in her hands, rubbing the edges of her thumbs over the smoothly carved features. The man had called it a *Bauta*, pinning upon it a name not unlike those in the shop's window. It seemed fitting to her, simple and elegant. And very Italian.

She paced into the crowd, once again noting how practically everyone was masked, walking the narrow streets, laughing, chatting, dancing, drinking wine. The scene allured her, begging her to don her own mask and become one with the people of Venice.

Slowly she brought the mask up to her face. Thick black ribbons hung from the edges, tickling the sides of her face. At once she realized, quite ridiculously, that the ribbons needed to be tied around her head in order to hold it in place. But once she placed the mask against her face and peered through the eyeholes, she realized with surprise that this wasn't necessarily so. Painlessly, startlingly, the mask adhered itself to her cheeks and forehead, as if in some way had become part of her face.

She struggled with it, willed her hands to pull it away, but couldn't budge it. Without warning, she felt the strength in her body draining away...along with her very consciousness as she was suddenly transported to a place much different than the one she now occupied.

Even if she possessed the ability to pull the mask away from her face, the scene before her wouldn't allow it. *How can this be possible?* She beheld a dark, quiet place, a street so narrow it could barely admit two people walking side by side. She moved very quickly down it—or felt herself moving—all the way to the end, where it twisted through a network of back passageways and narrow staircases. At the foot of one staircase, she tripped over a paint can, her leg scraping harshly against a rusted grate fallen from the shattered window above. She screamed out in pain...

...and pulled the mask from her face.

Once again she was in the center of the crowd, not too far from the square where a group of masked men were tossing paper streamers at a number of cowering, giggling women. Feeling a bit dizzy and disoriented, she looked down at the mask in her hands, the ribbons now knotted together as if someone had snuck up behind her and tied them as she held it against her face.

I saw something... she thought. *I saw myself. And I was running. Running from...from what?*

"Only one way to find out," she murmured aloud, feeling not so much afraid as curious to see if it would happen again. Heart fluttering like a captured butterfly, she draped the ribbon around the back of her head, the mask against her face…

…and peered out through the eyeholes.

Again Sarah found herself not as an attendee at the Carnival of Venice, but as a woman stricken with terror, running from something terrible, something dark, something shadowy and ominous leaping through the moonshadows toward her. In pain, blood trickling warmly from one knee, she climbed to her feet and staggered through a winding succession of cobblestone streets, old brick buildings crowding in from both sides. Gone were the bright lights of the Carnival—the sights, the sounds, the aromas. Now only darkness and desolation existed in streets so confined she imagined them shunning light on the brightest of days.

From behind her came a sudden, heavy breathing.

Nuh…nuh…nuh, like a chugging train, it came toward her, unstoppable. Terrifying.

She wanted to turn, wanted to face down the thing that had chased her here…but she knew, somehow, that her feelings of fear weren't her own, that she was experiencing and sensing another consciousness, one that had somehow bled into her very own awareness, was actually *controlling* it, relating to her the fear, the complete, unequivocal terror of the moment that someone else was feeling, or had already felt. Even as she ran, Sarah realized she was witnessing a crime, possibly a rape or murder, through the eyes of the victim.

She turned to look at the thing chasing her, a thin shadow leaping from the darkness into a pallid shaft of moonlight, a figure wearing a black mask, the nose elongated like that of some cartoon witch's, the scowl matching the aggression of the figure's arm as it swung upwards, the shimmering blade of the knife in its grasp silhouetted by the white face of the moon.

Not looking where she was going, she tripped and sprawled forward, hands spread out to help break her fall.

The mask slipped off her face.

It skidded three feet before coming to rest at the foot of a table outside a sidewalk café. Her senses became overloaded at the bright lights and sights and sounds of the carnival. She had to shutter her eyes as her pupils adjusted to the overwhelming glare.

I'm back...

Two masked people dining at the café stood from their chairs and helped her to her feet. She nodded her thanks, not saying a word as she looked down at her knees and saw a twin set of abrasions.

Blood trickled from one knee, just as it did in her daunting reverie.

She adjusted her backpack, again looking at the diners, everyone around her, masked...all of them, like aliens from another planet, she a stranger in a strange land, lost, weary, unsure of where to go. Lively conversation surrounded her, the Italian language so familiar and yet so foreign in this moment of extreme confusion.

"Miss?"

The voice startled her, causing her to jump.

A masked man stood before her, countenance ivory-white, highlighted with dark eyebrows and rosy cheeks, very feminine in appearance. *La Gnaga*, it was called, she knew, having seen one just like it on display at the shop. A wave of confusion plagued her, and she had to take a deep breath before attempting to speak.

The man offered the mask back to her. She set her gaze upon it, now frightened of it, *horrified*, unable to take it, much less continue looking at it.

"This Bauta is yours, no?" the man said, holding it out toward her. She wanted to say no, to be rid of it now, to never be near it again for fear of it landing on her face once more—for fear of witnessing the scene of horror in the dark alley.

But it was hers. All the masked faces peering at her from the café saw her fall, saw it fly off her face.

She nodded, briefly, but didn't take it from the man.

"Allow me." The man stepped forward, and in an unforeseen move, reached out, looped the knotted ribbon around the back of Sarah's head, and pulled the mask back down over her face. Gasping, she brought her hands up to stop the man...

...but saw only the dark of the alley through the eyeholes of the mask. Her first, most immediate thought was to yank the mask from her face. She raised her arms, gripped the edges…but was unable to loosen it.

Fear had her paralyzed.

Fear, and the encroaching pound of footsteps directly behind her.

She spun and gazed up at her attacker, the steady position of his head blocking out the moon. She saw in clear detail the mask he wore, the nose protruding, the glisten of its black finish reflecting a distorted image of her screaming face.

In the figure's hand, the knife, its blade six gleaming inches of steel igniting the immediate scene, as if powered by batteries, raising up…up…up. Her hands shot up defensively, grasped the elongated nose of the mask, yanked upon it. The man behind the mask grunted, *nuh…nuh*, his hand momentarily frozen, buying her a second, maybe two, allowing her to pull the nose of the mask again. A slight cracking sound filled the dead silence of the moment, as though a tiny firecracker had gone off nearby. She fell back, the nose of the mask in her hand, she gazing up at the man, his mask having slid down his face, revealing his features…his *familiar* features—dark, hollow eyes, scruffy goatee, mussed hair—a split moment before the knife came down.

She screamed…

…in agony, the mask falling from her face as she plunged to the ground, blood seeping through her clenched fingers as she gripped her neck. The sounds of the carnival were distant, garish lights pouring into the street from between two buildings.

Before her, a storefront, the door open, allowed her a promise of aid as her final moments began to bleed out onto the street.

She staggered into the store, her plea for, "Help" barely discernible as the word whistled through the slice in her neck. "Please…"

She gazed up…saw the masks on the wall. And then, the shopkeeper in the leather apron, smiling once before hiding his dark hollow eyes and scruffy beard behind a mask missing its nose.

The last thing she saw before the bloody carving knife plunged into her neck was her own mask lying on the floor before her, its features somehow changed ever so slightly to mimic her own, dying features.

Room 412

"Here's your key, sir. Room 410. Elevators are to the right."

"Thank you," I said, returning the young girl's smile. It was the first conversation I'd had all day, and frankly, it felt good to simply talk to someone, regardless if the exchange had only been a few pleasant words with the hotel's desk clerk.

I'd been traveling all day, since early this morning. First the flight from JFK to Omaha, which had been delayed at its scheduled stop-over in Chicago for nearly three hours, and then the drive from Omaha to Grand Island, which also took longer than anticipated. I'd ended up smack in the middle of rush-hour, and believe me, these cornhuskers don't take to offensive driving as much as us city boys do. They pretty much stick to their lazy ways, even behind the wheel, no matter if they're early, late, or what. Once I battled my way out of the city though, it was pretty much smooth sailing to Grand Island — all three hours of it.

The stale smell of a hotel hallway is always welcoming odor on a business trip, today being no exception. I was tired and hungry, and needed to wind down; I had two meetings to attend at the Grand Island Convention Hall in the morning, and since a promotion was in the cards, a good night's sleep was foremost on my mind.

I stopped in front of Room 410. Finally.

I slipped my keycard into the lock and entered. The lodging held no special detail: brown carpeting, cheap art with contrasting floor-to-ceiling curtains, paisley bedspread. I placed my bag in the mirrored closet and immediately tested the bed, stretching out my limbs to work the tightness from my muscles. Good. The bed was soft and comfortable, and would provide for good sleeping. I twisted my neck and looked at the clock; nearly 9:30 and I still hadn't eaten any dinner. Hardly any lunch either, just a pretzel and cola at O'Hare. My stomach groaned, protesting its emptiness.

I ordered a grilled chicken dinner from the room-service menu, then took a shower. By the time I dried off and changed into a pair of knit shorts and tee, my food had arrived. I ate voraciously, cleaning up every last morsel of chicken, broccoli, and rice from my plate, washing it down with two cups of decaf. My mouth felt pasty afterwards and I regretted not getting something cold to drink, so I scrounged up some change, grabbed my keycard, and set off in search of a vending area.

I bought an orange soda and a package of cupcakes from the machines next to the ice maker at the end of the hall. I gobbled the cupcakes as I paced back, eyeballing every nondescript wooden door along the way, 420, 418, 416, 414, my tired mind wondering as to who settled within the rooms, where these mystery people came from and what kind of business they had here in Grand Island. I shuddered for a moment, suddenly suspicious of the unknown occupants and whether they might be standing just behind the doors, staring at me through the tiny peep-holes as I walked by.

I passed room 412.

I heard a voice.

Help...

I stopped, gazed curiously at the door, my heart tremoring with surprise. Call me crazy, but it *felt* at that very moment as if the voice I heard—mind you, not an amplified utterance from a television, but a *spoken voice*—had called to *me*. I stood still, listening intently, but found only silence. At once I assumed that the whispery beckon had been contrived from within my own fatigued imagination.

I peered at the tiny peephole, a hazy point of light returning my gaze. I took a step closer, turned my head in attempt to hear something from within, a rustling from inside perhaps: a confirmation of occupancy. But I heard nothing.

I looked up, the door only inches away.

The tiny light in the peephole vanished.

Someone was looking at me.

Immediately I ducked away, aware of the embarrassing truth. The occupant in 412 had seen me loitering at their door! Mortified, I quickly utilized my keycard and slid back into my room, shut the door and attached the chain. I then peered out my own peephole to see if 412's occupant had come out in search of me, but the view was limited, the span of it narrow and warped. So even if an individual *had* emerged from 412, I don't think I could have obtained a decent glimpse unless they'd stood directly in front of the door.

Like I had.

Unnerved, I pulled away and slipped into bed, hugging the television remote. I watched the local newscast with blank disinterest, trying to shrug off my mind's sudden preoccupation with room 412. Soon I shut the TV and rolled on my side, staring at the LED display of the clock on the nightstand. It read 10:47.

Long moments passed and I listened to my breathing, unable to find sleep.

Then, from amidst the shadowed silence, there came a sound, emerging suddenly and unexpectedly. A sharp rhythmic noise.

Thump...thump...thump...

It came from room 412.

It sounded like a fist, someone gently carrying out their boredom against the wall behind my bed. I ignored it at first, figuring its maker to grow weary of the incessant routine, but its persistence soon had me tossing and turning in bed, and I found myself armoring my ears with my palms as its ceaseless rote tempted to water torture my mind in the minutes to follow.

Suddenly I could take it no longer. I yanked the covers down, scampered up and grabbed the edge of the headboard for support, pressing my ear against the wall. I don't know why I did this, I guess I was just hoping to hear the muffled voices of those in occupancy, or the sounds of their television. But I found the room to be silent except for the *thump...thump...thump...* against the wall, now a bit louder than before, the three or four second intervals of dead silence between each occurrence strongly suggesting the room's vacancy.

My mind ran amok. *Then what of the voice I heard in the hall? Could that have come from another room? If so, then who or what produced the thumping noise?*

I slid back down under the covers, pulling them over my head. Here in my vulnerable privacy I blamed the intrusive thumping on a loose water pipe, denying my initial premise that its source had been man-made, whether by finger or fist or through inanimate supplement. I swallowed a dry lump in my throat that tasted of orange soda, reaffirming to myself that my intuitions had been wrong, that indeed someone in the room above or below was taking a shower, that they would soon be finished and the thumping would cease.

Beneath the covers, I waited for the thumpings to stop.

But they went on and on and on.

I closed my eyes and wished for sleep to come, trying unsuccessfully to think solely of my meetings in the morning, and not of the mysterious thumpings issuing from room 412.

I tossed and turned for nearly two hours. Cool sweat spilled from my body like rain, dampening the sheets that were twisted into knots from my restlessness. Outside, wind and rain came.

The thumping had grown louder.

It was *torturing* me.

I decided to place a call into room 412.

I opened the light next to the bed, picked up the telephone handset and placed it to my ear. Slowly and methodically, I pressed the three numbers on the keypad, *4-1-2*, careful not to trip up as I did not wish to awaken anyone else by mistake; no other should needlessly suffer sleeplessness as I had tonight.

The phone rang in my ear. With slight delay, I heard it ringing in room 412.

I waited. And like the thumping, it went on and on and on.

I let it ring perhaps a dozen times, not knowing whether my toll was being ignored, or if indeed no one had occupied the room. *But how could that be?* The thumping, it *was there*, as real as my restlessness had kept me awake. *Certainly some individual produced this noise, the motive behind it clearly mustered through effort to drive madness into me!* I was beginning to scare myself, thoughts like this making me feel as if my mind had begun to erode: each thump and each ring of the phone chipping away another little piece of my sanity with every stroke.

I pulled the phone from my ear.

Halfway to the cradle, I heard a click. The phone stopped ringing in room 412.

Someone had picked up.

I hung up.

Damn! Couldn't I have waited another second, another ring? My momentum in preparing to hang up had forced me to disconnect the line! Or was it my fear? Perhaps a dreadful combination of the two? Does it matter?

Dear God, why am I so afraid?

I tried to get a grip, to convince myself of my intelligence. I reminded myself of all the years spent traveling for this company, to places even more so desolate and lonelier than Grand Island. *Why then, all so suddenly, am I buried in fear tonight? Terrified of this thumping? It is a thumping against my hotel room wall, and nothing more. There is nothing to be afraid of.*

But a piece of my mind tried to convince me otherwise. That there *was* something to be afraid of.

Its source.

Thump…thump…thump…

Again I attempted sleep, gazing pointlessly at the clock, watching the minutes creeping at a pace no faster than the hours it took me to arrive here. Finally, I squirmed up in bed and put on the light.

I stared at the phone for what seemed an eternity, then picked up the handset, shivering as I did so. I had to know. I had to establish a rationale to these impacts that so threatened my sanity.

A dial tone met my ear.

I punched in the room number, 4-1-2.

It rang, from the earpiece and through the wall.

Someone picked up on the second ring.

Whoever it was, they did not identify themselves, or say "hello". I waited, thinking for a moment that the line had simply disconnected. I hesitated to utter, my breath caught in my lungs. I felt horrible waves of discomfort. I sensed the presence of someone at the other end.

My heart nearly stopped as I realized something.

I could hear the thumping through the phone. *Indeed I had a connection into 412!* My heart pounded, my mouth went dry. Finally, I found the spirit to speak.

"Hello?"

Something followed my summon. Not a voice, but more of a stiff blare of static, as if someone *had* spoken but the signal proved too weak and distorted to appropriately carry a voice.

"Hello, can you hear me?" This time I spoke a bit louder.

The line disconnected to a dial tone.

I pulled the phone from my ear, utterly confused. Had someone been there? Indeed, the thumpings had sounded in the phone, and I did *sense* a presence at the other end. Perhaps the connection *was* bad, that the person in room 412 couldn't hear me and had simply hung up the phone.

I dialed again, now frantically determined to make contact.

The phone picked up on the first ring.

A storm of static met my ear, hissing waves rising up and down in volume like swooping winds, carrying with them a barely audible whisper—a voice—lost yet trying to find its way out from the tempest. Indeed, I could hear a voice, but could not make out what it said.

Thump...thump...thump...

"Hello?" I called. "Can you hear me?"

I nervously picked at a fingernail in wait for a reply. Then I wondered: how on earth could the voice of the person in room 412 be veiled in so much interference, when the ambient strikes against the wall transmitted so clearly? That didn't make sense.

"If you can hear me, I'm sorry to bother you, but..."

Like an animal attempting to free itself from its captor's jaws, the voice broke through the static.

Help me.

The same voice I'd heard in the hallway. I *hadn't* imagined it.

The phone disconnected and I was once again left with a dial tone.

My heart raced and I started thinking clearly for the first time since the thumping began, assuming that somehow the phone lines had gotten crossed and were either picking up a local radio broadcast or some nearby cellular activity. It *had* to be. I could form no other postulation. I called the front desk, something I should have done from the onset. A woman answered.

"Hello, this is room 410," I said. "I was wondering if you were having any reports of problems with the phones?"

"None that I'm aware of sir." She was courteous and seemed honest, even though I didn't receive the answer I desired. "Are you having trouble with your phone?"

"Just a moment ago I tried to make an in-house call, but couldn't get through."

"Would you like me to try the connection for you?"

"Yes," I said. "Room 412 please." It sounded strange coming from my tongue.

"Hold on." I heard a shuffling of papers and then a moment of silence. The phone rang through the wall from 412, nearly startling me. It tolled six or seven times, then stopped. "Sir, there's no answer on that line."

I shuddered, orange soda gurgling in my throat. "Are you sure?" At this point I really didn't know what else to say and was probably sounding a bit crazy. After all, it was the middle of the night. I thanked her and depressed the receiver. I then let it up and dialed into 412 again.

The phone rang. I heard it ring in 412 too.

It picked up on the first ring. Silence.

"Hello?" I said.

Waves of static. In the background: *thump…thump…thump…*

"Hello? Can you hear me?"

Within the storm of whiteness I heard the voice, now repetitive, like a scratchy record skipping on a Victrola:

help me…help me…help me…

"What is it? What's wrong?" I was in a panic and could barely control the shudders rippling through my body. Blood sped in my veins at break-neck velocity, and I knew at this moment that I wouldn't find sleep tonight.

"Can you hear me?" I was yelling now and could have sworn I heard my voice echoing back to me from beyond the wall, as if traveling full-circle from the phone in 412.

A strong wind swept across the window, vibrating the sliding doors in their tracks. The thumpings grew louder. The static blared in the phone, a violent storm. The voice in the phone *screamed*. I could hear her. A woman, in distress.

Why can't I hear her through the wall?

I had to do something. I smashed the phone down, picked up my keycard and ran from the room. The door slammed shut behind me, leaving me basked in silence. Eerie, foreboding silence.

And there I stood in front of room 412, gazing groggily at the peephole, its pinpoint of light staring back at me, empty and devoid of life. My mind swam in crazy circles, and I made great attempts to understand what it was in God's name that had me assuming such abnormality in an otherwise unimpressive situation. Easily an individual under normal frame of mind could explain the night's events with conventional rationalizations. The thumping, a pipe in need of repair. Or perhaps a laboring air-conditioning unit efforting to release its flow. And the phone, crossed lines, a stray satellite signal.

So does my refusal to accept such standard explanations predicate a grounds for insanity? Perhaps, but my feelings are passionate, and I stand determined. I had no choice but *to know* for sure the very rationale to such intrusion into my life, my life that up until mere hours ago had been completely normal and carefree. My life that now gave promise to madness.

I knocked on the door.

No answer.

I don't know why, but I tried my keycard, as if compelled by unseen forces. I came to the realization at this very moment that most if not all of my curious actions tonight had been prompted by something strangely mysterious, almost supernatural.

The key fit into the slot. The tiny light on the lock changed from red to green.

I pushed the door open.

And here I beheld the source of the thumping against the wall.

The room was cool, the windows having been left open, its curtains billowing in the night's stormy winds. The bed had been moved to the center of the room.

A female body hung lifeless from three exposed pipes in the ceiling above where the bed had been. The head was twisted in an impossible angle, eyes bulging from their sockets, tongue swelled and protruding from the lips like a slab of meat. The woman's skin looked soft and pulpy, bearing a milky tone that reminded me of a fish's belly.

The body swayed in the breeze entering through the open window, its weight thumping every few moments against the naked wall.

It was horrible, the sight of the body and the deadened strike of it against the wall, so dreadful to experience. And yet, so remarkably secondary to what I noticed next. I could only gasp and cover my mouth as the emotion of fear as I knew it took on a whole new perspective. Suddenly I was suffering a terror at a level previously unfathomable, to near-death perhaps, and I virtually fainted at the truth of what *was*.

She had used the phone cord to hang herself. It was strung over the pipes, wrapped expertly around her neck, the handset twisted madly in its knots in a position so that the mouthpiece gently touched her swollen blue lips. I gazed away only to see the abandoned connection in the wall where the phone line had once derived its signal.

Paralyzed, I waited in silence, staring at the empty phone cradle sitting on the nightstand in room 412, listening to the thumping of the cold body against the wall.

And I listened still for her pleas for help, pleas that I soon realized were echoes from a life so desperately seeking help. A life where not a single living soul had been around to hear them. Until it was too late.

Err

Henry Sellers strained to see the thin beam of sunlight that dug its way through the near-permanent cloud cover of high noon. *It's a sign*, he convinced himself, turning to see June as she pored over the LCD pamphlets from Chroma-Key Splicing Technologies. *Surely by now she's got them memorized.* Good thing too. He wasn't as optimistic as his wife.

June considered Henry with the same teary-eyed stare he'd grown accustomed to over the years. Natural childbirth had been something they'd only read about in the history books, yet the maternal instinct in her failed to abandon her like childbearing had all of earth's females almost two hundred years ago.

It had been coined The Great Spay, a premature and wholly insensitive label that stuck despite the utter disregard it had for all humans. There were dozens of other names for the event that had changed the world nearly two hundred years ago—all of them familiar and no less terrifying—but The Great Spay had come first and remained.

June said, "Our three-year wait has finally arrived. Are we really doing this, Henry?"

What choice did they have? Both he and June (well, all humans on earth at this point) were "conceived" synthetically through alternative DNA & RNA splicing, epigenetics, genomic mechanisms, and dozens of other un-pronounceable techniques that when combined single-handedly saved the human race. What remained of it.

We can walk away June. Just live out the rest of our lives together on some island in the Caribbean where the sun is reported to shine nearly four hours a day.

But Henry...our parents did it. So, we can too.

Chroma-Key Splicing Technologies, founded two centuries ago, had remained the only corporation with the experience and technology to allow select couples to create their own child. *If it weren't for Chroma-Key,* Henry thought time and time again, *humans would be extinct by now.* The private corporation appeared just two years after the skies had turned gray, with much thanks from every God-fearing person (and future parent) on earth. But Henry had always leaned more toward the conspiracy theories that abounded after every human female born from that moment forward had no ovaries.

Henry said, "Three years of tests, five years income. Having a successful child these days decimates every prospective parent's everything. Money, gone. Home, gone. I really hope this pays off, June."

"There's no turning back now."

Henry nodded, adding an uncertain smile. "He'll be one of the world's greatest athletes."

"From your mouth to Chroma-Key's ears."

There had been rumors of couples entering the Chroma-Key facility, never to be heard from again. Henry had searched the Key-Web for endless hours seeking information beyond the images of smiling babies under sun-filled skies; although the sun seldomly broke through the dark skies anymore, it didn't dissuade many would-be parents. No one spoke up against Chroma-Key. Why would they? *Chroma-Key is God.*

Aside from the conspiracy theories, there are exactly zero negative opinions on Chroma-Key anywhere. He contemplated this daily, knowing that somehow government and corporation had become one and the same long before they were born. Chroma-Key's headquarters and labs, located throughout most of Washington Key (formerly Washington DC), remained a mystery to most of the world excluding those who worked and lived behind its iron doors.

Henry shrugged it off to propaganda (and perhaps a bit of denial), relying solely on the millions of success stories from happy-smiling parents. He truly hoped that he and June would be happy and smiling one day too.

"Do you have your Keyscanner?" June asked.

Henry revealed the three-inch platinum square in sleight-of-hand manner. "Our entire lives, right here." Full medical and DNA scans had been uploaded into the gadget, background checks, whims and ways, every second of their lives recorded from the day they were born until this very moment by a chip implanted in their brains at "childbirth". Only the life-recorded—a prerequisite all prospective parents agreed to on one of many dotted lines—would be considered for in-home testing...and then there was three years of *that.*

Their Keyscanner lit up, vibrated.

Their ride was here.

Three hours on near-empty highways led them into the snarled roads of Washington Key. Henry marveled at how so many self-driving vehicles managed not to crash.

"It's said that nearly 20% of the country's 56 million people live in and around Washington Key," June noted blankly, her mind elsewhere.

Henry nodded. They'd had this discussion before. "And half of those live *inside* Chroma-Key."

"Building's big enough."

It came into view long before they reached the city limit, towering nearly two-thousand feet high, the top half perpetually buried in smog and cloud cover. Thousands of mirrored windows adorned the mile-long face of the building, many more miles of windowless structures trailing behind, connected by a series of magnetic tubes that propelled the internal transportation system.

Looks like a colossal millipede, Henry thought with forced amusement, wondering if it would swallow them whole, never to spit them back out again. Again, his mind ruminated over *the rumor*: of those entering the huge walls of Chroma-Key, never to be heard from again. *Was it choice, or something entirely different? Or perhaps it's just disinformation, propaganda? Maybe they were simply forgotten about after living out the terms of their pregnancies under its monolithic roof?* Given the NDA's every prospective parent had to sign, the rumors would remain.

What started as a drizzle turned into a steady rain as the vehicle pulled into one of dozens of entry garages lining a portion of the Chroma-Key building. The huge room echoed and rebounded with sounds of numerous vehicles making their arrival through adjacent entries. The doors to Henry and June's vehicle slid up and they were greeted by a towering bulk of a man in a black jumpsuit with a digital chest badge; CKST73462 identified him as a member of the Chroma-Key security team. At first Henry thought he (it) might be an android given the ocular implants that made his eyes glow slightly purple, but he ultimately settled on human after hearing his voice.

"Keyscanners, please."

Henry and June presented them. The guard scanned both with an infrared Key-eye implanted in his meaty palm, then said, "Follow me."

Henry looked around, saw other couples exiting their vehicles and being escorted into far-away doors by larger-than-life security guards. He drew in a deep breath, then reached for June's hand and gazed into her eyes. "Ready?"

They followed CKST73462 through a far-away door of their own, shadowing the silent guard through a series of dark hallways illuminated by integrated monitors displaying images of happy-smiling parents frolicking with toddlers in bright green pastures. Brightly lit cobalt arrows between the monitors eventually pointed the way to a door labeled "Examination Room 1111". The guard placed his palm against the camera-eye adjacent to the frame, granting them access. "A doctor will be with you shortly."

The examination room glowed brightly with white tiles and fluorescent tubes that looped across the ceiling. Two flat padded tables before them were divided by a wall monitor that lit up with the image of a young, polished male face, eyes a bit too large to be human. *Android*, Henry marveled, having read about how parts of Chroma-Key was entirely run by humanoid robots. He never thought that one would be performing the surgery on them.

"Hello, I am Doctor Blaine. Please remove your clothing and lay face up on the tables." The articulate words from the talking head were soft and monotone, albeit slightly off-human. Henry and June faced each other, silently seeing no alternative but to comply.

As they undressed, the doctor's voice continued. "This is your final exam. We will make certain there are no new health issues to be concerned about. Once confirmed, we will begin the genetic extraction. All the variables you have chosen will be knitted together to create your perfect child: height, weight, hues, intelligence, creative abilities, everything you asked for on the completed and signed forms will be added. You have a full record of what you ordered. Do you have any questions before we begin?"

June spoke up. "We're worried about the risks involved…"

The head replied immediately, as though on cue. "As with every Chroma-Key made child, there are slight risks. However, our success rate is 99.4%, meaning there is a very good chance your child will emerge exactly as ordered.

"And the other .6%?" Henry asked.

"It is entirely possible that one or more traits will not surface as ordered. I see you ordered blue eyes. There is always a slight chance — though unlikely — that your child, *a boy*, may have different colored eyes. We like to say that we've perfected the process, but there are sometimes surprises."

As soon as Henry heard the doctor say *a boy*, much of everything else said went over his head. *We ordered a boy.* He'd convinced June to purchase strong athletic abilities (that cost an extra five-hundred grand) and now Henry was imagining cultivating these skills in Hecksher Park tossing baseballs and footballs to a blue-eyed, brown-haired eight-year-old son that looked a bit like him and a bit like June.

I want to give our child something special…something our parents couldn't afford to give us. We're basic, June. Is that what you want for our son?

"Are you both ready?" the doctor asked, interrupting his reverie.

There was a moment's hesitation before both Henry and June replied in unison, "Yes."

"Please remain still." A small circular compartment in the ceiling appeared and a gas mask attached to a long tube emerged, winding snakelike to their faces. "You will be placed under a medically-induced coma for two days during which we will extract the requested genes from you both. These will be stitched in our lab and implanted into an artificial egg that will be inserted into June's womb. When you wake up June, you will be pregnant."

Henry had many questions, all of which dissipated as both masks swiftly adhered to their mouths as though alive and hungry, bringing deep sweet blackness into their lives.

Henry dreamed of bright flashes striking him like bullets in the dark, leaving echoes of pain on his body like week-old bruises. Every movement he attempted was a numbed stagger that forced him down on all fours after a few pained steps. He looked up. Surrounding him were happy-smiling mannequins, plastic parents donned in bright tourist florals cradling babies in pink plastic arms, each newborn face a near-featureless oval perforated with tiny, dark, wrinkled gaps for eyes, nostrils, mouths. The mannequins dropped their ghastly babies on the floor and watched as they crawled all over Henry, whistling "daddy" through pinpoint mouths. More came, burying him like ants on sugar, prodding with terrible clutching fingers and shrilling a discordant insect-like chorus. Henry attempted a scream, but only matching whistles emerged from his fear-stricken lips: *"June!!!"*.

"Henry? Henry?" The voice was June's. "Are you OK?"

Then, an unfamiliar female voice: "Mr. Sellers? Can you hear me?"

Henry opened his eyes. First he saw June, sitting on the bed alongside him. Then he gazed at the female android standing in the room with them, a top-of-the-line model nearly indistinguishable from the human counterpart it was designed to emulate. Its sparkling green/grey eyes contemplated them with impassive regard as though it had someplace else to be.

"Are you ready to see your new home?"

Henry nodded. "Ok. Yes, of course." He looked at June, who was now smiling from ear-to-ear. "Wait…June…are you…"

She nodded. "It worked. I'm pregnant."

After a few hours of tests where both Henry and June were privately subjected to various scans and probes, they were reunited in another exam room where the female android—dressed in the same silver jumpsuit that Henry and June were provided—briefed them on their next steps.

"It is time for you to see your new home. Are you ready?" Before Henry and June could answer, the android added, "As you know, you will live out the full term of your pregnancy here at Chroma-Key. During this time, you will be monitored and provided with the nutrients and practices to ensure your child develops to specification. Follow me."

Henry and June held hands as they followed the android down a long hallway toward a protruding oval-shaped door. As they walked, the android continued its pre-programmed pitch. "The Family Zone is filled with expectant parents like yourselves…

…happy-smiling couples…

…all of whom are working toward bringing their own perfect child into the Chroma-Key world."

Henry could hear the whir of the magnetic transport pod as it approached behind the oval doors. He took a deep breath as the doors glided open, offering them access to a small windowless pod as white and neon-sterile as the examination room. They entered and sat alongside one another, watching as the android sat in the corner seat and closed its eyes. A sign above the seat indicated it as an *Android Charging Dock*.

The doors whooshed closed and the magnetic transport pod took off, barely vibrating as it propelled them to another part of the Chroma-Key headquarters. They rode in awkward silence, the android opening its eyes one time in silent response to June's only question: "How many people live in the Family Zone?"

Henry placed his hand on June's belly, an attempt to offer some solace in this seemingly tentative moment. Once the car slid to halt, the android opened its eyes and said, "Welcome to the Chroma-Key Family Zone.

Our new home…

The doors slid open and revealed their new neighborhood.

Henry's heart immediately filled his throat with uncertainty and fear. In this moment, June squeezed his hand, but he couldn't comfort her. He could only stare at the awful sight before them.

The space they stepped into was a massive grid of cookie-cutter homes as far as the eye could see, each row bisected with gleaming white pathways. Far above, a faux blue sky with little fluffy clouds cradled an incredibly unbelievable simulation of the sun.

Happy-smiling families under sun-filled skies…but there's a problem here…

All the houses were clear, entirely see-through for all nearby occupants to see. Each diminutive structure was one floor, roughly 400 square feet, three small rooms constructed of thick, gleaming glass. As Henry and June slowly followed the silent android down one of the six-foot wide paths, Henry could plainly see the couples inside the matching domiciles. Some were seated on small beds with their hands in their laps, dark despondent eyes quickly glimpsing Henry and June. Others were sleeping or eating, showering or exercising. Every clothed person they saw wore the same silver jumpsuit, fitted to suit the various terms of pregnancy or body sizes.

Henry and June exchanged a worried glance. She mouthed silently, "What is this?"

"It's your new home," the female android replied, stopping in front of an empty unit as clear and identical to those surrounding it. In the home to the right of theirs, perhaps a dozen feet away, a young woman sat on the white floor in a yoga pose, peering peripherally at Henry and June through dark eyes that may have been holding back tears. June offered a little wave to which the woman pretended not to see.

The android placed its palm against a scanner on the front wall of the empty dwelling, revealing an entranceway that appeared out of nowhere, like a miraculous hole in the clouds emitting a rare beam sunlight. With a wave of its arm, the female android escorted them in…

…but remained behind as the glass wall reappeared, enclosing Henry and June inside.

"You will be provided with instructions on how to proceed." Henry and June watched uneasily as it paced down the hard white path, not knowing that this would be the last time they would have contact with anyone—*anything*—from Chroma Key for the next nine months.

The "Great Spay" was, for all human understanding, a natural event caught in an endless whirlwind of controversy for the last 200 years. 65 years after doctors discovered that no human female born had ovaries, natural childbirth had been completely eradicated. The nameless woman to be the last female ever to give birth died a few years later, with the last naturally born human passing on over 80 years ago.

Chroma-Key had been there to save humanity. Chroma-Key is still saving humanity.

After a short welcome message provided by the android image on their wall, Henry and June tried to communicate with the neighbors but were largely ignored. The yoga neighbor who they watched conquering positions despite being about 6 months along, mouthed, "I'm sorry," through tear-filled eyes, and was rightly electrocuted through the floor. Her husband was also shocked and released a pained howl of his own.

Tears filled June's eyes. "What are they all doing? Why aren't they looking at us? Why are we in glass houses? Why are they being hurt?" She had a million questions and Henry had answers to none of them.

They explored the domicile, three rooms with zero privacy: bathroom with shower and toilet in crystal-clear view for all to see, bedroom a full-sized mattress with just enough standing room between it and the clear walls surrounding it, a half dozen silver jumpsuits (like those being worn by every occupant of every glass house) separated into two rows: *male & female.*

"Please return to the living room," a female voice beckoned. Henry and June exited the bedroom and saw a Chroma-Key logo displayed on the wall of the main room. They sat on the small cushioned rectangle acting as a couch in the main room and faced the integrated screen, mimicking those visible in adjacent homes.

"Henry...the other people...they're all doing the same thing. Look."

Henry rose from his seat, stepped to the front of the home and peered out at the house directly across the way. He motioned to the couple with both hands...and an electric charge entered his silver jumpsuit from the floor. He howled in pain, tripping over himself, landing ass-first on the blank white surface, both fists grabbing his crotch. With hot tears blurring his eyesight, he crawled back to his seat alongside June, breathing heavily.

June hugged him and whispered tearfully, "H-Henry...are you okay?"

He nodded but no words came; the pain in his lower half wasn't the only shock he felt. *My God, what is happening here?* He trembled uncontrollably alongside June until the Chroma-Key logo morphed back into the same female android face that brought them here.

The android spoke: *"This is your afternoon reminder. Chroma-Key saved humanity. Chroma-Key continues to save humanity. You are playing an important role in evolving the species. It is imperative you submit to these guidelines...*

In unison, Henry and June blanched white and repeated, "Evolving the species?"

They continued watching the screen—along with all the other couples he presumed—but he and June were too afraid to face in any direction but forward. They sat for what felt like hours, listening to the directives, *obeying*, until the simulated sun set behind the glass city far, far away. Once darkness came, they were beckoned into the bedroom, where they were instructed to lay down and absorb the subliminal whispers caressing their ears from the persistent, wavering tones that entered the room from every wall.

Tears filled their eyes as they fell asleep their first night at Chroma-Key Splicing Technologies, Henry's mind torturing him with one of the many mantras he was taught that day in the seemingly unending message: *You are playing an important role in evolving the species...*

Henry awoke with a start, seconds before the Family Zone alarm blared and the imitation sun rose over the homes behind them. Throughout the last nine months his body had grown accustomed to the routine forced upon them. June not so much. She suffered terribly at the stark, unchanging living conditions, her brain fully stretched to capacity with Chroma-Key doctrines; she was one with them now, her soon-to-be-born child part of the unyielding and unsympathetic program.

"We will be fine, June," Henry instilled upon her for the millionth time, reminding himself daily that both their parents had survived the process and brought them into the world with no problems.

"How can you be so sure, Henry? We don't know what it was like to be part of the world back then…or part of the world *before us.* When childbirth was natural."

She was right. They didn't. Very few historical references of life over two-hundred years ago remained on the Key-Web. *Government and corporation had become one and the same many years ago.* And now here they were, nine months after participating in the Chroma-Key family program, enduring nine months of their principles, their mind-altering curriculum, the automated tests both painful and incapacitating, the tasteless food paste and tangy water delivered via the feeding tubes in the main room, the enforced solitude broken up solely by the rare permissions to watch and applaud other couples being released from their glass prisons that glowed pink or blue before they exited to bring their child into the world.

"June…everyone in the world today was born right here. We will soon be going home with our child. Our *son.* Just like everyone else."

"Ok Henry…I believe you…"

Over the months her voice had changed, had become detached. Her eyes now dilated orbs, devoid of emotion. Henry remembered the dream he had when he first arrived here, of blank-faced babies crawling on him, suffocating him. Tears formed in his eyes. Despite living—being imprisoned—here with June for nine months, in this moment he barely recognized her. Or their real reason for being here.

A splash on the white floor. June's water.

Within seconds, the opening they walked through nine months ago reappeared in the main room. The female android's image appeared on every family's glass wall, repeating one of hundreds of Chroma-Key invocations previously instilled in them. *Chroma-Key is God, Chroma Key will re-populate the earth with better humans, Chroma-Key is all knowing, all seeing. Please congratulate Henry and June, they are about to become parents to a boy.*

Their home glowed cobalt blue *(it's a boy!)* and the nearby neighbors began to applaud. As always, the applause increased in volume as it cascaded across the entire zone until everyone—thousands of people—filled the small city with the sounds of clapping.

Henry peeked out the opening in his home, looking both ways but hesitant to advance any further for fear of becoming electrocuted. June hobbled to the doorway, holding her belly. Henry supported her as she huddled alongside him but was too scared to exit.

She doubled over suddenly, both arms now wrapped around her stomach. "Henry…it hurts! Something is wrong!"

Henry stuck his head out the door. In the distance, the android that delivered them here nine months earlier appeared, pacing briskly toward them. He could see an unmoving and wholly creepy smile on its face. As it arrived, it said, "Please follow me."

Henry and June exited and slowly followed the android as it headed back toward the transportation hub. Everyone in the Chroma-Key Family Zone continued clapping, peering at the couple about to become parents—the only time any interaction between Parent-Zone inhabitants was permitted—as they followed the android out of the area they lived in (as prisoners!) for the last nine months. Soon the clapping stopped and everyone they left behind returned to their regularly scheduled programming, undoubtedly envious of the couple who was about to re-enter the real world with a baby in their arms.

The smile remained on the android's face as it faced Henry and June. "It is time for you to become parents."

They arrived at the same oval doors that granted them access here less than a year but seemingly a lifetime ago. The doors slid open and they entered the transportation pod.

June stopped, hesitated, then collapsed to her knees. "Henry! It hurts!" Blood mixed with amniotic fluid leaked down her legs and puddled on the floor.

Henry looked down, saw small, silver fish-like scales floating in the gummy mixture. "What in God's name…?!"

The android's left hand pressed a spot behind its ear. "We have an Err. I repeat, we have an Err." This odd mention morphed into a series of clicks and whistles interspersed with odd-sounding words in a language that was wholly unfamiliar.

Now in a panic, Henry tore his terrified gaze away from June. "What is an Err? What are you saying?"

Ignoring him, the android sat in the corner charging seat and closed its eyes.

"Hey! I'm talking to you!" The doors closed and the pod began to travel...not sideways but dropping down—the fluttering in Henry's stomach confirmed this. He leaped from June's side, grabbed the android by the neck and repeatedly slammed its head against the *Android Charging Station* sign behind it. Mercury-like liquid exploded from the back of its head in a shimmering spray, tendrils of smoke materializing as thin black wires wriggled from the open wound like tiny tentacles. "Help her, damn you!"

June cried, "Henry, please...*help me!*" before fainting into a motionless heap on the floor.

Henry slammed the android one more time before kneeling next to June. Her pregnant belly expanded outwards, stretching the material of her jumpsuit into a globe-like shape. It was at this moment he felt the travel-pod cease its downward momentum.

The doors slid open.

At once several beings wearing customary silver jumpsuits grabbed Henry and June by the arms and pulled them out of the pod into a large, brightly lit room. The beings, although much more human than creature, were visibly not of this earth. They stood as bipeds with many features like that of humans but with black eyes slightly too large and slightly too far apart. Their Albino hair was short and identical amongst them, exposed skin on their arms and faces milk-white and translucent. Henry could see dark gray veins tubing across their necks in crisscross patterns.

Henry attempted to break free but the alien holding him was strong and unwavering. Behind a glass partition in the room he could see more humanoid creatures scurrying about, moving back and forth in their silver jumpsuits as the whistle-clicky alien language he'd heard via the damaged android resonated about the room. As June was pulled away and placed on a rolling stretcher, Henry observed the terror in her eyes a moment before a gas mask was placed over her mouth, subduing her into unconsciousness.

"What are you doing to her!!" he screamed, watching in horror as the humanoids tore away her jumpsuit and revealed her distended belly. His mind shouted frantically, memories and judgements whirling about as though caught in a vortex, very slowly bringing forth hints of comprehension and a horrible realization amidst the horrifying situation.

Chroma-Key saved humanity...

...no, they didn't...they destroyed it...they...THEM...these unknown beings who have kept themselves secret for over 200 years...dear God...The Great Spay...it was their *doing...*

Chroma-Key continues to save humanity. You are playing an important role in evolving the species...

...and they rebuilt the human population to their own specifications, on their own terms...and we humans let them do it...I let them do it to me...and June.

Chroma-Key is God...

And yet Chroma Key and its inhabitants—these beings playing God with all humans on earth—could not do anything about what happened next.

June gave birth, but not to anything resembling a human. From her womb crawled a diminutive beast with eyes at its temples that orbited in rheumy-wet sockets as they explored its new world for the very first time. It had a snout like a mole's and lips that would've looked more at home on a tentacle, save for the mucus-coated fangs snapping at the air. It wriggled violently in a puddle of shimmering fish scales, emerging halfway out of the womb as one arm grasped blindly at the air, the other tearing through June's bloated belly and making room for a segmented tail to twist free.

The alien holding Henry released him to assist in the fray, shouts in Alien-speak and English now commingling with one word in common: "Err. Err. Err..." He heard it, over and over, pulling his agonized gaze away from June to a shifting digital image on a nearby wall of a massive spaceship resting above an expanse of gray clouds, tendrils of gray vapor stemming down to what used to be New York City.

An image of the Great Spay: one of its conspiracy theories, doubly proven correct, right before him.

Henry screamed for June as she died giving birth to their son, a single memory from nine months prior skipping endlessly in his brain before a gas mask was placed over his mouth: *As with every Chroma-Key made child, there are slight risks...*

"It is time to visit your son, Henry," the android image on the wall said.

Many months ago, after June had died giving birth, he never expected to ever leave the small accommodation they put him in. But things were different here than in the Family-Zone. Upon waking he was immediately made comfortable, and as time passed was sometimes fed real food outside of bland processed goo he had grown used to while stationed in the Family Zone. Here there were no directives, no glass walls, no punishments. He was permitted to exercise once a day in a rec room, although he had to do it alone. The isolation was harsh, with his last memory of June dying in childbirth haunting him every day and leaving him utterly despondent.

The nights were more difficult, fractured sleep rife with nightmares disrupted by strange animalistic howls and inhuman whoops echoing beyond the walls of his room.

The only thing he looked forward to were the daily visits with his son.

There are rumors of couples entering the Chroma Key facility, never to be heard from again...

The rumors, the conspiracy theories, they were *true*. He still didn't know what this alien race was called, or if they were responsible for humanity's origins...but they appeared two hundred years ago and terra-formed the earth to conform to their species. And at the same time, they altered the course of humanity, for what ends he could only guess.

What he did know for certain was that they were not perfect. Their process, for all its successes *(99.6%)*, was also prone to error...

...*Err*...

An alien arrived and escorted Henry out into the hallway leading to the Err Zone, where the .4% were kept. They passed many doorways like the one he emerged from, behind them people—*fathers*—just like him who once signed on hundreds of dotted lines but were never heard from again. Henry wondered if there were any couples in them but didn't see how any woman could survive a childbirth like June's.

They reached the Err Zone entranceway. The alien peered into a retinal scan and the doors slid open.

Ten feet ahead, behind a clear protective barrier, was a jungle packed with trees and foliage under a faux blue sky filled with sunlight. The Err Zone was massive, not unlike the Family Zone, only this place had no glass homes. It was bursting with possible habitats for the creatures inadvertently created by the alien geneticists at Chroma-Key. The *errors*. He didn't see any of them through the thick foliage, but he could hear them now, roars and chirps and bellows and grunts echoing in the immense chamber.

"Please call my son," Henry asked. He had yet to definitively name the boy-creature, but wittily thought "Errol" to be fitting.

The alien escort, stoic in its movements, passed a hand over a control board outside the barrier. It howled into what could only be a communicator of some sort and then stepped back to monitor Henry's daily meeting with his son.

It appeared from the dense foliage, prehensile tail enabling it to move quickly and efficiently through the trees as it made its excited approach. The creature—Errol, he supposed—was now a much larger version of the thing he saw ripping through June's belly months earlier.

It dropped from the closest tree and scurried on all fours to spend time with its father.

It *knew*. It recognized him. It leaped forward and banged on the clear glass barrier, whistling "daddy" through its suction-cup jaws. And Henry could see amidst all the horrific characteristics it possessed, through the clear intelligence its part-human brain displayed, through eyes that turned blue after a few weeks' time, a slight resemblance to June.

It has her eyes, her cheekbones…

The creature…

…my son…

…stepped back, picked up what appeared to be a coconut, and threw it farther and higher than any human would be capable. It then raced away at an incredible speed, chasing after it.

Athletic ability. That cost me 500 grand.

Tears filled his eyes. He turned and faced the watching alien.

"At least you got something right."

Anxiety

A nxiety exists in everyone. It is a learned talent, like the ability to tap into one's own psyche and draw out an extra-sensory perception proficiency. We thrive on it, allow it to command the very essence of our lives. Succumb to its dark temptations, to the quality of life considered flawed and insufficient. Cognitive Behavioral Analysis, anti-depressants—ways to mask the pain. Still, beneath these shrouds of dependency, anxiety lies blossoming, waiting for the veil to be lifted so that it may once again attack the mind with more determination than ever before.

For some, it's a license for suicide.

For others, euphoria.

Cognitive Behavioral Analysis had proved to be no true practical methodology for Shane Whitcomb's recovery other than offering him the ability to matter-of-factly discuss why he dreaded the world he lived in. His therapy sessions had gone much deeper than that, examining every grain of fear gimmicking with his nerves and mind. In this age of medical dependency where individuals looked high and far for a magic pill to cure all their physical woes, Shane Whitcomb joined the ranks of those spiritless teeterers woefully lining up at the psychologist's office in desperate search for normalcy. A stroke of poor fortune it was that Richard Allis had been the doctor he found.

They had their first session three months ago.

"Good afternoon...I'm Doctor Allis." He did not offer his hand to Shane.

"Hello. Shane Whitcomb."

"What do you do for a living, Shane?"

"I work in Manhattan. Used to, actually. In the Garment Center."

"Sales?"

"Piece goods. I took a temporary leave because of this...this thing."

Allis poured himself a glass of water from a Poland Spring bottle. He looked like the type that drank a lot of liquids, ate fruits and vegetables, exercised. Not a worry in the world other than to keep fit and decide when to fuck his trophy wife. He offered some water to Shane.

"Nothing for me. Thanks."

Allis tasted it as if it were fine wine, seemingly committed to find flavor in its sterility. "You sure? It's cold and good."

"I'm fine." Dumb, Shane thought. The water would have felt nice on his coated tongue. He yawned in effort to catch a deep breath; he prayed he didn't start hyperventilating.

Allis studied his water for a moment, and Shane used this time to observe the man: perhaps twenty years older than his thirty-two. An odd choice for fashion: new boat shoes, khakis, short sleeve button down shirt with vertical stripes. Over it, a tattered sports jacket—its best days long past—draped loosely upon his angular shoulders like a damp bath towel on a door-hook. His face was drawn-out and prosaic, the eyes muddy brown with milky ringlets edging the perimeters, a hint for the need of cataract surgery. Heavy glasses pressed juicy red spots into the skin on the bridge of his prominent nose. Mouth thin, wet from the water. Hair, gray and thinning.

He reminded Shane of a college professor. The office added to that. Three walls lined with texts that could very well have been the same book. And just how did Allis derive his worldly pleasures? Via woman? Man? Child? God? Savvy thoughts, indeed; typical for a man in Shane's sensitized condition.

"I'd like to take some notes. Is that okay?"

"You're the doctor."

Allis nodded. "You should be seeing a psychiatrist."

"Why?"

"First impression tells me you're in need of medication."

Shane hadn't considered this.

Allis droned on. "It's unprofessional of me to make such an assumption. But I see it in your eyes. They're hungry. In need of something influential to quell the turbulent waters."

Odd statement. Was this the doctor's way of trying to appear clever? Shane tried his luck at a grin, but Allis' face remained stoic in his effort to impress.

"You look familiar. You say we've never met?"

"I don't think I said that." Shane began to wonder about Doctor Allis. "I did say that I was never here before. That doesn't mean we've never crossed paths at one time." More silence, the doctor staring, Medusa-like. Perhaps *he* was on drugs? Shane added, "I thought you were going to take notes."

The psychologist grunted, reached into his shirt pocket and pulled out a cigar. He bit off the end and lit it with a Zippo. Not a common maneuver. Doctors didn't smoke in front of patients, did they? Then again Allis appeared to not consider himself a legitimate doctor. Real doctors prescribed medicine for the sickly, not words of encouragement for the needy, so he implied.

He blew out a stream of blue smoke. "I asked if I could. Doesn't mean I will."

Interesting. "Fair. Ball's in your court."

Allis broke his stone face. "Shane, let's talk in generalities for a moment. Mental health. Do you really believe there's anything corporeal in it that will make you feel better?" His voice rang slightly bitter, perhaps even contemptuous.

"Corporeal?"

"Real. Tangible."

"I was hoping so."

"Hmph. I could nurture you with a little Freud, sprinkle it with a dash of Jung and wash it down with a half glass full—or should I say empty—of Weekes. Regardless of the research, you must realize that there's never any true assessment to the complications we suffer in our minds. We therefore choose to rely on choice words to provide us with the will and desire to carry on. But understand this: it's all a sugar-coating. Beneath the rosy layer lies a monster. The devil. To the extreme."

"The devil?"

"Our mental health. It's the devil in disguise. I'm sure you'll soon agree."

"I never really—"

"It's a dog with a happy tongue and waggly tail that'll bite your fucking hand off when you go to pet it."

Shane could only nod in forced agreement. The analogy was harsh, way over his head.

"And when it crumbles, we seek out a prescribed methodology that unbeknownst to us maims us even further. You see, we should be more terrified of our inner mind than of the anxieties forcing us to seek its counsel!"

"Why?" Strangely, Shane was intrigued by the doctor's reckless technique; was this the start of some radical form of therapy?

"Because no one walking this earth is perfectly sane. Deep inside the human mind exists the unbridled potential to snap under pressure. Although we may never reach this grand level, a tiny part of it leaks out in all of us, allowing us a small taste of what it would be like to completely lose your sanity. Hence, anxiety. A sampling of madness. When we seek comfort in the remedies of mental health, we rely solely on the deception of linguistics to soothe our instability, when in fact it still exists flourishing infinitely beneath the weak layer of persuasion we place there."

"The devil in disguise?"

"Exactly!"

"So...is that what we're doing now? Sugar coating the rotten parts?"

Allis smiled, eyes suddenly on fire. "Sure, Shane. We are. Walking hand in hand with the devil. Nurturing it. Hoping it leads us in the right direction."

Interesting. "And which way is that?"

"Toward the things that terrify us, the things we don't understand. To assist us in confronting our fears. Strolling through the dark instead of waiting for the lights to come on."

Shane thought about it. Mental health, cognitive behavioral training: soothing the irreversible acids of insanity so that we may possess the capabilities to face the things that fully terrify us. He was beginning to grasp Allis' roundabout approach. *Anxiety is the fear of fear, mental health a loose companion of fear itself.*

"So, you discuss your intimacies," added Allis. "And provide a blanket of comfort. Unless..."

"Unless what?"

"Unless we eliminate the anxiety."

"How do we do that?"

Allis took a puff from his cigar. The ashes on the end were an inch long.

"We choose to face the devil itself, and kill it."

There is nothing in this world that can compare to anxiety. If it were possible, in a voyeuristic fashion, to read any one individual's mind at any chosen time, their thoughts would flaunt the issue with great profundity. Certainly other more tangible reflections would creep into perspective, such as the current presidential election, the victor in last night's ballgame, the rising prices of gasoline, or simple cogitations initiated by the incessant exchange of pleasantries. But peel away these illusions, and rearing its dreadful head like a disease of the heart, is anxiety. And yet, while the cosmos press on and the nature of all that is universally divine goes fully ignored, human beings unceasingly deliberate over their immaterial pessimisms and tribulations. It happens everywhere: on the job, in the bathroom, while sleeping, while making love. A rite with no true passage repeated like the unavoidable finger picking away at a festering mosquito bite. Our fears. We go back to them time and time again until we no longer maintain any tolerance for them. That's when a life powered through the bitter course of anxiety takes hold.

And that's when we explode.

The next few days for Shane Whitcomb were customary. And then again, they weren't. Casually he went about his newfound business, taking off another week of work, spending a good deal of time cowering under the blankets and suffering true fear with no *real* threat: uncontrollable heart palpitations, tightness in the chest, tingling in his hands, nausea. Like the sun rising, the physical symptoms were there, tormenting.

On the internet he conducted some informal research on Allis. Graduated Harvard Medical, 1978. Full Honors. A pioneer in his field, garnering accolades in his research on Behavioral Psychology.

He found out nothing else, nothing about the *man* that was Dr Richard Allis, Ph.D. That terrified Shane. Yet, it intrigued him; he wanted to understand him. For the first time in months, Shane Whitcomb felt the first twinges of desire.

There are two types of fear: first fear, the subconscious response of the mind upon thinking the body is in danger—that something terrifying and threatening is happening. It forces the individual to take to flight as its only means for survival. Second fear is the shocking notion that such utter discomfort can arise for no observable reason at all.

That opens many, many doorways. Finding the right one is the arduous part.

"Hello there," said Shane.

Allis turned around. His eyes were black, pupils dilated. He'd been thumbing through the psychology section with no purposeful intention, it seemed. Why he was here, Shane could not guess. Didn't he have other clients? Or was this a lunch break?

"I'm sorry if I frightened you."

He looked different, preoccupied. "I was wondering."

"About?"

"About why none of these 'brilliant' men and women have discovered what I have." He swept his arms towards the bookshelf. They began a lengthy conversation. Shane didn't know why he approached Allis in the bookstore; it'd been strange enough to keep his company during therapy. And truthfully, Allis was intimidating. His ceaseless talk of the devil had reached a grand level of complication — a simple analogy blown way out of proportion. Yet still, when Shane sighted him, he wanted more, a taste of the man outside the insipid walls of his office. To find out whether his affinities held any ground beyond the stale, theoretical environment of his chamber.

Thankfully there were no analogies this day, but he did discover more about the man that was Doctor Richard Allis. He looked up to no one, and followed no leaders—political or religious. He appeared unable to discuss or contemplate any subject without pessimism. The extent of his grin went no further beyond a flat unreadable display of pitiless humor, present only when discussing the sad throes of weak-minded individuals fruitlessly tracking their faltering sanities. To Allis, Shane discovered, all that mattered was anxiety, and the joys of exploiting the fear in it.

Shane found it stimulating. He developed an appreciation for the renegade attitude with which Allis dismantled the universal practices exercised in sweetening the ailments of the nervously ill. It had been quite troublesome at first to have him slam Shane's initial perceptions on how to cure his anxiety—Cognitive Behavioral Analysis was a great waste of time. But after five weeks of sessions, the injurious decry of Allis' convictions began to titillate. He had effectively eaten through Shane's sugar-coating to disclose an unsettled state of mental health.

Yes, it scared Shane. But it also excited him. His fear was suddenly free. According to Allis, he could use it any way he chose.

"There is so much more to fear than just fear itself," Allis tenderly emphasized. "You are beyond anxiety and now have fear to guide the way. Do you feel your heart beating faster? Do you feel the adrenaline sucking the life from your endorphins?"

Shane nodded.

"Do you feel the utter unsteadiness of discharging serotonin?"

Shane nodded.

Damn, he did.

Everyone fears. Of thunderstorms, of snakes, of heights, of the dentist, of the future, of failing, of dying. Fear is an internal alarm, a system to alert us of harm's way so we can take self-protection. But some people have powerful fears and anxiety of things or situations that are not immediately dangerous and which take possession of the person's body, mind, feelings and actions.

For most, it is terrifying.

To others, an electrifying exploration into uncharted lands.

Nearly three months into therapy, Shane entered Allis' office and found an attractive woman in her thirties seated on the black leather couch. Anne Devot was another one of Allis' chosen clients, Shane would later discover. Allis initiated an anxiety/fear/mental health discussion in which the three of them listened, argued, and reveled in its fascinating implications. The session continued on for hours with the three of them present. Things grew intense. Shane never knew how long Anne was seeing Allis before their assembly, but it seemed she wanted out by the close of their second group go-around.

"I'm tired of being afraid. This therapy has its intents, but I don't necessarily find answers in its purposes. Isn't there any validity in subjective banishment?"

Shane found pleasure in Anne's sharp appeal for a more affirmative prescription to her anxieties. Presumably she'd thought about it for a while, but never found the opportunity—or guts, really—to ask Allis. Shane thought, *not only is she masturbation-applicable, but she's smart too.* Too bad he didn't have the balls to put a move on her.

"The *only* truth lies in the faculty of our anxieties," Allis replied. "Smell it, taste it, *feel* it. The bittersweet knot in your gut that calls your name and begs you to flee the moment wherever you are." Remarkably influential guy, Allis was, twisting Anne's thoughts back into his own predisposed arena. Pointing out the fallacy in her impulsive notion. He was good.

"It's not helping me."

"Is there no pleasure in your pain?"

"There's only fear and panic and anxiety. And nothing else."

Allis' eyes narrowed. He hesitated, staring at Anne, then said, "You're not telling me everything. You're hiding something."

She stayed still, pointing her gaze to the floor. When she raised it, the slightest sheen of tears coated her brown eyes.

"I'm right?"

She nodded.

"Tell me."

Shane felt uncomfortable. He bit his bottom lip, eyes going back and forth between Allis and Anne Devot.

"You tell *me,*" Anne stipulated.

Allis' face contorted with scorn, as if hit with a blow. "My anxieties are intimate to me!" he shouted. "Nothing you could ever understand! I could very well tell you the things my brain symbolizes as panic, but they're mere words, simple comparisons to the real terrors at the crux of my identity."

The room fell in silence. Shane wanted to talk of his fears, but held back. The session ended with not a single confession.

What happens after one experiences a nervous breakdown? When we can no longer tolerate the panic, the anxiety? Do we die? No, of course not. No one has ever *died from anxiety.*

No one has ever died from their own *anxiety.*

But they have through the command of someone else's.

Women were an enigma to Shane. He never understood their thinking. Conflicting and elusive. Anne Devot possessed these qualities, and it didn't surprise Shane one bit when she didn't show up to their next scheduled rehabilitative triad.

Shane had an odd feeling (by the pompous look on his face) that Allis had been using Anne for some odd, ulterior motive. Perhaps therapy was his initial intent, but her sanity—and Shane's, for that matter—was of no ultimate concern to the good doctor. There was something self-serving in it. Shane wanted to know what it was.

Before he sat down, Allis said, "I was fucking her."

"Anne?"

"Who else?"

"I don't know. You could very well be sleeping with many women."

"She was very passionate."

"So why did you stop?"

"Did I say I stopped?"

Where was this going? "You look...sad. Let down." A guess.

Allis paused, grin pursed with defeat. Front exposed. "She stopped because she was afraid."

"Of what?"

"Her husband."

Shane felt his heart flutter, a knot in his gut. He prayed the anxiety didn't show in his voice; Allis would capitalize on it. "Did he find out?"

Allis shook his head. "No."

"Why was she afraid of him then?"

"Because there would be no hiding that she was pregnant."

Shane's stomach turned. "With your child."

Allis nodded. "Her husband had a vasectomy years ago. She wouldn't have married him otherwise."

Shane was stumped. "Why?"

"She's deathly afraid of childbirth. Even more so of abortion. Anything that has to do with her uterus. An odd and quite distinctive fear, I'd say. Freudian? Perhaps, but quite unique in the sense that we're talking about a woman, purely heterosexual, who would rather die than have something *alive* growing inside her."

"You must've known this before you slept with her."

Allis nodded. "The issue was discussed quite extensively in therapy."

"So why weren't any precautions taken?" Shane, exploring personal territory. And taking a chance.

"Because I wanted to exploit her ultimate anxiety. I wanted to see how she'd handle it."

"Is she...?" He didn't want to imply an adverse reaction to Allis' secretive misdeed.

"She's safe. And she will live."

Shane stared at him as if in a spell.

Allis leaned over. "Shane, it may be time."

"For?"

"For *you* to face the devil, and kill it."

Fatigue, exhaustion, heart palpitations, chest pain, rapid pulse, dizziness, faintness, distorted vision, hyperventilation, aching muscles, cramps, stiffness, irritability, depression, insomnia, nightmares, loss of memory, lump in the throat, nausea, diarrhea, depersonalization, increased sensitivity to light and sound, stiff neck, burping fluids, numbness, tingling, tinnitus, jitteriness, tension, sweating, trembling, facial twitching, frequent urination, apprehension, unwanted thoughts, a fear of going crazy.

The mind is a powerful thing.

Allis crossed the professional line once again, this time by offering Shane to join him in indulgence: Dewar's and sodas, cigars. Then, the sharing of a joint—a sweet mellow cannabis that filled the air, their lungs, their minds, all softened with influence. The drugs, alcohol, it made Allis quite even-tempered, his talk of the devil and anxiety loosening into a comfortable chatter of sex and its pleasures.

"The THC in marijuana bonds to the GABA emitters in the brain, the serotonin producers. It arouses them, thereby increasing more of the pleasure-inducing chemical, elevating our awareness and the level of satisfaction we experience, regardless of the stimulus. When sexual incentives are introduced, the intensity of joy experienced reaches astounding levels, to a point where orgasm seems ecstatically impossible, yet achievably desirable."

After an indefinable amount of time, curiosity got the best of Shane.

"So how *do* we defeat the devil?"

"You wish to gain complete control of your mental health then?"

"I'm highly intrigued as to your motivation, Dr Allis. The whole process that's led me to this point. Surely you don't expect me to back down now?"

"Quite honestly Shane, I've yet to decide if I want to show you how to do it."

"Because?"

"Because it's major-league stuff. Not for the unprepared."

"So you're saying I'm unprepared then?" Allis—clearly exercising his twisted vernacular. All part of the process.

Allis smiled. "No, I'm not.

"Then?"

Allis' eyes were like stone pebbles. "It involves Anne Devot."

"The mother of your child."

"You could say that."

"What about her?"

"She's in the house. Right now. Been here for a couple of days."

"Where?"

"In a room. She's hunting down her devil."

Shane felt giddy, the walls of the room oscillating. He wasn't sure if it was anxiety or the pot. "So...*she* was prepared?"

"She had no choice but to be prepared."

"I'm prepared, doctor. Show me how to kill my personal demons."

Mommy, there's a monster in the closet!

Yes, baby. There is.

Slowly, Allis led Shane upstairs. He spoke of nothing as they moved down a long hallway, past a number of closed doors into a bedroom on the left. The smallish space took Shane by surprise, empty except for a solid pine chair bolted to the hardwood floor. He questioned the purpose of the stark environment.

Silently, sneakily, Allis answered, pressing a cool wet tatter of cloth against Shane's nose and mouth. Harsh vapors seared his nostrils and lungs, burned his eyes, weakening his call for panic. A curtain of blackness seeped into his blurred sights, ran deep into throat and lungs, sending the world into chemical shadow. His heart, pounding in tempo with a rushing headache. Legs turning to sodden tea-bags. He collapsed on the wood floor, saying to himself: *this is no anxiety*.

The abrupt glare of the television screen flashed into Shane's dreamscape—a free-floating world where monsters are willingly defeated by simply thinking their demise—causing him to cast off the final moments of his stupor sooner than he wished. If it were only that easy to stamp out the iniquities of the mind, Shane thought, then the world would be free of the devil and the fears it sheds upon its rightful seed. In a powerless attempt to move he discovered the cool tight grip of metal shackles about his wrists and ankles, link chains connecting them in a marriage of confinement. The sound of the television had yet to be turned on, so it seemed, the chaotic image of static snow enough to convince him that a signal may soon be coming into view.

He was right.

Shane shuddered when he saw the face of Richard Allis on the screen, the loose features telling the tale of a man who at last unearthed a cure to his own anxieties—had defeated the devil, taken command of his own state of mental health. Damn, he was *smiling*, and despite the crisis at hand, Shane had to smirk at the crooked teeth, mussed hair, flushed cheeks. Eyes, wild and black, snake-like. It had taken months, but the doctor had finally broken his stone composure.

The image of Richard Allis spoke, no designation indicated, as if the message could have very well been intended for anyone happening upon it:

"There is indeed a much greater fear than fear itself, of worrying with respect to those things that never happen. Now, the fear of those things that DO happen! That's one damn scary possibility! Be prepared. I am going to make it happen. And when we're finished you will thoroughly understand that anxiety means absolutely nothing at all when the body has something real to be terrified of.

"Can you think of something that really scares the fuck out of a person? I can…"

The screen went back to snow. Shane watched the hectic display until his eyes teared and dried on his cheeks. He squirmed, the restraints tightening as he ineffectively fought their grip.

Time passed. Minutes. An hour. More.

Dizziness tickled his brain; he imagined himself a prisoner on a boat, unable to recapture his equilibrium. Again blackness crawled in from the corners of his sights. If it weren't for another scene on the television blinking into view, he might have surrendered to it.

At first he had trouble theorizing as to where Allis might have concealed the camera, but quickly realized that the image of the person restrained and struggling in the bolted chair was not of himself.

It was Anne Devot.

She wore a stark white tee-shirt that ran long to her knees. Feet naked. Hair tossed and disheveled. Eyes squeezed shut, teeth clenched—a combination of attributes signifying an abandonment of hysterics, a submission to a rational acceptance of predicament. Her spirit had been split open, Allis now prodding and poking it with venomous fingers.

How long did Allis say she was here? A day? More?

Before her was a table. Shane could see a puddle of clear liquid on its surface. In the foreground, on the floor, a plastic tumbler lay on its side. On the wall in the background hung a sheet, red letters sloppily spray-painted upon the white surface:

Is the lesser of two evils the best course of action?

Shane yelled for help, for himself, and then for Anne Devot. But the house swallowed his pleas, and he nearly shouted his voice away until his thoughts ran ragged. What if Allis kept him here forever? Would he die of starvation? His stomach purled at the mere thought of sustenance, and he knew it must've been twenty-four hours since he'd last eaten. Periodically Anne looked directly into the camera, and Shane conjured up a variety of questions. Could she see *him*? Did she know that *he* was watching her? Certainly she assumed Allis to be the voyeur, no? His thoughts fell away like worms, sluggish and slippery, difficult to hold. Nothing steadfast or certain.

With nothing else to do, Shane continued to watch Anne Devot. Her head turned from side to side. Staring at a point beyond the camera's reach. A door?

Time passed.

Anne nodded off and slept for nearly an hour when something startled her stiff. Her eyes darted open and quickly pinned an unseen spot. They followed something across the room until a man wearing a rubber clown's mask came into view. He wiped the spilled liquid from the table with a small towel, then retrieved the plastic tumbler. He filled it with what looked like water, set it on the table before her, then placed a small white pill, oval shaped, next to the glass. In the silence of the scene, Anne's tears returned, her mouth a twisting, soundless barrage of curses. Allis (Shane assumed the masked man to be the doctor) was stoic in his actions, creeping behind Anne to free one hand from its bind. He stood at the side of the view, pointing to the glass—and the pill.

Clearly, Shane realized, *all she has to do is take the pill, and he'll release her.*

But what exactly will the pill do to her?

With her free hand, she knocked the glass over. The contents sprayed the table. The pill dropped unseen to the floor. Shane could see Allis shake his clown head with dismay, ignoring a screaming Anne as he grasped her wrist, twisted it behind her and refettered it.

Then he did something interesting. Sidling up beside her, close to her ear, he must have spoken, and for the briefest moment pointed to the camera. She looked, stared straight into it, tears pouring from her eyes.

She shook her head, slightly, and mouthed the words, *I'm sorry.*

Allis walked to the camera, and the image went back to snow.

Eight hours later, the scene repeated itself. Exactly. Anne refused to take the pill. Allis pointed to the camera before shutting it off.

He never came to Shane's room.

Shane was very hungry.

Every eight hours, like clockwork. Two more days. Anne grew haggard, clearly frustrated. Shane's hunger turned to starvation, the discomfort choking him with bitter acids, then agonizing his gut with pain after the acids dried up. In a semi-hallucinatory state, he couldn't be certain if Allis had fed Anne anything, but he had strong doubts. He wouldn't let her touch the water unless she took the pill; that much was clear. Another day without water and they would both die.

In the next session, Anne took the pill.

This time clown-masked Allis nodded, as if congratulating her accomplishment. He walked from the camera's view, leaving it to catch Anne Devot in the apex of anxiety, crying, tongue swollen and dangling from her mouth like a damaged kidney, body limp with fatigue, hunger.

Anticipation.

An hour later, Shane saw the first droplets of blood. Two stark red spots where the tee-shirt gripped her inner right thigh. More blood came, like water overflowing a sink, running along the front edge of the chair then dripping to the floor, splattering her legs, her ankles and feet. She thrashed, doubled over, face contorted in agony, arms wrapped around her lower abdomen, hiking the shirt up to her hips, revealing the blood and gore between her legs, the pre-birth of her self-aborted fetus oozing out her once sanctified uterus.

The deed completed, the camera went dead.

Allis, mask free, came into Shane's room soon thereafter. Shane used every last bit of energy to peer up at the doctor. "Where is she?"

"Downstairs."

Worrying about Anne's welfare was important to Shane, but secondary to his own destitution at the moment. "She did it for me, didn't she?"

Allis nodded. "I told her you'd starve watching her. Ultimately, she did what she had to do."

"She saved my life."

"Barely."

He wanted the conversation to end. "I need food, water."

"And you shall have it," Allis said. He stepped from the room, only to return moments later holding a small metal saucepan. The thought of nourishment made Shane's mouth water, regardless of—

First he saw the red smears lining the inside edges. He prayed for sauce, raspberries, anything but...but...

Allis said, "Time to kill your devil."

Shane closed his eyes. Allis held the pan down on his lap.

He took a deep breath, and without thinking once of his anxiety, used both hands to feed Anne Devot's abortion into his eager mouth.

There is no greater pleasure than to experience vicariously the anxiety of others.

Richard Allis, Ph.D.

The Alley Man

It was summer and twilight was fading beyond the skyline of the city. Lester wandered into the alley, lungs reaching for air, frayed boots challenging puddles thicker than stew. The world behind him quickly drifted away—the people who brushed by him, the cars that glided by him, the subway trains that awoke him so many times like thunderstorms in the middle of the night.

He stopped and cautiously scanned the area ahead. Long and dark, the alley emulated a looming, forbidden place...a mouth that wanted to swallow him whole. On each side, abandoned buildings towered into the dark star-lit sky, the shattered glass from broken windows high above scattered beneath his feet and beyond. The dead end, only slightly visible in the dull gray moonlight, merged the two opposing structures, creating a menacing impasse to the narrow passage, like the throat of a giant monster. A small green dumpster, mottled with graffiti and jagged patches of rust, hunkered in the far left corner.

Firming his grip on the worn duffle bag he held, Lester set his sights on the dumpster. With no trash overflowing, the reek was bearable; he'd smelled worse in the past. Perhaps this wouldn't be such a bad place to spend the night?

He reached the rear of the alley and noticed a small crevice—about two feet wide—between the dumpster and the wall. *Perfect*, he thought. *It's just perfect*. From here, most of the City's ambience was absorbed into the porous night. It always amazed Lester how peacefully quiet it got between a pair of tall buildings.

"Hey...you...out...there..." The voice was deep and gravely, not loud but carrying a distinct tremor that suggested its owner was angry—that Lester might be invading space.

Lester took a step back, squinted, listened intently. A steady breathing whispered out from the lightless area between the dumpster and the wall. Sensing a pair of eyes on him, Lester tightened his grip on his duffle bag.

"You be tresspassin' on pravit' property!" shot the voice, a little louder than before. Lester brought the bag up and hugged it to his chest with two hands, just in case this sudden and unanticipated encounter turned aggressive. In the distance, the wails of police sirens leaked into the quiet of the alley.

"Where are you?" Lester asked warily.

"This is my home...so you gots to get outta here..." The voice trailed off into a series of sickly gasps and wheezes.

Lester craned his neck, tried to peer further into the shadowy corner. His eyes adjusted to the darkness and he was able to make out the blurred form of someone crouching down. "I'm...I'm just looking for a place to sleep. I'm very tired." He hoped the mysterious dweller wouldn't give him a hard time. This was a "good" alley—quiet, not too smelly, and barely occupied. Most of the alleys in the city were overcrowded and downright disgusting. He would probably get a rare good night's sleep here.

Lester pressed his right hand against the rear brick wall and bobbed his head slightly back and forth in attempt to glimpse the alley man, but darkness still shrouded the unknown inhabitant. He then hunkered down and nestled himself in the opposite corner, eyes glued to the dark crevice. After a few seconds of uncomfortable silence, there was a shuffling, and from amidst damp gloom, a figure emerged.

It appeared to Lester that the alley man had spent a great deal more time on the streets than his own four months. Like Lester, his clothes were tattered and torn. But they were much dirtier, layered upon his body like oily rags atop a service station pump. There wasn't the slightest hint of skin beneath the filth on his face. His hair was a mess of tangled strands. He coughed and a thick stream of mucous shot from his nose into the thatch of moustache and beard covering his mouth.

"You got a name?" the bum gurgled, leaning forward, examining Lester wide-eyed, as if *he* were an oddity.

"Lester." He pressed back, repulsed at the unsightliness of the vagrant. "You?"

The tattered vagrant was silent, eyes darting back and forth between Lester's face and the duffle bag. "Jyro..."

"Huh?"

"The name's Jyro!" He coughed and something purled in his throat, but thankfully nothing showed. "So whattya so quiet about, Lester?"

"Nothing, I..." Nervous, he turned his head away to face the distant street.

Jyro shuffled on his knees, inches away from Lester. Lester could smell God-awful breath on him, a repugnant mixture of whiskey and something rotten. "What's your story?" Jyro asked.

"My story?"

"Yeah, what's brought you down?"

Lester took heed and swallowed hard, half afraid, half nauseated. Perhaps it would be best to talk. No telling what the alley man might do. "Well, I...I used to be a doctor. Up until about a year ago, that is."

Jyro let out a half-laugh, half-snort sound. A little more "stuff" flew out, this time from his mouth. His grunts of amusement quickly skewed into a labored cough.

"Really, I was..." Lester shook his head with frustration.

Jyro stopped hacking, took a few moments to catch his breath. "How long you been on the streets?"

"Four months."

"Ha! A newcomer! Welcome to Hell!" Jyro took his sleeve and wiped the spittle from his mouth.

"You?" asked Lester.

Jyro cut off his laughter almost immediately. His eyes bulged wildly. "Nine years, Lester. Nine years on the street...but your story first!" Again he leaned forward. "What's brung you down?"

"Well, like I said, I was a doctor. A chiropractor. I...I had an affair..."

"Whooo-weee!" Arms waving. More spit.

"...with one of my patients. About two years ago. It all started so innocently. She was just a patient at first, but an attractive one. One day she asked me to lunch. One thing led to another, and, well, it carried on for quite some time after that. But I never told her that I was married. After almost a year of sneaking around, she found out."

Jyro remained eerily silent as Lester continued his sordid tale.

"First she went to my wife, spilled the whole story. That led to a divorce. I lost time with my kids and a good deal of my savings. Then she filed a lawsuit against me. Sexual harassment, misconduct, the whole shebang. I lost the case and was ordered to pay millions to her, which of course I didn't have. As a result, I lost everything, including my practice. I was finished. Eventually I couldn't afford to pay rent, and had nobody to turn to. My family, my friends, they all disowned me. I was disgraced." He looked down, shifted his position a bit. "So here I am now, four months later."

Jyro stood silent, motionless, eyes bulging crazily as he stared at Lester. He leaned forward, face only inches away from Lester's. "That's some tale Lester."

"It's the truth."

"The bitch should see you now. It would make her proud!" Jyro laughed out loud and again the coughs immediately took over. Lester caught another windful of rancid breath before the decrepit vagrant turned aside to finish his hacking frenzy.

When Jyro finally quieted, Lester asked, "So...what's your story? What happened nine years ago that's kept you on the street all this time?"

Jyro's face turned expressionless. The gesture made Lester feel uneasy and troubled. Then Lester then saw a gleam in Jyro's eyes that wasn't there before, a hint of life that shined out from deep within his desolate gray eyes.

Jyro smiled evilly, and said, "Nine years ago, I killed a man, a friend of mine. Sliced his throat wide open. That was after I raped and murdered his wife in his bed. He came home and I was waitin' for him. I walked out his front door that day and I've been hiding here on the streets ever since. I ain't ever killed anyone since then, but I stabbed at a bunch of people over the years to get a hold of some money. I gots to eat, you know."

Lester, his face a sudden mask of sweat, looked up at Jyro, now looming over him. He clutched his weathered duffle bag tightly.

Jyro must have seen this because he asked, "What's in that bag of yours, Lester?" He then reached into the pocket of his tattered jacket.

Lester saw a glint of fiery silver shine out.

A blade.

Oh my god...

Jyro was quick to move. Lester had only a fleeting moment to protect himself, and like a flash the knife slashed across his forearm as he raised it to defend himself. His eyesight blurred. White hot pain assailed his body. He then felt the duffle bag slip from his grasp, and as he gripped his arm in agony saw Jyro hobbling away with all his worldly possessions.

Bleeding badly, he pressed a hand against the wound, but the blood was flowing fast and in no time seeped out from between his fingers.

He heard a commotion.

Not a minute after Jyro sliced and ran, Lester heard that now familiar raspy voice shouting, "He's here, right here at the end of this alley!"

Jyro, still holding Lester's duffle bag, was being escorted back into the alley by two uniformed policemen. Held tightly by each arm, the vagrant was wriggling uncomfortably in their grasp, feet dragging as he tried to keep pace.

"That's him in the corner! Right there! I was jus' sittin' here mindin' my own time when...when this guy right here jus' came over and attacked me. He tried to steal my bag! I had to defend myself! I thought he was gonna kill me, so I had to defend myself! That's what happen, it did!" Blood still seeping through his fingers, Lester stared up at Jyro in utter disbelief. One of the policemen asked Lester, "Is this what happened?"

Lester was silent first, then, still staring at Jyro, said, "Yes, it's true. I tried to steal his bag."

At first Jyro's face went blank with confusion. Then a gap-filled smile appeared. "That's right! You see! I had to defend myself!" he yelled, twisting his head back and forth, spit flying everywhere.

One of the policemen grabbed the bag from Jyro's grasp. "So what's in here, old man?" he asked Jyro.

Jyro sneered viciously at Lester. Lester sat silent, gazing back at the lying thief with disdain.

"Everything I got, that's what." Jyro answered.

Lester grinned at Jyro as the cop unzipped the bag.

The sneer quickly left Jyro's face as a pair of handcuffs were slapped on his wrists. "Hey what the…"

He twisted around to look at the open duffle bag.

Stuffed inside were the severed body parts of a woman who once had an affair with her chiropractor.

The Potato

"When's mom coming home?" I asked, biting my bottom lip.

Dad patted me on the back. "You know she won't be home until late tonight. C'mon, sport. I'll let you ride in the front seat."

Mom works as a reporter for the city papers. When she has a deadline, she usually stays late, and each time dad and I do something special. This time I'd been hoping for a trip to the amusement park, or even the library. But with all the talk about the potato Old Man Jessup had grown on his farm, Dad had other plans for us.

"She'll be mad."

Dad laughed. "I promise not to tell if you don't."

I reluctantly slid into the front seat and buckled up.

"You know, it's supposed to be the size of a small car," Dad said excitedly, pulling away. "At least, that's what your mother says."

Mom has been to the farm three times already, taking pictures of the potato and interviewing Old Man Jessup for the story she's been working on.

Dad whistled as he drove. I rode in silence, gazing out the window, watching the trees zip past. Autumn leaves colored the landscape, falling from the trees like confetti. Soon the trees thinned out and the plowed farms took over, extending colorlessly as far as I could see.

Finally, I asked, "How'd he grow it so big?"

Dad turned right onto a dirt road. A rotting wooden sign up ahead said: JESSUP'S POTATO FARM, the letters etched in black. "Mom said he uses a special fertilizer, one he makes himself."

We shook along the dirt road until a small gravel lot came into view. Three cars and a pickup truck were parked along a worn wooden fence, next to an open gate that led into the fields. To the right was Old Man Jessup's house. It looked haunted, with broken shingles, dangling shutters, and cracked windows. A rotting scarecrow stood crookedly alongside the rusted mailbox at the foot of the steps.

Dad got out and walked toward the fence, looking out to the fields. "C'mon, sport. What are you waiting for?"

I climbed out and stretched under the cool October sun. A horrible stench filled my nose. "Ugh…what's that smell?"

Dad smiled. "Probably the main ingredient in Old Man Jessup's fertilizer: cow manure."

My stomach felt suddenly queasy.

I looked at the old, two-story farmhouse. *I bet there's ghosts inside*, I thought, then squeezed my eyes shut, cursing my overactive imagination.

"What's wrong, sport?"

"This place is creepy."

"And it's also going to be very popular." Dad leaned down next to me and placed a hand on my shoulder. "When mom publishes her story about the potato, people will come from miles around to see it."

"Why do *we* have to see it?"

"Because it'll mean a lot to mom if we do. She's been working on this story for almost two weeks."

I frowned. "Joey Carlton told me that Old Man Jessup boils squirrels and feeds them to his sick wife Emily."

Dad laughed. "Joey Carlton's right about one thing. The farmer has a sick wife named Emily. But he doesn't feed her boiled squirrels."

A young couple with matching denim jackets emerged from the gate. Both wore crooked smiles on their faces.

"So is it really as big as everyone says?" Dad asked.

"Huge," the girl replied. "But hold your noses. The thing *stinks*."

"C'mon, champ. Let's go check out how big this potato really is."

We entered the farm through the gate, following a hardened path along rows of potato mounds nearly a foot high. The rows disappeared into the distance, thousands of potatoes attached to the roots beneath them.

I wondered aloud, "How come there's only *one* giant potato, dad?"

"Well, I suppose Old Man Jessup only wanted one. Think about it. If there were a whole field of giant potatoes, they wouldn't be very special, would they?"

"Billy Holliday from Mr. Guthrie's seventh grade science class saw it last weekend, said it was as big as a cow."

"Really?"

"Yep. And Aubrey Jarvis told me during recess yesterday that it was as big as the Jolly Green Giant's turd. Said it looked like it too."

Dad laughed. "That Aubrey thinks she's funny, doesn't she?"

I nodded, swallowing a lump in my throat.

We approached a small group of people gathered about ten feet to the right of the path. The smell grew even worse as we stepped into the field. I held my nose, but could still taste the awful odor, manure and...something else. Something *rotten.*

"Over here, folks," a raspy voice called.

I recognized Old Man Jessup from a photo mom had taken of him. In the picture he'd been standing next to the giant potato, just like he was now, wearing mud-stained overalls, a quilted flannel shirt, and a straw hat that sat crookedly upon his head. His skin was all brown and wrinkly, like a crumpled lunch bag that had been smoothed out.

I glanced at the potato.

Wow. It *was* huge.

I suppose if the Jolly Green Giant had dropped a turd, then it would look just like this. It was about as long as a cow, and as tall as my shoulder. Fat too. The skin was coated with dark mud (or manure), and a number of huge gnarly eyes protruded from it, like comic book zombie hands rising from the grave.

A terrible chill seized the back of my neck.

The old farmer spoke, his expression cold and grim: "I'm guessing it weighs about a ton, but could be more."

"How'd you do it?" a teenage boy I recognized from town asked.

"Secret's in the fertilizer. When you farm all day long, you have a lot of time to think. Eventually I came up with an idea of how to feed my crops, and make them grow. So I tested it on this here potato. Used a bit too much, I guess." He laughed.

My dad asked, "Do you plan to make more giant potatoes?"

"Naw," the old farmer said. "One's all I need."

At that moment, the wind picked up, sending a cold chill down my spine. Dark clouds seeped in over the sun, darkening the fields.

For a moment I thought I saw the large, claw-like eyes of the potato move.

I gasped.

Old Man Jessup looked at me with his dark scarecrow eyes.

"Something wrong, young man?"

"Well, uh, the eyes. They look like hands. And...and I thought I saw them move."

Everyone laughed. Everyone, except the farmer.

Dad rubbed my shoulder. "My son has a very active imagination."

"I'm sure he does," the farmer said, still staring at me.

Afterward we went to Dairy Queen, but I didn't have much of an appetite. I only managed to choke down half my ice cream cone. The stink of the farm and the monstrous potato had seeped into my clothes and skin, and was turning my stomach.

Dad was pretty impressed with the potato, though. Couldn't stop taking about it, in fact. He was probably just excited about mom's story, which he said might be published nationally, and if so, would make us a lot of money.

Speaking of mom, she didn't make it home for dinner. Dad called her office, but all he got was her voicemail.

"She must've hit some traffic on the way back," he said. "Either that, or she's trying to finish up her story."

"Sure..." I replied quietly, thinking only of Old Man Jessup's giant potato.

I woke in darkness, gasping, terrified. I dreamt of the potato. In my nightmare it had come to life, crawling on its claw-like eyes out of the field and through the woods, all the way to my house, where it pounced my mom as she arrived home from work.

I heard a scratch at the window.

I screamed.

Dad came running into my room. "What is it, champ?"

"The-the potato, Dad. It's out there, trying to get in."

"The potato? C'mon kiddo, did it really creep you out that much?"

"Yes. Where's mom? Is she home yet?"

I saw Dad's face pale. "Not yet." He looked at the digital clock in my room, which read 10:15. It wasn't unusual for her to come home this late when she was finishing up a story. But Dad still looked a bit concerned. "She should be home soon."

Something thumped against the window.

Both Dad and I jumped. Tears of fear filled my eyes. "See?" I cried. "The potato. It's out there!"

Dad peered at his reflection in the glass, then cupped his hands against the window. "Stay here," he said.

"Where are you going?"

"To see what that noise was."

"Was it the potato? Was it?"

Dad laughed. "I don't think so. Probably a raccoon. I want to make sure it's not rummaging through the garbage pails."

I leaped from bed and followed him through the living room. He opened the front door and put on the porch light. "Wait here, buddy. I'll be right back."

I didn't want him to leave me.

He rubbed my messy hair and went outside.
He never came back.

After three minutes, I peeked through the door. After five, I cracked it open and called for him. When he didn't answer, I put on my jacket and sneakers—which looked and felt odd with my pajamas on—then grabbed a flashlight from the coat closet and stepped out onto the porch.

I was trembling uncontrollably, never more scared in my life. If my dad—and maybe my mom—had been captured by the monster potato, then they would need my help.

In the distance, in the moonlit woods at the side of my house, I heard a grunting noise.

"Dad!" I screamed.

I ran down the porch steps, and without stopping, raced into the woods. There were sounds up ahead, twigs snapping, leaves rustling. I kept on running, following the flashlight's beam, dodging trees and sidestepping thorn bushes, my mind conjuring up images of the monster potato, its many claw-like eyes clutching my father, shoving him under its massive bulk (*weighs about a ton*, Old Man Jessup had said). Rolling over him. Crushing him.

I emerged from the woods.

Chilly foul wind blew in my face.

Oh no...

Old Man Jessup's rickety house stood a hundred feet away.

The lights were on inside.

I clicked off the flashlight, and with trembling legs, scurried across the back yard to the door at the side of his house.

I peeked through the cracked window.

And saw my mother.

The potato, I thought. *It did get her. I was right.*

She was in a chair, bound and gagged, struggling to free herself. I heard a man's shout, and then a grunt. Biting my bottom lip, I was about to open the door, but stopped as Old Man Jessup staggered backwards into the room.

Oh no!

His hands were tucked beneath my father's armpits.

I saw my mother's face cringe. Tears sprouted from her eyes.

The farmer dropped my father's body down onto the wooden floor.

Deep red blood stained his hair.

Oh no! My parents were in big trouble...and it was up to me to save them!

But what could I do? I couldn't just walk in there!

Everything felt like a nightmare. This couldn't be real! But it was real, I knew, and I immediately stepped away from the door, running to the detached garage as quickly as I could, guided solely by the light of the bright white moon. Here, I hoped, I could find some sort of tool to protect myself—to use as a weapon against Old Man Jessup.

The double doors to the garage were open, and I slipped inside.

Pale light beamed in from the broken windows above, allowing me to see Old Man Jessup's pickup. Behind the tailgate was a huge steel basin, much bigger than a bathtub, probably used to feed livestock. Next to the tub was an old gas-powered forklift, used for moving bales of hay. Then I noticed a few empty bags of cement mixture a few feet away.

I turned the flashlight back on and glanced into the huge basin. It was lined with a dark, dried substance, as dark and smelly as the potato in the field. Cement, and manure. *And the tub is about as big as the potato itself.*

Wait a second...

And in the same shape.

I gasped.

Holy crap! The potato wasn't real! It was made of cement!

Upon closer inspection, I saw that there were streaks of blood in the dark substance. For a fleeting moment, I thought back to when I first saw the big potato, how the eyes had looked like claws.

Oh my god...

Not claws. *Hands. Feet. Arms...*

I located a tire iron next to the basin, and traded the flashlight for it. It, like the basin, was caked with cement—clearly the farmer had used this to stir his mixture.

Then I noticed that it was also stained with blood.

No...

Heart pounding, blood pumping, I slipped back out of the barn and raced toward the house.

I looked through the window.

My parents were still there, Mom bound to the chair, Dad writhing on the floor, his head wound leaving streaks of blood on the linoleum.

Old Man Jessup had his back to the window. He was busy with something on the kitchen counter.

I zipped around to the front of the house.

Heart slamming, I placed a hand on the doorknob, turned it. Open.

I slipped inside.

The house was hot and humid, despite the cool temperature outside. It smelled faintly of the foul odor in the fields. I paced across the living room, the floorboards moaning beneath my sneakers.

I heard a groan up ahead. A shuffle. A clang. I held my breath, listened.

A thump.

I stepped forward, gripping the tire iron, hoping and praying to get the first blow in. *This is crazy*, I told myself. I'm going to get myself into trouble too. As I reached the end of the hallway and peered into the kitchen, I saw that I had a chance.

Old Man Jessup was still standing with his back toward window. From where I stood, off to his left and slightly behind him, he couldn't see me.

He was holding a small hatchet.

On the butcher block before him was a squirrel's hide. Joey Carlton was right.

Only once I took a second look, I realized it wasn't a squirrel's skin.

It was a hairy hunk of scalp.

My father's scalp.

"I suppose one potato isn't enough after all," the old man said to my father, who along with my mother still hadn't seen me yet. "I guess, now, I'll be needing *three*." He laughed.

"You madman," Dad shouted groggily from the floor. "What have you done here?"

The farmer grinned crazily. "I really hadn't planned on Emily's grave falling off the truck. Or should I say, grave *stone*?" He laughed again, chopping the scalp in half. "Fell right out of the tub I made it in. Figured I'd just leave it in the field—easier than burying it."

Oh my god! Old Man Jessup had killed his wife, then chopped up her body and mixed it with cement in the steel basin.

I stepped into the kitchen, tire iron raised. I wasn't all that strong of a kid, but I was sure I could inflict a good deal of pain if I hit him with it.

Old Man Jessup spun. Saw me. Bared rows of creepy yellow teeth. His scarecrow eyes were dark and savage. Hay-like hair fell in tatters about his wrinkly face.

"Make that four!" he screamed, lunging at me, hatchet raised high.

I whirled away, toward my mom, who was screaming now. Dad struggled vainly to move across the floor.

I slipped on a wet patch and fell to my knees.

The old farmer, unable to move very fast, also slipped on the wet patch—my father's blood—and collapsed on top of me.

Just as I held the cement-coated tire iron up.

The old man howled as the tire iron sunk deep into his stomach.

I cried as his blood poured out, all over my trembling hands.

It went like this: Old Man Jessup had cracked. His wife Emily had grown sicker and he'd lost the strength of mind to take care of her. So he killed her, using the same tire iron I eventually used to kill him. As

I'd guessed, it had been his idea to cut her up and hide her in a block of cement before burying her in the fields. But he hadn't planned for her grave—the potato—to slide off the truck in the field.

Before he had a chance to move the forklift into the field, my mother—doing a story about our town's farmlands—saw what she thought was a giant "potato" and told Old Man Jessup he'd stand to make a pretty penny if she could write a story about it. At first he agreed.

Then the cement dried. But not all the way through. And parts of Emily Jessup began rising to the surface, creating "eyes" on the potato. Old Man Jessup knew that if a lot of people started coming to see the potato, someone would notice the eyes weren't really eyes at all. That's why he kidnapped my mom. To stop her from writing the story.

When I made the comment about the eyes looking like hands, Old Man Jessup saw me as a threat too, and came to get me. Only Dad had interrupted that plan, and got himself a too-close haircut that for weeks made him look like, well, Mr. Potato Head.

To this day, I still lie in bed at night, my overactive imagination frightened of the noises in the woods outside my home.

Sometimes I can still smell the ghostly stench of manure and Emily Jessup's dead body floating from the farm her husband failed to bury her in.

And we *never* serve potatoes at dinner anymore.

11:11

The APB came over at 11:11.

It was so frighteningly ironic. You see, I have always considered that time as the witching hour, forever wondering as to how many evil misadventures befall at exactly that moment. I have also regularly queried myself as to why 11:11 is repeatedly observed by chance; it seems that many a subtle glance at the clock reaffirms the most wicked moment in time. Now, you may ask if I've witnessed evil at every instance of 11:11 encountered. My answer to you is no, not in the past, I have not. Not once.

But this time, this 11:11, I did, and it was fated for me.

I was summoned to investigate an unusual circumstance at what I call "the crossroads", that is Waters and Johnson streets, a truly infamous intersection in a loathed section of town where crime is rampant and disease and poison dictate a lifestyle that runs amok amongst the inhabitants.

At the northeast corner of the crossroads sits the James housing project. It is a sad excuse for shelter and the origin from which the complaint came. A resident there reported a foul smell emanating from one of the apartments.

The "neighbors" did not associate with one another unless there was a dispute over money, food, or drugs. Only death would cause them to notice one another in a light other than hate. I was certain that this foul odor was a death, unquestionably a murder, and that those living around it hopelessly wished it away for they did not need another premonition of their own ultimate forthcomings.

And it was not a recent departure—that I was also convinced of, for if an unpleasant smell in that environment provoked the residents there to grumble, it most certainly would have to overpower the dense putrescence presently flourishing in the air.

I arrived at the tenement at 11:23. I was alone and should have called for backup, but this was my time, my 11:11, and I did not want to burden another to endure the ordeal predetermined for me.

Comfortlessly, I got out of my car, shut the door behind me and faced the exterior of the building. Within the light of the full moon splaying upon the intimidating structure, I sighted empty eyes gazing at me through broken windows, like hungry wolves in the night stalking their prey, seeking hope for one more night of survival.

Peering straight ahead I ignored the jackals and ambled prudently along the littered cracked pavement leading into the ominous moon-shadow of the building. Soon after, I set foot through the graffiti-embellished entranceway.

My footsteps echoed in the hallway like the sound of water dripping in a cavern, the cadence of my stride periodically interrupted as my shoes sliced through garbage and grime. Bacteria and germs thrived within the humid, malodorous atmosphere, creating a milieu that rang the dinner bell for any rats and cockroaches nearby.

Apartment 7A, the scene of the crime. There were eight floors in the building. The small elevator was waiting for me on the ground floor and I entered. I managed to find the button for the seventh floor amidst the multiple layers of urban art, and depressed it. The car slowly rattled up, shaking loudly. I feared that it was going to give way at any moment and crash down, leaving me abandoned, helpless upon the ground, the scavengers soon helping themselves to my belongings, the perverts surely violating me.

The elevator came to a halt on the seventh floor and the doors opened. I came into view of a young girl, maybe fifteen or sixteen years of age, seated on the darkened hallway floor opposite the elevator. She was bathed in filth and rottenness. Her glazed eyes contemplated me and no attempt was made to hide the needle positioned in her left hand.

Then the stench hit me.

I wanted to vomit.

It was very bad, the unmistakable reek of death.

"You come about 7A?" the girl slurred, drool commingling with the white curds of foam that had accumulated in the corners of her sore ridden mouth. "She's dead in there. Ya smellit? And she got twins, two babies, but they ain't cried no more."

I looked at her pitifully. "How long has it smelled like this?" I asked.

"Dunno … long … time." She shut her eyes and passed out, her hand still firmly gripping the needle like a napping child holding its bottle.

Room 7A. Three doors to the right. I moved sluggishly down the hall, the violent stink of death thick, assaulting my senses in such a way that I could taste it. Oh, something seemed different, it felt very wrong, and I feared for the worst as I, step by step, came closer to the door of death.

My career in the force has yielded me the misfortune of death firsthand on a few occasions, but this was different, a death that was meant for me to experience; to hold, touch, and caress. To feel the cold within, to live the rest of my life with this moment of death as my brother, my personal agony, my obsession.

My 11:11.

I placed my right hand on the knobless metal door and pushed. Locked. I knocked. No answer. With no other alternative, I pulled out my gun and stood a few feet back. Shaking nervously, I fired at the lock. The shot reverberated throughout the tenement like the National Anthem at a ball game. I looked around and saw that no one had come to investigate from their rooms. Gunshots are commonplace here and decidedly ignored by those behind the safety of locked doors.

I placed my left hand on the door and pushed.

Still warm from my gunshot, it creaked open.

It was at this moment that I recalled what the teen-age junkie in the hall had said.

"She got twins. Babies."pWhat was I going to find? Three dead bodies, one big one and two little ones; small humans, sprawled, decaying next to their mother's body, their futile quest for love and nourishment long abandoned, willingly turning to death as a means for quietude?

I readied my gun although I knew that all crimes here had already been long committed. I looked around. The apartment was in complete disarray, but burglary could not be assumed for most living quarters in the tenement looked like this. The living area was devoid of the source of the smell, leaving me just one more room in the tiny flat.

I grasped my stomach and stopped to choke back a second wave of nausea as the syrupy fetor of rotting death violated my senses even further.

I needed to get this over with and go on with my life.

Trying to ignore the thick aroma filling my lungs, I walked three steps to the doorless frame of the bedroom and went inside.

First I saw the feet. Two milky pedals protruding from the far side of the bed, the toes black and green from decomposition; the remainder of the body was hidden from view. One step closer revealed more of the corpse, up to the calves. Another step, blackened knees. One more, death white thighs, swollen and discolored in blotches. The body appeared to be nude.

Then, I heard something.

On the floor, in hiding with the upper half of the torso, a whimper.

I stopped, afraid to investigate further. My heart stammered, and I prayed for peace of mind after this was all over. I listened. Quiet. Utter silence. I convinced myself that it was an envisioned sound, an unrealistic, subconscious hope for life amid death.

But it was not my imagination, nor unrealistic, for I heard it again and recalled for the second time that the woman had twin babies. Could they still be alive?

I held my breath and walked around the side of the bed to view the rest of the body. Shock gripped me and held on tight as the sight before me nightmared its way into my line of vision and toyed with any residuum of sanity I had left. An anomaly so bizarre, so grotesque, I had trouble deciding if it was an act of God or the work of the Devil.

The woman lay dead, the pale white of her skin scourged with patches of black and green. Six bullet holes riddled her upper chest, their circumferences spreading wide with decomposition. Her mouth and eyes were open, a last emotion of fear forever frozen in time.

Nestled at her side were her babies, their faces and bodies splattered in many shades of red.

Still alive.

At that dreadful moment one of the babies crawled atop the body and began to suckle one of the gunshot wounds in its parent's chest, burrowing its entire mouth and nose into the diseased flesh. The dead woman's breasts were flattened and pale, devoid of all nutrition.

The other turned its head and contemplated me with blackened eyes, and I could see, *feel* only despair and insanity impressed on the babe's bloodstained face.

Dear God, it was all too obvious to me. The nurslings survived by feeding on their dead mother's blood.

I radioed for help. Immediately after, I vomited.

Paramedics attended to the babies while police and detectives questioned, answered, and contemplated.

A paramedic walked by me and I grabbed his leg. He looked down at me, a surprised look on his face.

"How long?" I asked.

"Excuse me?"

"How long has she been dead?"

"Well ..." he said, "I can't say for sure right now, but it looks like a week to ten days."

I never mentioned that I had witnessed the infants' act of survival instinct. The mystery remains to everyone as to how they survived all that time.

The following day, the Captain sat me in his office for questioning regarding my find. I seated myself in front of his desk, prepared for a tedious session of detective formalities and paperwork, anticipating his first question and my answer for it.

"At about what time were you called to investigate?" he asked.

"11:11."

The Juggling Jester's Final Appearance

Myron "The Juggling Jester" Higginbottom scowled at the black-and-white film playing on the smudged, thirteen-inch screen in his trailer. *It's a wonderful life, my ass.*

He peered guardedly around the cluttered space, then, using the flat end of a makeup brush handle, crushed the forty-milligram Oxy Crazy Javi sold him on the worn Formica counter. *It's got a lickable surface.* A third of Myron's paycheck went into Javier's pocket...that talentless taco who less than a year ago had swum naked across the Rio Grande and, without even the clothes on his back, eluded border patrol and manipulated his way into the dim limelight Big Man Charlie's Traveling Little-Top proffered to small-town crowds across America. Fucking guy couldn't hold a candle to the Juggling Jester in his prime! But that was then, and the Universe thought otherwise now, and continued to pay Crazy Javi off handsomely while Myron gazed emptily from the sidelines, his days of juggling knives in the spotlight bowing out to tossing rubber baseballs to rhesus monkeys, his once-revered position center stage bottled-up in Crazy Javi's rapidly growing shadow.

"This used to be *my* trailer," Myron grumbled, peering over his shoulder at Javier (who, in addition to the Little-Top limelight, also procured half of Myron's living space) before snorting the grainy powder into his right nostril (the left used to be his go-to before it started snotting blood). He washed it down with a few swigs from the pint of Wild Turkey he kept in his duffle bag, then locked eyes with

Javier and expelled a long, whispery, unpleasant *ahhhhhhhhh* right in the migrant's face.

"You remind me of this all the time, Cabron," Javier replied, slowly and with a prickly snicker. The trailer used to have a star on the door, and Myron's name used to surround it, *Myron the Juggling Jester Higginbottom*, before the star fell off and the letters peeled away, leaving room for Charlie the Little-Top bossman to sticker *Crazy Javi* on it in giant, shiny gold decals (undoubtedly nicked from some South Texas Dollar General).

Myron would never forget what the greasy pigman had said: "Javi is funny, *Mo-ron*, and he's half your age. No boo-boo-fingers to cry like a man-baby about." Big Man Charlie twirled his handlebar moustache, snapped his threadbare suspenders, then retrieved a spit-soaked cigar from his shirt pocket and shoved it in his mouth. "And Javi's getting half your pay, take it or leave it!"

He took it. Right on the chin. And in the balls. And he kept on taking it, like a champ, a chump, both in and out of the spotlight. He struggled without success to ignore his Mexican adversary, thought about reporting him to the authorities, but didn't even know where to start. Myron Higginbottom could do nothing but long for a gift from the heavens—*anything from anywhere*—to help bring back a fragment of his former splendid self...a means to eliminate the pain: years of Little-Top mishaps resulting in broken ribs, sprained ankles, torn ligaments, and open wounds, all heartily challenging his body's rapidly deteriorating healing response.

And now: younger, funnier, healthier Javier.

Myron belched loudly, declaring his agonies to be "nothing a little toot can't fix." He sniffed loudly, pinched his nostrils, then wiped away the mucus-y discharge with his tattered sleeve before peering dead-eyed at his withering reflection, soon to be hidden beneath the daubed guise he'd worn nearly thirty years. His security blanket, thank the good lordy-Jesus he still had that!

He applied the white grease base, not as smoothly as he often did, but in clumpy layers, heavy uneven streaks on his brow and neck that looked *just fine* to his Oxy-cloaked eyes. It wasn't an easy feat, night after night, getting the makeup just right. Not that it mattered, of course; no one gave a shit what Myron the Juggling Jester was supposed to look like. And the crowds. In just the last year, *fuck the economy*, they'd thinned to scraps, just like the hair on his head, once full and hearty, now dispersed into diminished clumps. The Little-Top would soon become the No-Top if things didn't pick up soon. Myron knew it, and so did greasy pigman Charlie who, doubly impressed with Javier's acrobatic skills, wetback or not, hired him to take over Myron's place center stage.

The Little-Top was *always* on tour, south in the winter, north in the summer, small town to small town Monday through Wednesday, set up on Thursday (rain or shine), with shows running all weekend long, provided the local yokels saddled up their Durangos and showed up. Myron again wondered how he could possibly keep up now that Crazy Javi was running foolish circles around him. Years of injuries had slowed him to molasses, helped only by his new addiction, credit to friend and foe all rolled into one. *Rolled up like a stinking burrito*, he added to his jumbled thoughts, peeking over at *It's a Wonderful Life* and the black-and-white murk clearing the way for Clarence's note to George inside Tom Sawyer: *Remember, no man is a failure who has friends...*

The Mexican is my friend. If he hadn't come through with the Oxy, I'd be six feet under now. Bet your rubber nose on that...

He applied red greasepaint on his lips and cheeks in wrathful splotches, jagged with no attention to contour or detail. On splotched the green around his eyes, used in the past to accentuate, now to inadvertently alarm—draw attention to the man he'd become in this moment, slate Oxy-cleaned of airs and postures, the empty-headed routine he'd clung to all through the years snuffed out. It was time for Myron "The Juggling Jester" Higginbottom to shine, to put his real self out there for today's world to bear witness to.

He shifted his bulk, the creaking barstool beneath him meant to fit a man in shape. The bones in his knees and back howled, graveyard hounds, near-unbearable pain resounding across pneumatized bone and threadbare muscles. He needed *more*. Now. He could hear them.

People, shuffling into the tent, draft-beer voices and Timberland footfalls packing the bleachers. His heart began to pound, gummy blood erupting in and out of it, a compressed stress-ball bubble. An audience! Worry rained down on him, *deluged* him. The first pill hadn't kicked in yet! Or maybe it did? Oxy worked diabolically, *greedily*, gripping the user's nervous system like sharp, puckering tentacles.

"Hey wetback...got any more candy?" He couldn't face his frenemy and retched at his own monstrously colored reflection instead. Javier's response was silent...but satisfactory, red satin fingers gifting a pearl-white pill upon the chalky, countertop residue: a lifesaving buoy in an ocean of desperation.

"Pay me after the show," Javier said. "I need to finish getting ready. It's almost showtime." He disappeared behind the sheet-acting-as-a-curtain separating their lives.

Myron didn't thank him, and instead hastily crushed the pill into a gritty powder and shored it up his nose. With no second thought, he licked the countertop clean, then washed away the bitter taste with three more gulps of Wild Turkey. In this moment of bodily vandalism, Javier billowed through the curtain donned in full-on gear, a brand-spanking-new, exploding-with-primary-colors costume, it too conceivably pinched from some small-potatoes mom & pop shop. A string of drool descended from Myron's gaping mouth, red-stained and quivering undetected as he gazed in jealous awe at the Mexican's finely applied makeup. Fucking migrant had mad juggling skills, the dexterities of an athlete, and just look at that top-notch paint job, completed in mere minutes: a scary-slash-funny amalgamation that would in some way, Myron knew, enrich every emotional role he shifted into.

As Javier exited the trailer, the crowd noise *loud*, Myron brushed a few more unconventional colors on his face: olive drab, pumice, sienna brown. A massive turd at once appeared in the mirror before him, something King Kong might shit out: a warped bastardization of his former guise. But...pill number two, plus all that extra goodness on the countertop, and shots four through six, were all starting to make his reflection look good. As good as The Juggling Jester in his prime.

Maybe even better. It was as if Myron had somehow retained Javier's fine makeup skills to produce the best possible version of The Juggling Jester.

Look at me! I look just like I did thirty years ago! Young! Full of vigor! And that paint job, wow! Watch out Javi...here I come!

Finally, fucking *finally*, Myron Higginbottom felt good, great even, just like he did all those years ago. He smiled at the perfection smiling back at him from the mirror, brimming with a level of confidence he hadn't felt in years.

Good enough, and confident enough, to start juggling knives again.

He donned his curly blue wig and cockscomb hat, ineffectively wiped the sweat and makeup from his palms on his costume, then winked at the young, healthy, handsome clown staring deceitfully back at him from the mirror.

Showtime.

The bannerlike stripes of the Little-Top tent whipped in the breezy air, giant ribbons snapping at Myron as he made his approach across the dirt field. His eyes burned and he rubbed them, ruddy swirls of makeup dyeing his hands gray, painting the whites of his eyes red and black. He moved through clown alley, listening to the crowd applauding, screaming "Crazy Javi" in unison as the migrant juggled bowling pins atop a unicycle. Burp and Hiccup, the Littleman Twins, were performing mini-cartwheels around Javi as he adeptly circled the ring.

Myron opened the rusted storage locker filled with supplies and grabbed six rubber baseballs. He gave them a practice juggle without fault. Brimming with confidence and feeling no pain, he peeked out at the crowd. His heart galloped. Wow! The audience was huge for the Little-Top: a few hundred people packed the bleachers shoulder-to-shoulder like hardcovers on a bookshelf. It'd been years since "The Juggling Jester" performed before a crowd this big.

And the painkillers! They were finally doing their magic! He felt happier than ever, super-thrilled to be—

...in an altered state of mind...

—the performer he once was, looking and feeling great, brimming with confidence, God-bless Oxycontin, God-bless Wild Turkey. A celebrated entertainer who regaled crowds night after night, juggling six knives at once and never once injuring himself...until the day he did. Only then did greasy pigman Charlie demand he switch to something he couldn't lose a finger doing. *It's either that, or sayonara Moron. Your choice.*

Without second thought, Myron shelved the baseballs and trotted unsteadily back to his trailer. Fuck the baseballs, and fuck those stinking monkeys! Pain? What pain? It was *gone*, unmistakable now that he was hunkering down and rifling under his bed in search of the burlap satchel there, inside, six matching chef's knives, props once an integral part of his performance. He washed them in the sink, nicking his ring finger and not feeling it all: the pain nor the trickle of blood that mixed into the makeup on his fingers. He tied the satchel with the knives to the end of a broomstick, then shouldered the bindle hobo-style and wobbled effortlessly back through clown alley.

Javier was still on the unicycle, but instead of juggling bowling pins, he was now blowing an airhorn, Myron's cue to hit the ring. The skit they'd practiced had Myron juggling six baseballs while Crazy Javi circled him, trading them two at a time. It was a crowd-pleaser everywhere they went, and an ideal lead-in to Myron's comical one-clown-two-monkey routine.

Myron took a deep breath, ready, willing, and feeling able. *Thank you Oxy and thank you Wild Turkey, that match made in reprobate heaven.* He promenaded into the ring, waving his makeshift bindle-full-of-sharp-surprises like a war flag, catching Javier's face as it went from grins to grimaces, greasy pigman Charlie on the sidelines, scowling his disapproval at Myron's unexpected improvisation. The crowd, on the other hand, applauded and howled at the unhinged-looking vagrant-clown who wasted no time in winning them over by shoving the unicycle-riding clown out of the spotlight. Javier gave it a good go, but lost his balance and tumbled awkwardly to the ground, much to the delight of the crowd.

They love me...

The Littleman Twins launched their little statures into damage-control mode, somersaulting alongside Myron like wayward tumbleweeds. Myron grimaced as strings of still-wet makeup bled across his eyes…through which he saw a few small faces in the crowd shifting from happiness to confusion, mirth to uncertainty. Myron tore open the burlap bag and removed the half-dozen eight-inch steak knives, damp steel unpolished (and unsharpened) since last year still glinting in the swirling spotlights. From the outer edges of the ring, pigman Charlie watched on, dumbly absorbed and rightfully curious as to what Myron was up to.

The crowd loves me, so why not Charlie?

Myron smiled, then closed his eyes, and in his mind's eye recalled his younger-and-much-more-entertaining self charming crowds nearly a thousand strong, the genuine smiles on their faces a testament to his former abilities…and in his mind's eye he retained those abilities once again. Before Javi could stop him, all three spotlights centered on Myron, clarifying the sweat on his face as it ran through the thickly and messily applied makeup, more of it now running into his eyes as he tried to blink it away, one of the spotlights hitting him square in the pupils, blinding him…but the Oxy spoke in unison with the alcohol: *it's all muscle memory!* He could juggle rubber baseballs with his eyes closed, so why not knives? But, with his eyes closed, he wouldn't be able to see the smiles on the faces of *hundreds* of people watching him —

…some of them aren't smiling anymore…some of the children look scared, some of the adults too, everyone visibly uncertain if the sudden spectacle before them was part of the program…

— so he squeezed his eyes shut and went for it, the knives going up in a semi-circle, following each other back down, into his left hand, tossed to the right, back up and back down, over and over in a smooth and continuous motion, wash, rinse, repeat, simple as that.

I'm doing it! Sweat and makeup trickled down his face but it didn't stop his Oxy-tuned brain from *hearing* the crowd, multitudes of laughter littered with random gasps of anticipatory shock —

…they love me, I'm jugging six eight-inch knives, they love me, I'm the Juggling Jester…

—abruptly moving into half-laughs of the raucous variety, half-gasps of authentic shock—

...I'm doing it, I haven't dropped a knife, muscle memory baby, no more pain, no more pain, NO MORE PAIN...

No knives hit the ground. He did it! Was *still* doing it, transformed back into the venerated clown he once was, miles away from the pathetic jester he'd become. Up and down and up and down the knives soared and landed, soared and landed—

...they love me...

—until someone, Crazy fucking Javi he imagined, leapt in and stole away his glory. The grip on the collar of Myron's costume was strong, yanking him four steps backward and down onto his platform ass. He could hear the crowd collectively gasp and murmur...could hear the knives hitting the hard soil around him, *one-two-three-four.*

Myron opened his eyes and through webs of paint beheld a quieted crowd, close to three hundred men, women, and children, faces aghast with the unsympathetic reality of what they just witnessed, mere seconds ago prettily painted with curious merriment for the odd clown in the triple spotlight, now forever traumatized by the monster that same clown had become—the monster their minds would forever fear.

Still seated, still staring at the fearful crowd, Myron's besieged mind could not comprehend what was happening.

Javi appeared before him, hiding a wicked smile only Myron could see. "Cabron...you okay?" He winked.

Myron scowled and snarled, "Why did you stop me? I didn't drop any knives!"

Javi looked at Myron's hands. "That, you didn't."

Myron looked down at his hands. His Oxy-sharpened ears had heard four knives fall to the ground. He again muttered, "I didn't drop any knives..."

He hadn't. There was still one in each hand. But somewhere in the early seconds of his improvised act, he started flipping them so that the blades landed in his grip, dull but still sharp enough to cause serious, *pain-free* gashes. *Thank you, Oxycontin; thank you, Wild Turkey.* One into the other, over and over, too many to count, up and down and up and down, deepening the numbed wounds into bone-glinting chasms, blood pooling in his hands like stigmata, red corkscrews cascading across his forearms, spatter staining his threadbare costume and paint-massacred face.

Myron "The Juggling Jester" Higginbottom could do nothing but sit in place and stare at the horrorstruck faces promising to blame "The Juggling Jester" for the fear of clowns that would haunt them for the rest of their lives.

The greasy pigman Charlie, with Javier's assistance, shoved Myron back into his trailer. The disgraced clown crumpled into a heap on the floor, then looked up at the pair, Charlie, snarling and pointing, "Pack up your shit, Mo-ron, and get your stupid fucking ass out of here!"

The door slammed and Myron sat alone and pathetic, staring at his hands and the knife blades still clutched in each. He squeezed. Blood spurted, but...*still no pain!*

He climbed to his feet and looked in the mirror. Smiled. His makeup...it was still perfection, expertly applied, the skin beneath devoid of wrinkles and moles and fatty deposits—a young, talented, witty, funny and pain-free Myron "The Juggling Jester" Higginbottom, at your service. Still holding the knives, he danced a little dance in his trailer, pleased to be the strapping young lad he once was.

The audience, they were scared of you, of your FACE!

His breath ran suddenly short. A twitch of pain emerged, first in his hands, then elsewhere as it rode his re-emerging nerves from head to toe. *No, no, no!* He stumbled back to the mirror, the TV alongside it now playing Lon Chaney's *The Phantom of the Opera*. His face...it was still young, the makeup impeccably mirroring his facial acrobatics.

"The crowd! They loved me!" he shouted at his reflection.

His reflection answered: *No, they didn't! They were terrified of you!*

With this, more pain and the sudden realization that the Oxy was starting to wear off. He looked back into the mirror. The fine features of his perfect makeup began to run and swirl, like a rainbow of oil on saltwater. He rubbed his eyes, begged out loud for his former self to return, but his altered state was already leaving him, *FUCK YOU OXY*

AND FUCK YOU WILD TURKEY!, bestowing upon his stricken gaze the colorful slaughter he had made of his face.

"No, no, no, no, NOOOO..."

He looked at the gored pits of his hands, bloody and congealing, knives still slackly clutched in each.

Tears burst from his eyes, and in this moment he decided that today would be the final appearance of the Juggling Jester.

"He leave yet?"

Javier looked at Charlie, shook his head.

"It's your trailer now. Kick his squatting ass out of there."

Javier nodded, then felt around in his pocket for another pill. This time he would give him Oxy, instead of LSD, one for the road if he was up for it. It would be worth the expense to be rid of the miserable old geezer.

He opened the door to the trailer, looked inside, then back at Charlie.

"Boss? You're gonna want to see this."

Charlie trundled up the stairs and peered in alongside Javier.

They'd hoped it was makeup spattered everywhere, but knew better. It was blood. Myron lay in a puddle of it, still breathing, blood belching with each gory exhale. His face was gone, both fists still gripping the knives, covered in blood, threads of flesh dangling, the makeup-and-blood-coated mask of skin laying alongside him, staring up from the floor, accusing Charlie and Javi.

Charlie grimaced, speaking his only thought out loud: "What the fuck was that with his makeup tonight?"

Javi knew the truth, but kept it to himself, and instead replied, "It was the Juggling Jester's final *appearance*."

Slugfest

"Coming down pretty hard now," Shirley said.

I nodded in agreement, mindfully watching the sheets of rain pounding the windows. Rivulets trickled down, melting the beams from the headlights creeping along the interstate. The Quik-Mart sign out front flickered on and off and swayed in the torrid wind like a Thanksgiving Day float. I hadn't seen a storm this fierce since the last twister came through about three years ago.

The weather had been treacherous for most of the night, and it still showed no signs of letting up. I got to work late, the ten-minute drive nearly taking me half an hour. I'd put myself on the night shift—eight to four AM—and had just finished up my second cup of coffee. Not a soul came in since I arrived almost two hours ago and I was thinking of having a beer to help pass the time along.

"Forecast's calling for rain all night," I replied, repeating what I just heard on the radio. A crash of thunder sounded, rattling the windows. Lightning lit up the gas pumps out front. I watched as the rain battered my '82 Buick, heavy drops splattering the hood like bursting kernels of popcorn. I wondered if it would be worth staying open for the remainder of the night—it seemed doubtful that anyone would come in at this point. I'd only seen a few trucks pass on the interstate in the last half hour.

Shirley poured herself another cup of coffee then put up a fresh pot. I decided to have a beer and grabbed one from the cooler.

"Hey Shirl, I'm thinking of closing up early. What'dya say if no one comes in by midnight, we skeddadle?" I looked at my watch. Ten-thirty.

Shirley smiled. And it was perfect too. She hadn't the greatest looks in the world, but she could light up a room with those perfect teeth and dimples of hers. She'd put in three years for me here, and damn if she wasn't the best employee I'd ever had. Countless losers had come and gone, but not Shirley. Even when things weren't going well for me and Mary, Shirley spent hours talking to me, putting reason back into my life. It hurt to know that I'd lose her someday. I only hoped it would be for the right reason, that she would meet a great man, someone that would take care of her like I knew I could if given the chance. If Mary hadn't been around, it would have been Shirley.

"We ought to wait for things to let up a bit," she said.

A gale whipped the windows, nearly shaking the building. The ceiling lights flickered. The Quik-Mart sign outside swayed like a tree. Cheerlessly, I nodded in agreement, doubting however that things would "let up" anytime soon.

She opened a package of cupcakes and gave me one. As we ate, I listened to the radio, reports of the storm. The noise of the rain slashing the roof and pavement damn near sounded as if the building would blow away any moment, maybe end up in *Oz*.

"You okay?" I asked, washing down the cupcake with a mouthful of beer.

She nodded, but looked scared. Hell, so was I. The storm—it felt powerful, and I wondered if we would both be trapped here forever. Crazy as it sounded, I wouldn't have minded being stranded someplace the rest of my life with Shirley, even if it had to be inside my store. As long as I wouldn't have to explain it all to Mary.

A pair of headlights suddenly appeared in the parking lot.

I hadn't seen anyone approach until the door swung open and Sheriff Allan Kane pressed in. He'd been soaked to the skin, and I wondered if it'd just been the short scurry from his cruiser that had him so wet. He spun and pushed the door shut as needles of rain forced their way in, prickling my skin even from the safe distance I stood at.

He turned and removed his sheriff's hat, which had a plastic shower-cap shell covering it. Wiping his forehead, he said, "Nasty. Damn nasty weather."

"Hello Allan," I said. "Nice night for a cruise, eh?"

Sheriff Kane had a grand reputation in our little town, where the worst crimes to be dealt with consisted mostly of bar fights and domestic squabbles. He had a knack to set calm to even the unruliest of situations by simply stepping into a room. The truth of the matter was that no one wanted to spend the night in the local pokey, where there would be no eats or comfortable sleeping for twenty-four hours. And if your tiff was bad enough that Allan Kane had to be called in, then it was worth backing off, as Allan was quick to send you to the lock-up.

"I was on my way home, had to pull off." He poured himself a cup of coffee from the fresh pot Shirley put up. "Couldn't see a lick."

"Any cars on the road?" Shirley asked.

"Hi Shirley," he said, smiling. Allan always feigned a thing for Shirley. Rumor had it that he was gay. He'd never been married, and once you reached a certain age around these parts without a serious prospect, then people started talking. Personally, I felt that the sheep had more to worry about than the women, but that's another thing altogether.

"Car went off the interstate about an hour ago. Since then, nothing but wind and rain."

"Everyone's playing it smart. Could be a tornado coming through." I walked to the window and looked out. Allan's cruiser sat next to my Buick. Both cars were getting reamed by the downfall. I noticed a few hailstones bouncing off the hood.

Then, from out of nowhere, a man appeared at the window.

I startled at the unexpected sight, not from the impetuousness of his appearance, but at the horrible condition he seemed to be in. My first thoughts were to shrug off his apparent state of distress as a weather-induced mirage, a distortion of the pane's watery runoff, but then he bounded in, confirming my initial glimpse: his suffering was as real as the beer was cold in my hand.

It appeared he'd spent some time outside in this crazy weather, his clothing drenched to sodden rags. His shirt had been torn at the collar and the skin on his face ran beet-red, a series of pock-like abrasions marring his left cheek.

"Hey Shirl, we got a fresh pot up?" I knew she'd just put the coffee maker into action, but I wanted to create a flavor of awareness, in case the stranger had some funny stuff up his sleeve. Suddenly, I felt grateful that Allan was here.

"You bet," she yelled over the din of the radio. A Garth Brooks song had come on.

I saw Allan place his coffee-free hand on his gun. I couldn't remember the last time he'd fired the thing, if he ever had. I guess it was just self-reassurance, that he was the big man in town.

"Hey fella, you awright?" he asked. He took a step toward the guy, placing his coffee down on the counter. I placed my beer next to his cup.

The man stopped and gazed at us. At once the anxiety I felt from the imposing storm took a back seat. The guy was in bad shape, his entire face having suffered those smallish wounds I first noticed on his left cheek. His eyes carried a blackness deeper than onyx, and I could've sworn at the moment they'd been witness to something staggering. He seemed to stare right through us.

"You hear me fella?" Allan raised his voice, cold and inquisitive. "What's happened to you?"

The man tried to speak, lips tremoring but unable to release any words. A few unintelligible murmurs eventually slithered out, then he pitched forward in an odd manner, as if kept by an unseen force, looking strangely like a jerking crash-test dummy in those slow-motion films. He collided with the gum and mints display, and it proved no viable support for his hands to grasp onto, promptly crashing down alongside him as he fell, splaying its candies all over the floor in a shower of flavors.

Allan and I ran over, pulling the metal grid away and sliding it down the nearest aisle. The man started convulsing, arms and legs jutting straight out and trembling as if running a charge of voltage. His eyes turned up into their sockets, revealing bloodshot whites. His chest had been exposed through his torn shirt and I saw a series of pustules there, not unlike those riddling his face.

Kneeling down, Allan holstered his gun and pulled the radio from his belt. He played with it for a moment, then pulled it away from his mouth. His sullen face had me concerned.

"What? What is it?"

"The storm. There's too much interference. I can't get through."

Shirley went behind the counter and picked up the phone. Her anxious finger on the receiver told the same story. The storm had cut off all hope of communication with the outside world, for now.

The man started hyperventilating, thick painful wheezes frothing from his lungs. I ran a nervous hand through my hair. I didn't know what the hell to do. I looked at Shirley and she just leaned over the counter staring helplessly. Injured—hell, he could've had some nutty disease, a strange case of the flu, maybe something worse. I had images of being quarantined inside the Quik-Mart for the rest of my life. Somehow this wasn't how I originally envisioned being stranded with Shirley.

It seemed Allan hadn't had much training in first aid either. His fingers searched the air, then he clambered up and pulled an asthmatic inhaler from the counter. He opened the packaging and tried to pry it into the man's mouth, but his teeth had clenched shut.

Then, I noticed something weird.

His pant leg had accordioned up like the stripped peel of an apple, exposing the milky white of his calf. The skin here had also undergone similar distress, riddled with open sores. I saw, nestled between two open sores on the side of his calf, a dark spotted slug. It slithered on the erupting skin, furling in and about itself, fleshy, wet and glistening, four inches long and showing two rubbery horns atop a lumpy head.

"Allan?" I managed.

The Sheriff tossed the inhaler aside and looked at the man's leg. "Ugh—"

But that's all I heard him say because at that moment every semblance of noise in the place—Allan's voice, the radio, the man's sickly wheezing—had at once been drowned out by a sudden torrent of hailstones pelting the roof, the windows, the cars outside. Everywhere, *rat-tat-tat, rat-tat-tat,* over and over, a great percussive storm beating out its rhythms in a symphony of chaos that pulverized every sound preceding it.

"*What the hell...?*" Shirley yelled, quickly pacing around the counter and sidling up next to me. I thought to myself that it had taken all this unanticipated fear and disarray to finally get her to seek solace in my company. I reveled in the moment of comfort I provided, then took to the windows alongside Allan to check out the storm.

"Don't let your eyes deceive you, my boy," Allan said mournfully. I fought a strip of confusion in his statement, then followed his boomeranging gaze beyond the window, saw, and understood.

The hailstones, they weren't bouncing on impact like most chunks of heavenly ice might. No, these babies went *splat* on the surface. They then duly uncurled into elongated, gelatinous strips and writhed about in manic twists and turns.

It was hailing slugs.

"*What is it?*" Shirley shouted, then stepped back from my side, fingers clawing at her reddened cheeks. I tried to offer her a comforting look, but she couldn't tear her eyes from the wicked phenomena outside. Neither could Allan. Remarkably the Sheriff had held his composure, and I could tell from the sweat beading on his brow that he was having a hell of a time trying to come up with an answer to the mess of questions rolling around in all our heads.

The slugs fell in a fury, whacking the roof and damn near covering the two cars out front. It had grown black outside and the size and consistency of the falling slugs increased, critters the size of golf balls slapping the concrete and twisting open into six-inch ribbons of wriggling, slimy meat.

Shirley let out a screech and I twisted to see her staggering back, shaking her right leg as if she stepped in dog crud. She almost toppled backwards but the counter caught her, supporting her weight. A small display of caramels spilled to the floor, along with my can of beer and Allan's cup of coffee. For a brief moment I wondered what was wrong but then I saw her peering downwards, hands shaking wildly, grin clenched in taut disgust. She kept on kicking her leg, and when I looked at it I almost fainted. A slug of considerable length and width was coiled around her ankle, twisting and slithering up her leg. It quickly disappeared beneath her pants.

"John, it *hurts*! Do something! Please!" I'd never heard her yell and scream like that and it pained me greatly to see her *suffering*. She needed help, even if it was just a slug.

But just a slug it wasn't. I'd gotten to my knees and slid her pant leg up to her thigh. "Jesus," was all I could mutter as I gasped at the sight of *them*. Two nasty critters way up Shirley's leg, the first at her calf, the other just below the knee. With two fingers I plucked the one from her knee; it made a suctiony sound as it came free. Shirley screamed as I tossed it toward the front door.

"Damn, it hurts John. Hurts so much…"

"Hold on," I said, then pulled away the other. Shirley yelled again, and I froze in shock as I held it out in front of me. Amazing, I couldn't believe what I was holding in my hand. The damn thing had *teeth*. A shitload of them too, as sharp as tacks, filling its round, puckering mouth. A flap of bloody skin dangled from its lower lip. Shirley's skin. I rolled my gaze back towards her leg. From where I pulled the slug away remained a nasty bleeding wound, like those all over the man that had come bounding in.

Which reminded me…

I spun around and beheld a crazy scene. Evidently, the injured man had dragged in more than his fair share of crawlers. I watched as they unearthed themselves from beneath his clothes and attempted to skim away, leaving moist and shiny trails on the floor. Allan was leaping about like a lunatic, trying to stamp them all out, doing his best to sidestep the spilled candy bars. His shoes were nearly lost beneath swathings of slug mush, and flat patches of gelatinous gore polka-dotted the tiled floor.

As Allan trampled the fleeing slugs, droves more slithered all over the downed stranger, sucking at his skin, crawling from his mouth and nose, one trying to force itself from his left eye. The poor bastard seemed to have stopped breathing, his body twitching at the limbs. A group of slugs had gathered at the puddle of spilled beer near my feet. I stepped back, nearly slipping on one that met its fate beneath my left sneaker. Shirley had crawled to the far side of the store and shrunk down in front of the slushie machine. Tears flowed from her eyes and when her sour gaze met mine she erupted in a terrified bawl. I raised my hands to try to calm her, but then I started to hear a spraying sound. I quickly twisted around to find Allan leaning over the slug-man, the inhaler now traded in for a can of bug repellent. His right arm was stretched out in front of him, the nozzle twelve inches away, coating the slug-man with a thick foamy layer of noxious stuff. I couldn't believe what I was seeing. It was a nasty sight.

"*Allan!*" I finally yelled, but he kept on spraying, his grin taut and maniacal.

I ran to Shirley and crouched down next to her, trying to offer her as much comfort as I possibly could through my shaky embrace. She hid her face in my chest as I watched Allan emptying the contents of the can on and around the slug-man.

He looked up at me, heaving, eyes wide and crazy.

Shirley pulled her head up, sobbing. "I-Is he dead?" she stuttered. Her tears were cool and wet on my shirt.

Allan nudged the unmoving man with his boot. "If he ain't, then there's no helping him."

I personally didn't know what to think at the moment. Here was the Sheriff of our little community, the one person who needed to be trusted and called upon during moments of distress, now a culprit of sorts. He certainly didn't make any effort to help the guy. But then again, he protected *us*. And himself. I guess that counted for something.

I shook away my rambling wisdoms, suddenly aware that it had stopped hailing.

Allan staggered to the front counter, hands gripping the edge, supporting his weight. His head slumped in anguish.

I threw a quick glance outside.

Abruptly I froze, utter disbelief nearly paralyzing me, a sight so grotesque I had to question as to whether I would come out of this alive.

The windows were completely covered with them. Slugs of all sizes and denominations. Black ones, white ones, red ones, some with stripes, some spotted. Many of them normal-sized, three to four inches in length, some of them monster-sized, a foot or more long, all of them bathed together in an orgy of slime so dense that not even the faintest kiss of night could be seen beyond their soft white underbellies.

"What do we do?" I yelled, not realizing that Shirley and Allan had not yet seen the union of slugs on the windows. Allan spun and staggered back at the sight, Shirley shrieked as if her heart leaped in her throat. What an insanity! These slugs, squirming in a riotous jubilation, their puckering mouths secreting a thick mess on the glass, some of the bigger ones possessing bulbous eyes at the ends of their horns that slapped against the glass, peering in at us. I shuddered, then took in the whole startling picture, beyond the few eyes I'd picked out, and saw a multitude of the buggy peepers skimming the glass at various locations. Looking. Seeing. They were *watching* us.

Allan started walking toward them.

"Allan, what are you doing? Get back here!" I retreated to the slushie machines, Shirley had taken refuge in the storeroom. I could hear her bawling through the closed door, calling for me.

Allan stood inches from the glass, neck craned forward, eying the slugs with morbid curiosity. "John, you see the eyes? They can see us."

"Allan, get back here." As much as I urged him, I was unable, like Allan, to rip my sights from those tiny eyes, eyes which moved and rolled around in an almost human-ish nature. They were freaking me out. Bad.

Allan placed a finger against the glass.

It shattered.

The sound the implosion made could've deafened a hundred men, a great crash that toppled jars and cans from shelves, shook the walls, set the slushie machine aflow. The wall of slugs plunged in atop of Allan, sending him to the floor. All around him the crawlers splattered the tiles, hunks of falling glass shattering into a dissemination of tiny shards. The storm's fury whipped about, sending magazines and newspapers flying across the store like birds.

Amidst the fury I saw Allan trying desperately to get to his knees, his face a mask of blood, hunks of glass sticking from it at various angles. He made a feeble attempt to crawl to me but in no time the slugs were upon him, slithering with an alarming, snake-like precision. Some of them leaped from the ground, arching their bodies like inchworms then bounding forward and attaching themselves to Allan's body, producing pig-like squeals as they did so. Many slithered beneath his pant cuffs and shirt sleeves, their trails evident by the moving wrinkles beneath the fabric of his uniform. He swatted at them in a maniacal manner, some meeting their fate beneath his hands. But they were too many. When he tried to scream, they crawled into his mouth, muffling his cries. When his eyes bulged, they ate at them, sucking at the vitreous fluids. Finally, Allan collapsed next to the stranger, blood dribbling from the multitude of slug bites on his exposed skin. His body convulsed, became lost beneath a solid layering of marauding slugs. He looked like a great piece of chocolate under siege from an army of ants. This all happened so fast that I had only precious moments to protect myself. The slugs started coming after me, at least a dozen of them slithering away from the two bodies—hunks of white bone had begun to show through the stranger's disappearing flesh—leaving silvery trails on the floor as they came. The first one to reach me was damn near the size of a football, so I did what seemed natural: I kicked it. It went flying across the store, hit the wall behind the register, stuck there for a few seconds, then plopped to the ground, leaving a sticky mess in its wake. Another had begun to nibble at my shoe, and I kicked it away. I backpedaled to the door of the stockroom, grasping at the knob. It was locked. I screamed for Shirley. More slugs came, staging their attack on me.

Finally, the door opened, and I fell into the stockroom.

I looked up and saw that Shirley had donned a pair of rubber utility gloves. After slamming the door shut—and severing a rather big, nasty one in half—she plucked the three or four crawlers that had started tearing at my pants legs and showed them their destiny beneath her shoes.

"Thanks. You all right?" I asked, breathing heavily.

"I was gonna ask you the same thing. What's happened to Allan? I heard the crash."

"Front window caved in. They started crawling all over it. It gave in from the weight."

"Allan?"

"They got him."

For a moment I thought Shirley wanted to embrace me, but then she held back, pulling her gloves off in frustration and burying her head in her hands. I cursed myself for the want of Shirley's comfort at that moment—there were two dead men in my store, one of them a friend. I should have been overcome with guilt, dismay, revulsion, a million other emotions. But selfishly, all I wanted was Shirley.

We remained unmoving and silent for what seemed a very long time, but was perhaps only a couple of minutes. The rain had ceased completely now, the screams and wheezes of pain from the store long quieted. Silence fell upon us, eerie and foreboding. I wondered if the slugs had finished with the two men and had begun their retreat.

Shirley sidled up next to me, her shoulder touching mine. I shivered. Then she said, "John, I hear something."

"What is it?" My ears still had a ringing in them from the window's implosion.

"The door," she said, her voice rising in a panic. "It's creaking, John. I-it's creaking."

I took a step forward, looked down, at the bottom of the door.

From the half-inch crack between the floor and the door a few slugs emerged, their amorphous bodies flattened and squeezing through from the pressure of what I could only envision as a million of the slimy fuckers pressing in from behind them. Once in the room with us, their bodies twisted and writhed about, reassuming their naturally globular state.

Shirley and I stood incapacitated, dread and the sudden complication of not knowing what the hell to do robbing us of our wits.

Shirley screamed.

The slugs continued to squeeze through. Those in the room began their approach towards us.

I shot wild glances about the stockroom, thinking crazily of Allan and his bug spray assault that had seemed to work. Maybe I could find a can in here...

Shirley screamed again.

I looked to the floor. They were multiplying, more of them making their way through the small space.

I heard a soft tearing sound, then a horrible squeal.

Of all the things that had gone wrong tonight, something had finally gone right. I couldn't help but smile at the sudden glint of light appearing at the end of this long, terrifying tunnel, a light that gave me—and Shirley—a promise of hope that we just might come out of this mess alive.

We had a weapon.

Salt.

The faint tearing noise I heard was Shirley ripping open the aluminum spout from a cardboard canister of Morton's Salt. We had at least a dozen of them on the shelves back here, we used them to fill the shakers by the popcorn machine. Shirley was standing over a foot-long meaty slug, shaking the canister, coating it as if it were a yummy treat. The slug let out a series of shrills like nothing I'd ever heard before, like a mouse under the paws of a playful cat, twisting and turning and convulsing before virtually melting away into a shriveled lump of orange jelly.

"You're a genius!" I yelled, rushing past Shirley to retrieve my own ammunition.

I gave her a kiss on the cheek, then proceeded to spray the floor with salt. The slugs squealed and shrank in agony, the salt burning them up like acid, eating away at their wet coatings and reducing them to clots of sticky matter. When all were defeated in the room, we attacked those pressing in at the base of the door, using up two whole canisters. The harsh combination of salt and melting slugs acted as a perfect sealant so that no more could get in.

When our attack had finally come to a conclusion, Shirley and I huddled together at the rear of the stockroom (armed, just in case we missed any). Shirley slept the night in my arms, and I stood vigil until the faintest beams of daylight leaked into the stockroom between the thin spaces at the sides of the door and the frame.

There really is no happy ending to this story. When Shirley and I emerged from the stockroom, all the slugs had met their fate under the heat of the morning sun, nearly coating the town in sticky orange goo. No one could explain the odd phenomena, and no one really talked much about it after everything was cleaned up. It'd been reported that the slugs fell as far as fifty miles away, and that they did a good number on the local livestock. I also heard that outside of Allan and the stranger, there were only another two fatalities.

As far as Shirley goes, I haven't seen or heard from her since. She left me that morning, and hell, I can't blame her for not wanting to come back. I guess my dreams of being stranded with her had kinda come true. I'd return those moments in a heartbeat just to know where she is now. Hopefully in the city, fixing to start a family.

Me?

I cleaned up the store, replaced the windows, restocked the shelves. Now, it's business as usual.

But, there was one small thing, something I failed to mention to anyone, and it's been on my conscious ever since.

You see, after the bodies had been taken away, while I cleaned the store, I found a something else. It was cradled under the counter by the cold medicines, hiding.

A tarantula, about a foot or so in legspan. It had a human finger in its mouth.

It met its fate beneath my shoe, but to this day I wonder: what will fall from the skies next time a bad storm rolls around?

Whatever it is, this time I'll be prepared.

The Radio

R obert kept all his dead father's things in the attic.
It hadn't been his intention to rummage through them. Yes, he *knew* they were up there, but their existence had merged with his environment, never seen and oft forgotten. Blame twelve hours of rain and another lost day in the fields to open this wound.

The attic was a cabinet of curiosities, a small humid place packed full of everything that remained of Edward Harris: his collectibles, his clothing, his *things*. There was an old 78 RPM record player sitting atop a stack of Mario Caruso records. Robert's father used to play the scratchy recordings all day long, sometimes well into the night. The crooner's voice would drill holes into Robert's brain, and no matter how much he begged to go outside, to escape the torture, Edward would answer him with a wrinkled hand (or two) across his face. Burdened with tears and the pain of his father's anger, Robert would flee to his room and bury his head, Caruso's piercing tenor sifting through the vents like aggrieved haunts.

There were black-and-white photos of his mother, a woman who left the family when he was six or seven years old. The snapshots were collected in the first four pages of a stiff clothbound album: a montage to a woman wearing a mask of eternal sadness, longing to escape.

A coat rack stood in the corner, and for a quick moment it looked like Edward approaching, wrinkled hand raised, primed to come down on Robert's arm or leg. Robert was startled at the memory, sucking in a lungful of stale dusty air, eyes wide and dry, burning as they pushed away from the shadowy illusion.

There was a pirate-like trunk, brass flourishes fringed with rust, the sleeve of a moth-eaten trench coat dangling free like the arm of a wounded soldier. Shadeless lamp bases lay piled beside it, decapitated corpses never to breathe life into a room again.

He hadn't been looking for anything in particular when he decided to come up here; memories of the past were painful, his father's things sorrowful commemorations of a time best forgotten. Still the question of *Why?* badgered him, the abrupt want to discover a reason for his actions unquenched. Just moments earlier he'd stood beneath the pull-down hatch leading into the attic, thinking of his father, thinking of his mother, trembling hand reaching up for the cord, pulling it, the foldaway stairs squealing as they stretched down to the floor.

A clap of thunder rattled Edward's things, dissolving Robert's desire to know a reason for being here.

From behind, a whisper.

Robert...

It might have been the rain pattering the roof, a gale of wind whooshing over the eaves, or the swish of a car's tires slicing through a thin puddle. Layered in the ambience, he heard his name being called, and with it came a sensation of repulsion, of reflexive alarm.

He spun and his eyes fell upon a radio. Like the Victrola, it was old-fashioned, a World War II–era keepsake his father might've kept since childhood. Despite its familiarity, he couldn't be sure if he'd seen it before. It was steeple-shaped, dark fabric mesh insets framed to protect the speakers. Two large plastic dials on the front jutted below a cylindrical rod where a third knob once existed. A cord snaked away from the back of the unit, disappearing into the shadows like a tail.

Oddly entranced, he stepped to the radio, footsteps creaking on the swollen wood floor. Had the whisper somehow, someway, come out of it? He felt strangely sure it had. Without further thought, he bent down and picked it up.

It was heavy, dusty, warm. Hefting it with both hands, he carried it across the attic and carefully descended the pull-down stairs, dusty springs moaning beneath his weighty effort to keep his balance. When he jumped down from the third step onto the hardwood floor, the springs made a loud *clang,* forecasting the clap of thunder that followed.

He carried the radio through the hallway, into the bathroom. He put it on the counter and by force of habit opened the medicine cabinet. Amber prescription bottles lined the shelves, honeycombs in a hive, the pills within nesting bees. His eyes played over them. Which pills was he supposed to take? When had he last taken any? From inside the bottles, the tiny capsules peered out at him—beckoned him.

Close it...

Robert's skin crawled, rough with gooseflesh. He quickly shut the cabinet and his eyes scanned the bathroom. Had the voice come from inside his head? He looked down. *Or was it the radio?* He felt frightened now, momentarily weak. He grasped the counter's edge for balance, eyes away from the radio now, out the window. Somewhere in the blowing fields out back, a crow began to caw—a piercing, panicked caw.

Moments ticked by. Slowly, Robert's eyes drew back toward the radio. There was a thick coating of dust on it. He extended his arm, touched the radio. Again, he experienced a crawling of the skin. He swiped his finger through the dust, revealing a polished gleam beneath.

More...

The voice startled him. Froze him. It had come from the radio, this time he was certain. He tilted his head down, leaning close to the dusty mesh, intent on hearing it again. Nothing. He peered at his finger, at the dust still on it...then swiped it across the top of the radio again, carving a thicker swath.

He listened. No voice came. But he could hear something else now. A low, condensed breathing: the muted pant of someone hiding in a closet or a box. Was it the resounding echo of his lungs inside his head? Or... He swiped the dust again. Now the radio made a sighing noise, suggesting an enjoyment in the cleansing.

He turned and yanked a mildewed towel from the plastic rack, ran the water in the sink and wet it. As he did so, a once-lost memory snagged his thoughts. From his childhood. Of his father, a drunk farmer who put Robert to work in the very land the window in the bathroom looked out upon. As the sun would rise and the neighbors began burning leaves in their yards, Edward Harris, eyes doused with the effects of Jim Beam, would haul Robert out of bed, put a boot to the boy's ass, and hurl insults at him as he staggered out the door into four acres of potatoes, squash, and stinking cabbage.

And then his mother—the woman who'd left all those years ago—a distant but clear memory of her returned too, of how she would sit at the kitchen table before a chipped-glass ashtray filled with cigarette butts, skin flaking from her slackened face, sunken eyes wearing their catatonia, staring right through him as he trudged past, hauling his tears and misery. His father's rule had come down hard on her also, evident from the screams and shouts that rode the wind out to the fields where he slung cow dung and mud. Then late in the afternoon when Robert's growing muscles could bear no more, he would return to the house, contaminated with the sounds of his father's scratchy Caruso records, the operatic tenor's wails penetrating his bones like a snake's venomous bite.

Here he recalls, somehow, seeing the radio sitting alongside the 78 RPM Victrola, absorbing the wailing music and the sounds of his father's iron fist coming down upon his mother...on him.

Once the radio was clean, polished wood handing over a murky reflection, he carried it into the kitchen and placed it on the table. Sunbeams pooled in through the window, drowning the room in golden light. Robert's eyes played over every inch of the radio as he concentrated on touching the life within.

He cocked an ear, close to the speaker, hand resting lightly upon the smooth surface. It felt warm, a baby's feverish skin. He pressed his fingers against it, feeling ill at ease, confused.

There was a soft scraping sound. And with it a twitter of movement, catching the corner of his eye: the weight of the plug, slipping down off the edge of the table, swinging back and forth, back and forth, producing a minute squeak. He recalled the cawing of the crow he heard while in the bathroom. Where had the bird gone? The fields out back were always busy with crows and their mortal enemy groundhogs, even in the rain. *Where had it gone?*

He grabbed the cord, running his hand down its smooth rubbery length, all the way to the plug. The connectors were warm. With their touch he sensed a presence, someone looking at him, not from the room's dark corners, but from the dense swell of air alongside him. He shuddered…then crouched down and plugged it into the wall socket.

Outside, lightning flashed. A clap of thunder. Static sputtered from the radio…followed by a pungent veil of smells, all vaguely familiar to him: the smell of a man's foul odor, the dirty stink of cigarette butts in an ashtray, the stench of shit in the fields. He turned and looked at the radio. The lone circular window was lit, a dim off-white cast the color of skin, except for a dark red slit that indicated the radio's frequency. It looked like a milky eye, the red slit its pupil, blinded yet still able to scrutinize.

He reached for one of the dials, gaze fixed on the cloudy readout. It stared back at him with unblinking need.

Static trickled from the speaker like drizzle from the sky.

Amidst the static, a whisper: *Robert…*

His fingers touched the dial. Static blared. His stomach burned, erupting with acids. To him, the voice was clear. Deep, resonant, slurred.

His father.

The phone sounded, right alongside him: a disquieting spew of noise that gave his heart a disgruntled leap. He quickly glanced at the phone on the wall, wondering who could be calling. He stepped away from the radio. Saw the number 13 on the LED display. Thirteen messages. He stared at the phone as the ringing continued.

Between the fourth and fifth rings, the radio's static blared. Riding atop it, like a weak overseas pickup on shortwave, the whisper demanded: *Answer it.*

This time, it was a woman's voice making the demand.

Staring dumbfounded at the radio, he picked up the phone. With the handset still inches from his ear, he uttered blankly, "Mother?"

"Robert? Robert? Is that you?" said Debra. She was his only friend in the world. She worked at Super Food, where he bought his groceries. Sometimes she would walk home with him because she lived with her parents a quarter mile down the road. But only when her shift was done. Debra didn't know that Robert had had her hours memorized and went there around the time she got off. But not of late, not since his father died.

He loved Debra dearly, as much as he did his mother and father.

"Hi…Debra."

"Robert," she said, voice twangy and agitated. "Where have you been? I've left you numerous messages."

He paused, uncertain. His mind looked back over the last few days and caught only snippets. The rest was dark, filled with static. "I've been around."

"Around? Robert, are you okay?"

"Yes."

"Have you been taking your medication?" she asked, her tone sensible and apologetic.

He didn't know how to answer. His eye caught the radio, its age-yellow window glowing brightly now, the red slash glaring at him. He saw it move of its own accord, static blaring until it stopped and his father's voice filtered from the speakers, loud and clear. *Tell her "yes."*

"Yes…"

"Robert…you haven't been to the store in weeks. You sure everything's okay?" The static moved from the radio to the phone line, her voice coming in scratchy and faint now, like an AM radio station falling out of range.

He saw the right knob on the radio turn. The slash moved, then stopped. His mother's voice seeped out now, along with her cigarette stench: *Tell her "yes."*

"Yes."

A pause. "Robert…I'm worried about you. You don't sound okay. I'm coming over there."

Music blared from the radio, the scratchy croon of Edward's Mario Caruso records being played on the Victrola. He could barely hear

Debra asking him, "What's wrong Robert? Robert?" This was followed by a loud crackle of white noise, her voice bleeding in and out and then away.

He stared blankly at the telephone handset, then hung it up and moved back to the radio. Again he smelled his mother's cigarettes, his father's stink, the reek of the fields—all seeming to emanate from the speakers. He turned the dials, prodded the shaft of the broken one too, trying to locate their voices again. They were *in there*, somewhere. He'd heard them. Had listened to them, had obeyed their commands. And now, nothing else mattered. All he wanted was to turn the knobs, stab at the power button, search out their signal. Find out what to do next.

At some point, either a minute later or an hour later, he heard the music again, the scratch of the 78 RPM phonograph clear and unmistakable. He held his hands up gingerly, away from the radio, as if just completing a house of cards.

His father's voice, over the music: *She's coming.*

His mother's voice: *She'll arrive shortly.*

Their voices whispered repeatedly over the operatic tenor's shrill wails: *Bring her to us.*

Rain continued to slash the house, wind picking up now, the static-like sound echoing the pulse-like bursts from the radio. When the rain calmed, so did the white noise from the radio. The crooning immediately returned, along with his dead parents' whispering voices: *Bring her to us...*

A knock upon the kitchen door.

Debra's voice punched through, disconcertingly aggressive. "Robert...you in there?"

He'd left the door open, and she tried it, not hesitating for a moment to enter the house. The door swung open, creaking hinges masking the *sleek* of the knife he removed from the countertop butcher block.

She was tall and bony, not at all pretty, her inherent interest in Robert justified. Her face was dazed and expressionless, eyes sleepwalker-like, unfocused as they fixed upon the radio sitting on the kitchen table. The music blared loudly, the operatic voice reaching a crescendo as he whipped the knife at her, the silver arc of the blade drawing a wide slash across her face. She shrieked. He slashed at her again, across the throat.

Debra struggled, fell back toward the door. Robert was there, closing it, keeping her inside. She collapsed to the floor, clutching her neck weakly. Blood pumped through her fingers. The wind and the rain keened outside, louder now, a high, piercing shriek. Mario Caruso's crescendo tapered down into a thin, dying wail, the voices of his parents still whispering in unison, *Bring her to us...*

Robert dropped to his knees before her, hands wrapped around the base of the knife. He stared at the radio.

"I love you," he uttered, then plunged the knife deep into her heart.

The rain continued to fall, slashing Robert's skin like nails. In the rotting cabbage field, Robert dug a trench.

Here he unearthed his father's body, buried only two weeks earlier. A few days after he stopped taking his medication.

Edward had been buried alongside his wife, her body now strips of skin, brittle bones, and tufts of rotted hair. The chipped-glass ashtray Robert used to slice her neck open was still clutched in her wasted hands. Right where he put it, all those years ago.

He buried Debra, next to his parents.

Right where they wanted her.

Robert sat at the kitchen table. His body was streaked with mud, with blood. He stared at the radio. Mario Caruso sung from it.

Outside, rain swept against the house. Lightning flashed the precise moment he placed the point of the knife against his wrist.

For a moment he thought about the pills in the bathroom medicine cabinet. Thought about going up there. Thought about taking some.

But then, from the radio, his mother, father, and Debra spoke to him, their voices a chorus of whispers: *Don't do it.*

With the knife's blade still against his wrist, he nodded, then waited for them to command his next move.

Banalica

I remember the very first time Juan-Carlos and I made acquaintance nearly fifteen years ago, when the mission first broke ground in Haslet, south of Baja. Father Sandi, head chaplain at my current post at St. Aquinas of Mercy, informed me of my transfer to oversee the final stages of growth at the new mission, Our Lady of Hacel.

Our Lady of Hacel was a modest tabernacle, erected in most proper fashion at the center of the quaint southern township, and I had been elected to assume all oversight of the sect. I believe the good Lord had been looking over me that day, granting my lifelong wishes to become a father of community. It had been perhaps the most glorious day in my career.

Juan-Carlos was the first to approach me the day I set foot in the new church. I remember the event so clearly, the gleam of the freshly polished pews reflecting the yellowish light from above onto his cloth-draped shoulders as I quietly paced down the center aisle—my aisle—for the very first time. He smiled and approached me with great open arms, and I had felt so dearly welcome at this start of my days at Hacel.

From that point on Juan-Carlos played a very special role in my life. Every day for fifteen years, through sickness and all, he made certain to welcome my entrance into the anteroom prior to mass, cloaking my neck with blessed rosaries, kissing the cross before draping them, crossing himself upon completion of the light ritual. He hadn't missed a day in fifteen years, had always been there for me, a true inspiration, and I in turn had become dependent to his waiting pretense as if God Himself had placed him there as a gift to ensure a cloak of sanctuary.

How badly his unanticipated absence one day tore my soul to shreds, and I experienced great difficulty proceeding through the service that followed, my hands trembling so badly that it became an anguish to simply place the host upon the tongues of the worshipers.

Following what was perhaps my least inspired performance, I unexpectedly located him as I entered my quarters. "Miguel," he greeted me, his voice solemn, preoccupied. I turned and found him seated at the chair I kept alongside my only window, the same chair I sit in daily to contemplate the possible evils in the world and how I might stifle their influence upon the faithful people. He gazed into the wooded area just beyond the quartered panes of glass, and I knew at that moment, a voice in my mind told me, that Juan-Carlos would be leaving the mission.

"What does the sun tell you today, Juan-Carlos?" As a philosopher, he gazed often into the day and night skies seeking logic in the exertions of the world. When speaking of the world, he never offered to reveal his travails even though I knew his principles at times suffered from great misunderstandings.

He placed his fingertips upon the glass. "*El Sol...*" he said, his breath fraught with fear, a patch of condensation forming upon a single pane. "He is wearied, but continues to struggle." I walked to the window and peered out. The sun was strong and vibrant, the woods bright and glorious. In this proximity, I looked for the first time into Juan-Carlos' face and saw tears streaming down his cheeks.

I knew not what troubled him, and dared not ask, allowing the brave man to work out his inner evils on his own. A confession I never solicited, only accepted if offered, and this day Juan-Carlos did not seek my counsel. He left not an hour later, placing the rosary around my neck and kissing me on my cheek before hoisting a single bag around his shoulder and departing on foot.

The mystery of his sudden departure ate at me for weeks. My confidence as a man of the cloth waned, and I wondered with great sadness how I had failed my best friend. I held his picture close to my heart at night in prayer for an answer to his deciding to leave—with great dismay I pondered the possibility of him deciding to leave the church altogether; the thought of which tore me to shreds. However, somewhere deep inside my soul, I felt this to be an unlikelihood.

Yes I realize that I, as a holy man, see the world through much different eyes than most—eyes filled with an unbalanced mix of uncertainty and optimism. The world holds many different types of people, those that love me, those that hate me, all those including myself, fragile human beings with no true understanding of life as it should be understood. We breathe, eat, love, hate, desire, and act out on our feelings in effort to appease the hankerings in our souls and the word of God.

This, I truly believed, is what Juan-Carlos had done.

St. Hugh of Lincoln in Taos fifty miles north of here acknowledged my petition and graciously initiated the transfer of a deacon by the name of Tomas. Tomas arrived six days later and briefly announced his presence at my parsonage, desiring a rest before attending confessional in the afternoon. I placed him in Juan-Carlos' empty residence. In doing this I perhaps resigned myself to the fact that Juan-Carlos would not be returning after all, even though I knew in my heart that the moment he left, his presence would never grace my church again.

Less than an hour later, Tomas returned to my door, his knocks urgent, almost burning. Although I had no acquaintance of the man and his traits, I knew that something was amiss.

"Yes Tomas? What ails you?" His face carried beads of sweat, his features drawn downward in a mask of consternation. He looked much different than the man occupying my room just a short while earlier.

He paced the room in circles, shaking his head, and I wondered for a moment if Tomas was burdened with personal troubles that I had not been made aware of. "I...I found something in the rectory."

My heart pressed against my ribcage with apprehension for whatever secret he had suddenly unearthed in Juan-Carlos' quarters perhaps held an indication to his hasty departure. I guided Tomas to my chair, the one by the window, and asked him to sit, in which he did, however tentatively. I kneeled alongside him and placed a hand on his shoulder. It was hot and damp, rigid with tension. It was then that he reached into his shirt pocket and handed me a sheet of yellowed parchment. I unfolded it and viewed a handwritten note penned in nervously shaken script. It had been addressed to Juan-Carlos:

> *Dear Juan-Carlos:*
>
> *It is with great hesitation and trepidation that I must contact you, but I foresee no other option at this time. God's grace has never failed to shroud you, and it is now that I must plead for your endowed blessings. Please hear my words, accepting them as truth and nothing else, for you are my only prayer.*
>
> *Banalica has succumbed to a great evil, and those unfortunate enough to have crossed its path have perished. Our crude fight, albeit a courageous one, has proved to be futile, and we now hide from its unrelenting grasp, relying on faith alone to deliver us from sure and certain death. I dare not reveal the true source of this evil that has invaded our tiny villa for fear that you will translate these messy writings as the ramblings of a madman. But I assure you I have not surrendered to any disease, be it mentally or bodily. We, the people of Banalica, are dwindling, and your empowerment of God is our only last hope, dear brother. Many have fled Banalica's domain (with success I cannot answer), many have perished, and those beyond the perimeter of evil have remained at a distance, for any man without the dignity of the Lord's blessings would dare not step foot in this town again.*
>
> *Please dear brother, return to Banalica and aid us in our battle against this evil.*
>
> *And brother, this is my third attempt in reaching you. I will try five times, at which time if I do not hear from you I will assume the worst has happened.*
>
> *Your brother,*
> *Roberto*

I read the letter twice, leaning upon the deacon's shoulder for support. I felt hit hard, and I could not fathom what this terrible evil could be. Evil rears its ugly head in many forms, in many potential menaces, plague, famine, disease, the list runs endlessly. Yet it still delivers an aftermath that affects all in its path with a similar burden: death.

A bitter tear ran from my eye, a lump of indignation forming in my throat. Juan-Carlos should have shared this plea from his brother with me! He should have beseeched my support! Now to sit here mute and speculate on the situation would be time and energy wasted. I would have to join my friend in his plight to extinguish this possible bane in order to appease my soul.

I would have to go to Banalica.

I waited until the following morning before leaving Haslet, as I knew the journey to Banalica would take much of the day and I wished not to arrive by moonlight. I traveled south for nearly three hours on a bus crowded with locals. The ride seemed agonizingly long, spent in sweat, and I read Roberto's letter over and over again to pass the time. I listened to the starving babies aboard wailing for their mothers' milk, swatted mosquitoes and flies, and watched the remaining passengers shake along in their tattered clothes and ripeness. When my stop finally arrived, the joints in my legs cracked and popped as I stood to depart the bus in the town of Cocina.

Cocina's streets bustled, the center of trade for the inland villas. It sat beneath the boiling sun upon a stretch of land that ran for nearly three miles along the coast. The entire length had been built up greatly over the years, incorporating nearly every provisional trade imaginable. I had visited here on other occasions, so the scene was familiar: piers jutting out into the waters, fishing vessels unloading their catches for the day. Chickens frenzied in their coops awaiting fate, squawking in the neck-grips of their purchasers. Sidestreet vendors peddling their fruits and vegetables for a few coins to purchase drinking water, or a few pounds of meat. And now and then, a car would race by, a wooden wagon in tow, clouds of dust spraying up from the wheels in whorling clouds, coming to rest on the dirty children playing in the streets.

It was here in Cocina that I hoped to find transportation to Banalica.

I immediately gathered that the presence of a holy man here in Cocina was a rarity, given the stares I elicited from most of those whose paths I crossed. I smiled periodically, nodding and moving for ten minutes through the marketplace until I locked gazes with a black man who leaned against a car that looked as if it had been left to die in the street.

"Good day," I said approaching him.

He offered a curt nod, nothing else. Sweat ran from his pores in rivulets.

I wasted no time. "Can you supply me with transportation? I will pay handsomely."

He grinned, exposing a mouth of empty spaces and brown rotting teeth that jutted from his gums like tree stumps. His gums bled red, a sharp contrast to his wet purple-black skin. "To Banalica?" he asked, eyebrows raised in question.

I felt a sharp twist of discomfort in my gut, and I remembered what Roberto had said in his letter, that those beyond the perimeter of evil had remained at a distance, that any man without the dignity of the Lord's blessings would dare not step foot in the town. I at once assumed that this man knew something of the evil Roberto wrote of.

"How is it that you know where I wish to go?" I asked him.

He folded his arms in a defensive posture, as if I carried a disease. "Many men of the cloth have traveled from great distances to go to Banalica. But none have returned. Only one *padre* remains in our house of God, and he has learned a valuable lesson from the *padres* that have tried to rescue those rumored to still be untouched in the villa. Banalica is an evil place, and those who enter bow down to the Devil, never to return."

He remained silent after that, closing his eyes in thought. I was trying to make sense of his statements when he said, "I will take you to within two miles of the villa. From there you can follow the road into town. It will cost you."

We agreed on a price and rode in silence. The ride was long, and the old vehicle did not handle the rough terrain very well. It shook along harshly, and I felt pains in my buttocks. I wanted dearly to solicit information from the black man, but he remained in prayer for the entire journey, lips trembling, undecipherable mumblings escaping his lips. Between his palm and the steering wheel a rosary dangled, half its beads missing. In my pocket I gripped Roberto's' letter, the sweat from my hand dampening the stale parchment. I closed my eyes and tried to sleep, but thoughts of evil kept my mind and body at bay.

We arrived two hours later at a nondescript spot where the brush grew thickly at roadside and the jungle towered just beyond its perimeter.

The man continued to pray, shaking presumably with great fear, and I hesitated speaking to him for fear of interrupting his invocations. But I had no choice, as the day was getting late and I needed to move on.

"Where do I go from here?" I gently asked.

He quieted, quite abruptly in fact, then said, "Straight ahead, about a mile and a half, this path will lead you into town. You must go now." Not once had he looked at me throughout our journey, and he continued to lead his gaze away, even in this conversation. I paid him and exited the car saying thank you, but received no acknowledgement. The car hastily kicked dirt up in my face as it turned around and sped back towards Cocina. I watched the car until it disappeared from my sights, then turned and began my walk to Banalica.

The dense growth flanking the roadsides had begun to clear some time later. I lost track of time but had kept a steady pace throughout, and by the looks of the sun, I still had another hour before dusk. The jungle finally cleared and I saw a small ranch at the forefront of an open road. Two modest sized dwellings sat next to one another and looked out over a fenced area. It was here that I beheld a daunting sight.

Apparently the ranch had been a chicken farm, and I say *had been* because the chickens here were nothing more than withered feathers and decayed skin laced over splintered bone fragments. If it weren't for the few feathers swaying in the late afternoon breeze, the casual eye would have had a difficult time identifying the animals these bones once defined. Although thousands of tiny bones lay about the weeds and dirt within the fenced pen, a great many had been intricately woven together to form grotesque gargoyle-like creatures, one atop each fence post at the side of the road. I paced to one and saw that the creator of these hideous models had taken great pains to construct them, as the bones were sewn together with strands of steel-meshed wiring from the coop. They served an appropriate welcome to the evil that was rumored to thrive here. I crossed myself and continued on.

The next thirty minutes had me passing similar sights, tiny ranches whose cultivations had succumbed to some hideous butchery, the livestock—cattle, goats, more chickens—slaughtered and maimed in such a fashion that I had difficulty fathoming the nightmarish sights as plausible in this waking world. Stakes had been erected, the heads of goats speared and staring at me through blackened worm-ridden eyes. Cows gutted, shreds of distended bellies giving way to fetuses long dried beneath the sun's rays. I had great fears of suddenly wanting to turn back, but forced myself to press on, as the tiny structures of Banalica's community were now within my sights.

Banalica was small, its inhabitants numbering less than two hundred. Each civilian worked to simply live, farming for food and making trips into Cocina to trade for luxuries such as fish and fruit. Here in this stretch, shanties stood alongside a lone dirt road, housing perhaps four or five inhabitants apiece. An open-air meeting place constructed of wooden beams and benches centered the town, and towards the end of the road by the outgrowth of the jungle, the church.

I stared hopefully at the much larger structure, but the uncomfortable silence here set alarm to me. Nothing but the wind stirred, and unlike the jungle where birds chirped and monkeys howled, Banalica slept, basked in stillness.

My thoughts came too soon, for something in the jungle discharged a terrible shriek, very loud, very long.

I nearly passed out from the start of the unexpected cry, and my body shook like a bundle of wires charged with high voltage. It went on and on, and I wondered how a pair of human lungs could sustain such a bellow. I kissed the cross at my neck, and then it ended just as precipitously as it started.

I realized suddenly that night was quickly pouring in, the sun dropping down behind the cloak of the jungle. I picked up my pace even though my legs ached badly, and approached the front of the church. I took the four steps leading to the entrance, peering behind me one last time before entering, swearing to my Lord that I thought I saw a great black shadow moving in the trees just beyond the perimeter of the jungle.

I entered the church. Darkness virtually enveloped the interior as I passed the threshold, and if not for the candles and kerosene lamps alight at the altar, I would have presumed this town to be deserted. I paced slowly up the center aisle, crude wooden pews carved from tree trunks at either sides of me. A series of bowed heads came into view at the first two rows, and I smelled something overly ripened, like rotting vegetables.

"Hello?" I quietly called, and the heads turned. There were a few sharp moans; apparently I had caused some alarm. A single figure rose up, and I paced forward thinking at first that it was Juan-Carlos, but realized quite soon that the individual only merely resembled my lost friend.

His brother. Roberto.

"Miguel?"

Although we had never made acquaintance, he recognized me, perhaps from photos Juan-Carlos had sent over the years. "I found your letter Roberto. In Juan-Carlos' room."

The younger brother bowed his head. Looking to the ground he asked, "How long has it been since my brother left?"

Immediately I felt a great trepidation, an ache in my pounding heart, and the prospects I had forewarned myself of during my travels here may have actually arisen.

Juan-Carlos never made it.

I walked over and hugged Roberto and he began to cry. As his tears soaked up in the fabric of my shirt, I gazed over his shoulder towards the others. No more than twenty people, they contemplated me with empty eyes and forlorn expressions. I saw great amounts of suffering written on their faces, each undoubtedly witness to perils distressing beyond any imagination.

Perhaps evil had indeed assumed control of Banalica.

In what form, I needed to find out.

Roberto controlled his anguish and pulled away. In his teary face I saw a man whose most recent days had been spent in agony, a messy beard covering half his emaciated features; puffy black circles like half-moons beneath soulless eyes.

"What has happened here, Roberto? Where are the rest of the townsfolk?"

"They are dead," he said forcefully, then grabbed my arm and added, "Come with me, Miguel."

He led me away from the others, leaving them to resume their prayers, and we sat in a pew a few rows back. "Nighttime has fallen," he said turning his gaze to the ceiling twelve feet above. "He will soon show himself, and you will see for yourself."

At once I associated his statement with those ramblings present in the letter that had brought me here, and I wondered regrettably if his written denial of being a madman might actually hold some truth. "*Who* will be here?"

He gripped my wrist, his bony fingers tight and hot on my skin. Sweat fell from his brow. "Dear Miguel, evil has risen in the jungle, and it has assumed control of Banalica. I am fearful to reveal the truth to you, as you may reject it as an invention of madness."

"Please…" I met his eyes with as much integrity as I could.

Then, he spoke. "Not one month ago, Banalica was a thriving community. We were happy. Suddenly the mutilations came, and all our animals within a week's time were dead. It wasn't until our people were victimized did we realize our true predicament." He paused for a moment, then confessed. "Miguel, I find no other explanation to give you other than…the evil from the jungle, it comes in the form of a…a *vampire*."

His last word came out as a whisper and my mouth dropped, but no reply came forth. I wanted to question his radical conclusion, but then I envisioned the slaughtered animals at the ranches, the bone-sculptures, and my tongue momentarily froze.

He continued, hands shaking wildly, tears flowing. "Many of our people have been snatched away into the jungle, I have seen it with my very own tired eyes. Some have attempted to flee, by morning, and I make no assumption as to how many have been successful in their plight for escape. Apparently it seems one has, as the letter you've received can attest. I've sent five letters with people who've chosen to brave the jungle on foot. So far only one letter has returned, with you."

I was about to force words from my mouth—anything that might humor the man—simply because I had difficulties deciding whether I should believe or doubt these frightened people shielding themselves within the church's armor, but I was cut short by a harsh scraping noise coming from above. Terror instantly struck me, not from the noise but from the shrieks of horror spewing from the mouths of all those cowering in the first two pews. Their shrieks quickly gave way to quiet apprehension—an apprehension of knowing that the possibility of death awaited them just beyond the frail walls of their shelter.

"Do not worry, we are safe here," Roberto said weakly, his confidence clearly overcome by fear. "He waits, tempts us, will scratch at the walls all night. But as long as you do not succumb to his hypnotizing beckon, you will live to see the morning."

The scratching grew louder, as if someone were attacking the roof with sharp knives. The curiosity of it had me in its grasp, and I wanted to investigate its source, despite Roberto's claims. The stench of garlic assaulted my senses, taking over the ripe odor of unclean bodies, and I looked over to see the townspeople donning themselves with roped cloves.

I felt somewhat incensed at this action, these people's brains being washed with folklore and not necessarily the truth of their real torment. "Roberto, whatever that is above our heads (*the scraping had grown to a point where it began to daze me, and amidst it I thought I heard something purring*), the reek of garlic is no serious defense. Faith and common sense is what these people need! Stamina! Not fairy tale logic!" My voice had turned to yells, and all eyes were set upon me. Above, the purrs had grown to grating, low-toned growls.

And the scraping went on and on and on.

"People! This is nonsense!" I yelled, somewhat in denial of the events suddenly taking place, also to distract myself from those terrible nails (I envisioned in my mind that the source of the noise above could very well be fingernails…thick dirty yellowed fingernails) splintering the wood above our heads. I launched myself from my seat and set foot down the center aisle to the doors, much to the discouragement of the people, who outwardly voiced their concerns.

"You'll die out there!"

"Stay in here! He won't come in!"

"Come back!"

And there were more, many more, and they probably held validity, but I ignored them, determined to make sense of this so-called evil in Banalica. I reached the threshold when Roberto grabbed my arm.

"Whatever you do Miguel, do not look into his eyes."

I almost scoffed at his request, writing it off to yet another whim of folklore, but the seriousness in his eyes nearly had me tranced, and I simply nodded, opened the door, and moved outside into the night.

At once a thrust of cold wind swept past me and slammed the door behind me. I stayed motionless on the top step, peering about the deserted town. The trees from the jungle sang, their leaves in concert with the wind. Circles of dirt flew up, and I instantly realized that the town was remarkably arid for such a temperate environment.

Then, just above and behind me, I heard the scraping.

Scrape...scrape...scrape..., each one sharp and long against the wooden exterior of the church, piercing my senses to a point where I felt as if they were cutting into my skin. Cowering a bit in fear of what I might find, I spun and saw the thing Roberto had spoke of. The vampire.

Perhaps not six feet away, the thing bounced and writhed on the edge of the roof above me, a man—or what used to be a man—with snow-white hair and ancient eyes whose sickly yellow corneas and black pupils stared pure evil at me. I swallowed hard as I found myself staring at this creature, this creature who looked older than time itself yet fidgeted with a kind of horrid, obscene glee, choking lunatic sniggers at me through rows of razor-sharp fangs, spanning a formidable pair of tenuous milky wings from its back that propelled their dark winds in my direction. Its taloned feet gripped the eave firmly, pointed-clawed hands twisting and dancing in the air, mesmerizing me.

At once, ever so slowly, it descended upon me...

My body was yanked away, back into the church. The door slammed behind me and Roberto was there, arms wrapped tightly around me. He held me like that for a few tense moments, then slapped my face as tears began to flow from my eyes. He pulled me further away from the door, and I stumbled along with him, feeling my hypnotic lethargy slowly slipping away. I realized with great dismay the peril I had just exposed myself to. Dear God, I had been tranced! I looked into its eyes just as Roberto told me not to, those terrible glaring eyes, and nearly fell victim to its evil, just as he said I would!

When my legs found their balance, Roberto led me to the altar where I sat and gathered my senses, trying so hard to get the image of those horrible demon-eyes out of my mind.

My strength soon returned, so did my lucidness, and I sat thinking, trying to conjure up a solution to this terrifying predicament—a plan that would grant myself and the people of Banalica freedom from evil.

My mind worked all night, and the scratching went on and on and on...

The night itself lasted forever.

The scratching stopped moments before the sun appeared. During the night, Roberto and I had gathered all the supplies we needed to carry out our strategy. We used the two kerosene lamps from the altar to see our way into Roberto's quarters at the back of the church where we located a bundle of rags, a jug of kerosene that was being used for the lamps, and luckily enough, an old wooden bed in which we were able to rend the legs into a few sturdy slabs.

"I do not possess the *bravado* to approximate myself for such a lancing," Roberto said fearfully, but I ignored him and his belief in folklore.

We carried the supplies out front where I tied a rag about the end of one of the legs from the bed. I kept thinking back to my coming face-to-face with the so-called vampire, and although the dreadful sight of the monster had had me mesmerized, I still refused to believe in any movie-induced pretense, merely blaming the sheer horridness of the monster for my inaction last night. "Listen to me close," I said. "No more folklore. Throw away your garlic. We are not to stake the creature through the heart, even though I'm sure it would indeed kill it, as it would any man. Tonight we keep our distance."

"Then how are we to accomplish such a task, Miguel?"

I grinned for the first time since I arrived here. "We find its lair and burn it."

About an hour after sunrise, Roberto, myself, and one of the townspeople—a young burly man named Jorge—set out into the jungle with all our tools in hand. We commenced north into the trees opposite the church, as my faint sighting of something dark there when I first entered the church yesterday had me deciding that it was in this direction we should be looking. The hours swept by us in our search, and the day had almost been surrendered to futility when Roberto called out.

"Miguel! Come see!"

In truth I had hoped our search would end unsuccessfully, for by this time my stomach yearned for food, and my muscles had tired. I followed his voice and found him and Jorge crouched near a small cave that had been crudely camouflaged with leaves. At the entrance a wash of blood served as its welcome mat.

"It may be an animal's lair, perhaps an aardvark," Roberto said.

"We'll investigate this spot, but carefully." In truth I had a bad feeling about this place, but did not wish to say anything until after we went in. We doused the ragged ends of the bed-legs and lit our torches. Jorge led the way, followed by myself and Roberto. We had to crouch to enter and walked nearly ten yards through a narrow passage guided solely by flame-light before we came into a clearing, signifying to us that indeed, we had found the lair of the vampire.

First I saw the bones, hundreds of them connected together not unlike the animal bones I saw at the ranch upon my arrival in Banalica. They too had been intricately meshed to form a great sculpture of some evil mind that ran nearly ten feet high and just as wide, situated at the center of the subterranean chamber.

It was constructed of human bones, skulls and ribs and arms and legs and all.

I shuddered at the sight and felt my skin ripple. My hunger dissipated and gave way to nausea. I tried to reassert my beliefs in the one God, the Holy Ghost, but somehow for the first time in all my years as a man of the cloth, I had difficulty simply conjuring heavenly thoughts. Indeed this was place of evil.

Slowly we paced around the sculpture, peering warily about. The underground chamber was quite large, and we saw situated at the rear the existence of two additional caves. Nodding to each other, we decided to stay together, our torches leading the way into the cave on the right.

The dancing flames revealed to us an empty room no larger than the one behind us: dirt walls, roots escaping from within, grubs falling all over. I glanced around thinking we had found nothing of concern here until Jorge stifled a scream.

I turned around and saw the man looking up, a twisted look of fear and revulsion painted on his face. Both Roberto and I followed his upturned gaze and immediately set our sights on the vampire, the same creature I had encountered last night, hanging upside down from the ceiling. It looked like a shadow in this dark place, the torch lights reflecting from its body in cinematic flashes, its clawed feet gripping a wooden beam running from wall to wall, its great wings enshrouding its entire body except at the feet—just like a bat.

"Damn," I muttered, staring up at the thing, my thoughts suddenly lost to a cloud of confusion: *is it human? Or animal? Or is it really a...*

"Miguel..." Roberto shook me with one hand, but I could only shake my head in denial at what I was seeing. "You must be strong!"

Nothing held more truth at the moment and I nodded, trying desperately to grasp my emotions. Yes, indeed I needed to be strong, but I also knew it would be no easy feat as I felt mesmerized simply contemplating the slumbering monster.

At that moment I realized Jorge was no longer with us. "Roberto, where is Jorge?"

"He moved off to investigate the other room."

We waited a moment in assumption that Jorge would quickly return. We had located the demon that had spent the past month terrorizing the people of Banalica, and felt no reason to look further. But when the time passed, and Jorge remained absent, we both moved to seek him out.

We exited silently from the antechamber of the vampire and paced over to the adjacent cave. In the back of my mind I kept reminding myself that from all our travels today it was growing late, and I wanted to put our plan into action before darkness took over and the vampire awoke.

When we entered the second room, I wasn't quite sure what in God's name I was looking at. But then, as the ensuing events unfolded, the horrible truth reared its ugly head.

This room ran much larger than the first, perhaps twice the size. At its center and trailing all the way to the rear wall was a nesting of what I could only interpret as cocoons: white, bulbous egg-like spheres, perhaps fifty or more of them, united together in a sticky conglomeration of fluids and solids. Some of them, the larger ones at the forefront of the mass, had begun to hatch, and from within more vampire-beasts emerged, heads ensconced in a layering of something viscous, their papery wings still wet and newborn, not yet feasible for flight.

I'll continue by saying that Jorge was dead. Well, perhaps not dead yet, but in the process of being taken alive. One of the hatchlings in front had Jorge in its grasp, razored claws rooted into his shoulders, sharp fangs buried deeply into a great tear in his neck; hence we heard no scream, as it had bitten away his vocal cords. Jorge's legs shot straight out in front of him like two planks, kicking up wildly as if electricity were running through them. And then the blood—so much of it, covering his mask of death and the mask of life of his attacker.

Roberto took an angry step forward and began screaming in Spanish, and this time, I held *him* back.

Thinking of my plan, I looked around and realized with horror that it was Jorge who had held the half-filled jug of kerosene. But it was nowhere near him—not that I could ever venture close to the horrifying scene to retrieve it.

"Here!" I heard Roberto scream, and I saw him dart back towards the entrance where the container sat; Jorge had placed it down before approaching the vampire ovum. He immediately ran to the egg-collective and started splashing the fuel all over them, tossing the container back and forth in a heave-ho manner.

At once, great screams echoed from the eggs, and they all began to tear open, quickly now, each and every God-damned one releasing its very own vampiric beast. Albino-like, tenebrous. Coated in embryonic wetness. Flattened wings, busily working their way free from their prisons into the new world. .

Roberto finished spraying the fuel and I walked over, holding my torch, preparing to set it down. But then something caught my eye, and I froze.

One of the emerging vampires, freshly broken free from its milky shell, was staring at me.

I felt my heart drop to my feet, heavy in pain. It was Juan-Carlos. Or what used to be him. "Lord have mercy," I managed. "My dear friend, taken by evil." The words came automatically as I stood there rooted watching my dear friend of fifteen years raise up and spread his wings out, a near six-foot span, and then launch a deafening roar along with the rest of the beasts: all of the missing people of Banalica.

Roberto had been wrong. The people of Banalica had not perished. They had found new life.

So *I* would be the one to put them to death, I thought, and placed the torch to the kerosene-drenched collective.

I watched with awe as it went up in great flames.

Screams erupted, pain, agony, bedlam, all evil things gone to hell and back, collected here in one single mass. I shielded my eyes as the flames multiplied, enveloping all the newborn vampires, watching in awe as their wings melted away. And then their fresh skins, sliding away from their bodies, and I held my breath as green smoke rose and the stench of sulfur filled the room. And through it all, I saw Juan Carlos' face staring at me, staring at Roberto, and it seemed to me that he was pleading for mercy, begging for our forgiveness.

I tossed my torch into the fire, forgetting all along my true purpose for coming here.

It was standing behind us as we turned around to leave.

The *great* vampire, the mother of all invention, looming over us, freshly awakened from a day of slumber only to find us—two priests—in its lair, burning its children. I tried desperately for prayer, but found no words of faith to break through my mortal fear. Roberto and I stood close awaiting the worst: our deaths.

The vampire howled a shrill so loud my ears popped and I at once went deaf. I expected it to immediately trance us with its yellow gaze, take us for its children, and I watched its scowling visage in assumption that no other alternative existed for me. But then it turned its head, shielding itself with its wings. Still howling.

Then I realized.

The fire. It was afraid of the bright fire.

Roberto still held his torch. He thrust it toward the vampire and it cowered, staggering backwards, wings turned. It staggered back through the cave and we pursued, realizing its vulnerability, chasing it out into the night where we saw it take flight like a giant bat, sending its dark wind into our faces as we stood by the cave's entrance.

Smoke filtered out behind us and we quickly made our way back through the jungle into Banalica.

With the assistance of the townsfolk, we built a bonfire outside the church and spent the night there, watching the skies for the flying creature, knowing deep inside that Banalica would now be safe from harm's way.

It has been six months since my experience in Banalica. I have relocated my plight of God to Cocina, where many of its *padres* have perished in attempt to rescue the faithful from evil.

With Roberto at my side, we wait, wait for word of some other villa that has been absorbed by evil.

And then, in the memory of Juan-Carlos, we will fight again.

Heirloom

Lucienne cast heavy eyes over the man's naked body. Smiled. "You know what I've always wanted to do?"

Grunting, she reached under the dinette table into the worn canvas duffle bag, pulled out the rifle and laid it between them.

To Lucienne, its power was definite. It commanded mankind.

She grinned, saliva trickling from the corners of her readied lips. "For so long I've wanted to..." she whispered. The man leaned forward, in agony, in ecstasy, desperate to unearth her deciding words.

But her sentence hung open, like the mystery of something wet in the shadows. She turned her back to him, did not reveal anything. Yet.

Instead, she ripped a long strip of duct tape and plastered it over his hungry, bruised eyes.

And then, gripping the weapon, aimed it at him, and smiled, ever so bittersweet.

The rifle was ancient, an heirloom passed down from grandfather to father, and then from father to Lucienne. A memento from her governed childhood, one sleek shiny barrel running eighteen inches, the grip serrated rubber, its bulk eight pounds of steel-grey manhood able to accommodate two spiral-cased bullets like deadly ovum in a hardened shell. Lucienne would sit like a doll and watch Father remove it from the worn canvas pouch it slept in. He would clean it, smoothing the oil upon its hard surface, her thoughts remaining somber, confused eyes following the graceful sway of his hairy fingers as they flittered about the barrel and stock, the aroma of cloth and oil hollowly contrasting her father's masculinity.

"You can look, but you can't touch," Father used to say, gently stroking the rifle with his woolly, withered hands. Her eight-year-old mind grasped the truth in his voice when he said that, the strikingly long rod itself a cold-hardened symbol of death—yet still, an image of Father's staunch virility. Mother, if she had been alive, would have frowned upon him, nodding and arguing that Father's rifle was an entity to keep a distance from, a force to never be reckoned with no matter what the circumstances. *Wisdom governs the female mind*, Mother once said. *Brawn, the man's.*

Lucienne nodded at the time, her silence an affirmation of her understanding and her knowing that she would never forget.

"Someday, my precious," Father would say, "this will all be yours."

Lucienne had been too young at the time to understand Mother's untimely death; she hadn't even known exactly what death was. She was only five at the time, and who explains to five-year-olds about death and dying? She'd heard some of the folks in the hospital mention the word "stroke," but Father always used the term *go away*. Whichever, she wondered how long it would take for Mother to be done with her death, and come back to her so she could ask questions about the food she ate and the clothes she wore. Father would have nothing to do with those things.

A few people had gathered in her home a day or two after Mother *went away*, all of them sitting quietly in the small living room and sipping wine. Father had pulled Lucienne aside, asking her if she wanted to say good-bye to Mother. She looked around at the bowed heads of those in attendance for some. No one coached her into making a decision, so she simply nodded.

Father picked her up and carried her down the humid hall into the bedroom where Lucienne had never really been allowed to go. Her eyes caught full sight of the ceramic and glass figurines that Mother kept on the dresser, the ones that Lucienne could never ever touch, even if she asked nicely. Father once told her that when Mother went away she would be allowed to touch anything she wanted, even if other people said it wasn't okay. Even Mother's figurines.

Strangely, Lucienne felt pleased that Mother had gone away. It seemed that Father was too.

You can touch anything you want...

A large, shiny box sat in the area where the bed had been. In it lay Mother, looking different than she usually did, so pale and still, wearing her lacy pink evening gown and patent-leather shoes, her makeup done extra-special. Lucienne felt a rush of blood racing through her body, an odd, fearful zeal that seeped through her chest, and then her stomach, and finally into the spot between her legs. This thing she was looking at was *death*. *This* is what all the pale-faced, wine-sipping grown-ups were talking about. They weren't talking about Mother, they were talking about *death*. *No wonder they did*, Lucienne thought. *It feels so good.*

She remembered how good it felt at that moment, to be in Father's arms, staring down at Mother, at *death*, and then at Father's hairy hand—the same hand than ran the length of the gun barrel as it cleaned the surface—as it massaged the spot between his own legs.

Yes, death feels good for all.

She returned her gaze to Mother, contemplating her flat and sunken eyes. Her cheeks, dulled gray and wrinkled, the dry, delicate fibers breaking through the weathered cracks of her lipstick. It felt so good to be there at that moment, peering upon her detachment from the world, Father there to reassure her that someday, if Lucienne listened, she would return from her death to be with her again.

Lucienne listened.

But Mother never returned.

The pleasures returned and culminated when Father cleaned his gun. He'd disappear into the woods behind the house for the entire day, Lucienne left home alone to tend the household necessities, cleaning the floors, doing the laundry, and making sure that the workbench had been adequately prepped for cleaning: a crisp sheet, cool pillows, perhaps a blanket on cold nights. Father would bring home an animal of some sort—a deer, raccoon, a pheasant—the skins stripped away to reveal the inner beings.

Father would carve the meat from the animal's bones, the sickly-sweet smell of viscera and gristle invading her nostrils in bursts.

Then afterward, Father would sit on the sheet Lucienne laid out next to the workbench and clean away the gunpowder staining the rim of the rifle's shaft, smoothing the oil up and down, up and down, as thick, biting fumes rose up and commingled with Father's richly striving musk.

"You can look, but you can't touch."

In due time he would slip the rifle away, its canvas casing swallowing it whole, and as he did this would press his thick, meaty hands against the jeans he wore in that feel-good spot between his legs. Lucienne would sit through his slow routine, truly enjoying the bulging image of the gun beneath its casing as it divulged its ultimate secret to her—an intimate purpose that only *she* could taste and understand. Father would stare at her then remove his jeans and lube himself with gun oil, and she would watch with great intrigue as his brow beaded furiously, sweat pouring from his pores, his grin growing tighter and tighter at the corners of his mouth, his jaws bouncing up and down in gross ecstasy.

Lucienne's mind would wander over the secrets the rifle revealed to her, of the killing stories, each and every tale a breach of solidity and persistence, a means of gathering dominance. Lucienne could find the capacity within herself to follow Father's lead, to take into her hands the power and finesse that Father displayed to her all those years.

"You can look, but you can't touch…"

Father would shudder one last great time and then hastily fire his own shot: his bullet softer, more yielding than those inside the rifle. But no less deadly.

Years had passed before Lucienne finally found the strength within her to make the demanding decision to bow down to her calling. She'd made every attempt to act accordingly, continually agreeable in answering to Father's call. She felt obliged to him; after all, he did feed her and provide shelter for her. And, he never really did *touch* her. But as the years pressed on and she grew toward adolescence, so did her anger, blooming within her body, mind, and soul like a flourishing cancer, spreading its poison through her blood until it finally erupted, its concentration boiling at the foundation of her heart, tainting her previous focus of well-meaning and goodness with something black and hideous. She could feel it. She could *taste* it. A complete transition, her life newly guided and influenced through venom and anger.

She had heard the gun calling to her from its place in Father's closet. Sleep had eluded her one night when Father cleaned his gun twice, and she followed its whispering beckon into his room—the room she hadn't been permitted access—quietly crawling on all fours into the closet as he slept, carefully lifting the gun from its canvas nest. It felt truly wondrous, more grand than the warm images of the gun oil slathering the slender barrel in any cleaning session. Heavy was its bulk in her pre-teen hands, hands that hadn't had the experience of touching much in her life.

...you can look, but you can't touch...

Here she had her first orgasm. An amazing pleasure, pounding through her body like crashing thunder in the mountains, utterly restful and flushing, her hands shaking so uncontrollably that she dropped the gun.

It went off.

The bullet ripped through the deadened silence, the mattress at once sending a storm of feathered stuffing airborne like a blast of snow, white as they went up, red as they floated down. A burst like a flower appeared on the wall behind the headboard, bits of Father's skull and brain adding texture to the wicked design now permanently etched into her brain.

She could feel herself breathing. Its cadence ran a rhythm with the surge between her legs. Nothing had ever felt so fucking good.

Shaking, she took the gun, the casing, the bullets, and fled into night, never to return, her mind at once conjuring the things she wanted to do with the rest of her life, knowing that everything she accomplished would be spurred solely to arouse passion, to create pleasure.

Father had said, *"Some day this will be yours."*

Today was that day.

The rifle had become her only companion, its cool, lengthy shaft her only lover, its casing, her blanket of security. Her environment had shifted from the backwoods of the country to the inventive streets of the city, the hustle and bustle of a million accents brushing by her, keeping their safe distance if she invaded their personal space. Lucienne lived her life in fear—she, still a virgin for all intents and purposes, the world around her ready and willing to rape her for the very meat on her bones.

She dreamed of Father nightly and everything he'd taught her, and she hopelessly desired returning to a day where she could realize his distant touch again. But was that possible? Perhaps. Physically, he had never laid a sweaty trigger finger on her. Yet still, he'd graced her with a pleasure that no other had ever equaled, a pleasure not precisely physical, but rather mental, fattened of strength and power that magically translated into something licentious. Now, in her early twenties, these explicit desires swelled to a pinnacle, forcing the need to create her very own ecstasy: a personal paradise not much unlike the Eden Father had secured all those years.

I could do it, for now, I can touch…

She gazed at her naked self in the mirror, at her alabaster skin, at her facial features which were remotely European, at her slightly waifish body, the hipbones slightly protruding, the bottom ribs visible beneath the swell of her breasts. She applied her makeup, circling her eyes with black liner, burying her full lips in deep red, setting purple-red pancakes into her cheeks like angry bruises. She filled all her piercings, eighteen in all: one in her tongue, one in each nipple, two in her navel, two in her left eyebrow, one in her lip, one in her clitoris, and nine at various places in her ears. She squeezed herself into a patent-leather dress, her ass cheeks resembling two black teardrops, her breasts pushed up and out so the very red-edges of her nipples were exposed. Standing tall on spiked heels, she adjusted the dress so her strapless shoulders were straight, her naked back stiff and proper, appropriately exposing the angular tattoo on her shoulder blade. Finally done, she stared at her tall, svelte body and tried to determine if her pain—her desire—would show to the outside world, if her bruise-colored eyes truly weighed down on her appearance like two open wounds.

There weren't any visible scars. But her pain: observable, tangible. *Good.*

Before escaping into the night, she retrieved the gun from beneath the bed and gently removed it from the casing.

She placed her blood-red lips to the tip of the smooth barrel, kissed it gently.

Smiling, she left to begin the hunt.

The place she chose catered to those black-shrouded clientele she'd become familiar with, those people whose androgyny equally matched their sexual preferences: it didn't matter what sex you were as long as you were willing to express yourself freely and comfortably, not too passively, not too dominatingly.

The night passed in common themes, sweaty prayers of ritualistic sex, the dance floor an orgy of reaching limbs groping the nearest flesh, exposed or not. Sweaty torsos writhing to the incessant thrum of techno beats, minds lost in the fervor of sustained moments.

Lucienne weaved through the club, her body in constant motion, not in dance, but in subtle pursuit of prey. She kept her methodology unobtrusive, her image inconspicuous, never allowing herself to be noticed lingering in one place by any one individual for any lengthy period of time. She continued on in this unassuming manner, head bobbing ever so slightly to the beat of the music, her legs taking short, self-assured steps, her back softly maneuvering the graceful sway of her shoulders. She was the hunter, she was *dominant*.

Her eyes finally locked onto the perfect target: a man, six-foot, middle-aged, not necessarily a true component of the surrounding lifestyle, but rather an individual seeking escapism from the hideously routine world. A broker perhaps, a lawyer, a businessman. Someone seeking to be hunted down for one night, to be made. He had a beard and moustache. Slightly overweight, a tired bulge squeezing over his belt.

He looked just like Father.

It had been months since the last one like this, an obvious target alone at the bar, unmoving except for beady eyes that searched the human mesh for a lover. She knew, he was the one. She had to have him.

His eyes locked on with Lucienne's.

She smiled kindly, feeling wet.

Then approached him.

They stood outside the door of her apartment, the man's eyes perusing the fourth-floor landing, his distorted features a testament that his common sense fell in clear conflict with his fleshly desires to press on into the adventure of the night. In the pallid light—dull but running much brighter than the chaotic darkness of the club—the man really didn't look that much like Father after all, and in that sense appeared to carry the possibility of threat. His forehead was much too furrowed, his eyes too round, his beard a bit too neat. But still, there was something about him, a sort of strange sadness that surrounded him: the same pathetic glee that had blanketed her father's hungry image when unwanted and uncontrollable desires beset him.

They went inside.

She instructed him to sit on the bed, his rotund body jiggling as the thin mattress sagged beneath his weight. She moved to the only table in the apartment, a small dinette, and sat at one of two chairs, two fingers exploring her wetness along the way, knowing and relishing all over again that she, like Father, had become a hunter, hungry and reckless, her cause pure defense from the enemy-past that had perpetuated her persecution.

That had still continued to tempt her.

When she looked up from her reverie the man was naked, a harsh coating of hair and moles riddling his husky glut. He smiled, teeth yellowed from morning coffees and years of cigarettes.

He stood up, smiling evilly.

Beneath the table, Lucienne slipped the rifle from its pouch.

He marched over to her and when he reached the opposite side of the table she showed him the gun. His eyes winced, his face blanched, cheeks trembling in sudden panic.

"Sit down," she instructed, and he obeyed. Tears clouded his eyes like a rushing tide. "You know what I've always wanted to do?" she asked.

"What is this?" the man asked, his grin showing a brew of fear and strange excitement.

Still holding the gun, she pulled a strip of duct tape from a roll on the floor alongside the gun casing and squeezed it over his eyes. He protested, albeit slightly. She ripped another strip and placed it over his mouth. Gooseflesh rippled his skin, the coarse hairs on his neck and arms standing on end.

Good. He was enjoying himself.

He mumbled something through the seal on his mouth. Lucienne answered him by pressing the barrel of the gun into the left side of his groin, just below the base of his penis, just above the scrotum. His penis hardened, his balls turned purple. Her body trembled with a rush of warmth, her nipples stiffening beneath the hot material of her dress.

"Hmph!" yelled the man, voicing his pleasure.

"Shut up!" Lucienne barked the words in the harshest tone she could induce. Using her free arm she plunged an elbow into his face, bruising the cheek purple. He tumbled off the chair and landed on the hard floor with a dull thud, his erection nearly tearing on impact. The sour tang of sweat rose into Lucienne's nose, an odor signifying to her the progression of lustful respect.

Perhaps he *was* the perfect target after all.

She pressed the rifle into the small of his back, running it and down the trail of gooey sweat leading into the fissure of his ass, the cold metal leaving red streaks pressed into his flesh. Placing the spike of her heel into the center of his back, she brought the gun up and placed it in her mouth, tasting his salt, tempting her taste buds, the cool twang of metal blossoming upon her tongue as she traced it about the shaft, flitting in and out of the hole. The man kept his sightless gaze to the wood floor, now stroking his purple erection and moaning incoherently.

Pulling the gun from her mouth, she quietly placed it upon the table. She then yanked the man up by the hair. Dragging him along, she pushed him to the bed, face down.

"Stay," she chided.

She retrieved the gun and utilized it to force his legs apart, exposing his anus. Curiously, she stared at the mahogany circle, its coarse hairs forested in crust, chunky dimples pocking the landscape of flesh surrounding it.

She hiked her dress up over her head, exposing her nakedness only to the mirror hanging on the wall over the headboard, aptly angled so that she could see herself and her current prey on the bed, his face wincing behind the duct tape. She tightened her grasp on the gun, blowing out a long, clogged breath. The man waited, breathing heavily through his nose, a tensed hand on his penis.

"Up on all fours," Lucienne demanded.

The man obeyed, shifting clumsily, his fat dangling obscenely. She prodded his great white ass with the end of the rifle, taking a poke here and there at his swinging testicles. The man moaned, in pain, pleasure, whatever.

She kneeled on the bed next to him, gripping his thigh for support, then flickered her tongue along the crack of his ass, deep into his anus, pressing the gun ever so closely to her lips. She alternated, swallowing the barrel of the gun, then lubing the man's dark, sour membrane, back and forth, back and forth, wholly participating in an ungodly ménage à trois. Tiring easily, she backed away, slapping the man hard on his buttocks. "Don't move."

She reached under the bed and grabbed the container of gun oil, twisted the top and squeezed a healthy dose of the shit-colored liquid on the barrel. It glistened as she lubed it up, her hand sliding up and down, up and down.

Just like Father used to do.

Kneeling a foot or so behind the man, she tenderly prodded the crack of his ass, leaving pukey streaks of gun oil on the shore of his flesh, greasing the surrounding hairs until she eventually ferreted out his soft hole. She took a deep breath, felt an orgasm nearing, then buried eight inches of the oily metal barrel inside him. He grunted, stroking his penis fervently.

Lucienne's life played back in her memory, her father and his hunting trips, her mother whose life Father had undoubtedly extinguished in order to carry out his profound desires. A lethal combination giving birth to her own sickening desire, the gun at its crux, her approaching orgasm its only aspiration.

The man gripped the edges of the bed, the sheets bunched in his grasp. By now the gun oil was burning the tender walls of his anus, but she showed no mercy, pounding furiously, eyes closed in prayer for orgasm, one gentle finger instinctively searching out the trigger. The man began to howl behind his gag, tried to pull away. Lucienne plundered forward, going deeper, her orgasm teasing her, but not giving in. She wanted it to last forever, her dripping flesh spraying upon his, staining the mattress, the smells of gun oil and musk and shit prevailing in the hot room.

She continued to pound. The man thumped in a panic, tried to wrestle away. But never enough to fully disconnect himself from the harsh encounter. Lucienne went deeper, both hands on the gun. Blood started pouring from the man's ass, streaking the barrel. His skin went from white to deep crimson.

His body stiffened.

And then the man came, his seed oozing from his urethra to the mattress in a weak globule.

He collapsed, ass in the air, permitting Lucienne to finish, to achieve her ecstasy.

She continued to pound her fury, unable to stop until she experienced the only love she knew. The gun slid in and out. Her muscles tensed, her flesh rippled. She felt her eyes roll up in her head. *Yes!* It came, a orgasm of proportions unfathomable, her muscles tightening up in great trembling quakes, sending electrical shudders throughout her body, from her head to her heart to her toes.

And, to her fingers. They, tensed, contracted...squeezed.

The explosion was muffled, felt more than heard. At the same shuddering moment her vagina sprayed its orgasmic juices, the man's body jerked forward in a deadened heap, an alarming spray of red blanketing the clear droppings of semen on the bed, splashing her naked body in a great river of release. The gun fell from her grip, and it slipped free from his anus, now devoid of contraction. She collapsed back, exhausted, clearing her face of the man's splattered gristle.

She stayed silent for a few moments, admiring tonight's effort as her beating urges waned. Just like the animals Father used to bring in from the woodland, her prey lay steaming on her bed, glistening entrails torn free from their cavity, slick blood pumping from various fissures. The putrid smell of death rising in swells. Gouts of blood and bile spilling from his mouth.

Another night, another successful hunt, the bullet unheard.

She rose from the bed and went to the kitchen. Removed the knife from the sink. The one with the twelve-inch blade. She placed it on the scarred dinette table.

Before skinning her prey, she would need to perform a task: clean her gun, Father's gun, grandfather's gun.

She would enjoy every stimulating second of the process, just as she did when she was a child, all those years ago.

Gila Way

The great demon known as Summer threatened to eat twenty-nine-year-old Jerry Smith alive. It held him tight in its grasp, simmered him to a virtual boil and gave no hint of letting go until he was fully cooked, both physically and mentally.

Jerry pressed harder on the gas, pushed ninety. Sweat streaked urgently down the sides of his face as if to keep pace with the speed of the car. Heart pounding, he pressed against the wheel, his grip vice-tight, muscles and teeth tensed as the beaten Nova roared like a great ancient monster, tearing down the highway, the wind whipping through its open windows as if trapped in the clutches of a heat-filled tornado.

He rocked his eyes back and forth between the road and the rearview mirror. Ahead I-15 intersected the sea of sand like a great black vein. Behind it vanished into a shimmering mirage that went seventy-three miles straight back to Vegas. He bit his chapped lips, watching carefully as the ghostly wave of heat shifted like a magician's handkerchief, revealing nothing but sand, asphalt, and cacti. No sign of *them*, no sign of Tony and Vito.

Without a sprinkle of forewarning a torrent of sand swooped in and slashed the windshield like an angry swarm of locusts. Innumerable grains reflected the shimmer of absorbed sunlight floating on the glass surface, creating a giant burst of sharp luminescence. Jerry shuttered his eyes, painfully blinded.

THUD THUD.

The Nova's shocks bounced. Panic seized him, heart pounding in his chest. He shrieked, slammed the brakes. The car skidded, tires screeching, burning rubber across the sweltering blacktop. He turned into the skid, doing his damnedest to regain control, but the car careened, shimmied as the steering wheel shook in his hands like a jackhammer. The stench of scorched rubber rose in the air as he finally opened his dazed eyes and glimpsed into the rearview mirror.

In the distance, a large, tire-mauled lizard rolled end over end down the road like a hot dog slipping from its bun, tumbling to a dead stop a hundred yards away.

The Nova's tires found their grip and Jerry felt the tension at once begin to escape through his gasps. He eased the car to about thirty-five and remembered the ride to Vegas. There had been a bloodbath of Gila monsters, one at least every mile sprawled in an impossible position at roadside. He hadn't thought at the time he would be donating his share.

He pressed back down on the gas.

The Nova's engine sputtered.

He startled up, a painful lump forming in his throat. He pounded the gas, banged the wheel. *Now is not a good time to start messing with me!* The car tried to resuscitate itself, surged, slowed, surged, slowed, like a city bus in traffic, but refused returning to getaway velocity. There was a startling gun-shot *bang!* Steam seeped from the edges of the hood. The engine made a chortling sound as if amused at Jerry's predicament, then exhaled one last wheeze before cutting out. Jerry Smith, almost lost in tears, sat stupefied, his hands white-knuckled on the steering wheel as the Nova rolled another fifty yards to a dead stop.

He sat motionless, forehead pressed against the wheel, in instant denial that his precious steel baby just died like a dinosaur on the verge of extinction. He wrestled with the ignition, pleaded with it to start. It offered a couple of coughs, then went mute.

Immense frustration cut into his body. He leaped from the car, feeling homicidal, banging the roof, the trunk, the hood, gushing a barrage of obscenities that no one could hear.

Soon fatigue suppressed his tirade. He'd been awake for thirty-six hours, and up until a few minutes ago wanted nothing more than to find a dark hole to crawl into and hide from the rest of the world. Now, as the bloated sun stared down on him with poisonous eyes, he scanned the barren landscape, praying for a sign of life, a soul savior to rescue him from the infinite sea of sand.

He tried to swallow but the lump in his throat blocked his effort. The sun beat its maddened rays against his chest, hot sand blew in his face. He questioned whether he would see another day.

He squinted back down the highway, searching for an answer.

There was someone in the road a hundred yards away.

Dressed in tatters, the odd figure picked up the trodden lizard and held it to the sun-scorched sky, as if in prayer. The stranger glanced in Jerry's direction then scuttled off the side of the road into the wind-whirled desert, cradling the dead lizard close.

Jerry yelled, waving his arms crazily, the gravel on the black asphalt gritting harshly under his sneakers as he jogged forward. The stranger took one last glance at him then vanished into the cloak of the mirage. Jerry stopped, kicked up a cloud of dust, his mind taken up with frustration. "Go on and make yourself a God-damned wallet, freak!"

He plodded back to the car, wondering if he'd been eclipsed with a supernatural something that brought on all his bad fortune. Three days ago, after months of thought and hankering desire, he left Louise in the middle of the night with all their money in tow—almost fifteen hundred dollars—trading in the Hell-bound trailer park in Steamboat for a few days in Vegas. Obsessed with wild fantasies of striking it rich, he became convinced of his game plan—blackjack first, then craps—and had tried to assure her that it was their only God-given chance to eliminate their problems and flee the park. All his efforts were in vain of course, caused countless arguments, heartache, and headaches, and resulted in his taking the trip alone.

blackjack first, then craps...

He immediately hit the tables when he got there, fared pretty darn well to start, turning the fifteen hundred into four grand within the first three hours. He felt that if he could just keep the streak going he'd end up back in Steamboat with a hefty bundle.

But his cockiness and drunkenness did him in, and he frittered all but sixty-eight bucks of it away in the next three hours.

Horribly depressed, he found a room at a dive on the edge of the strip called the Tree-Tree Inn. He was having a drink at the bar, wondering if sixty-eight bucks was enough dough to drink himself to death, when a *gentleman* in an expensive suit and thick gold chain introduced himself as Tony and invited him to play a friendly game of poker in the back room. *What have I got to lose…?*

In two hours Jerry Smith built up a debt of nearly thirteen thousand.

Tony and his partner Vito both had their backs turned when Jerry made a break for it. He was three feet from the front door before the goons realized he was bailing, and by the time they made it out after him, Jerry successfully mingled with the tourists en route to his car, parked a half mile away by the Crazy Horse Lounge. He was immediately on I-15 breaking speed limits.

Did I really see someone in the road, or was it an hallucination?

After an ineffective try with the car again, he got out, shielded his eyes and looked back down the road. The sun made Jerry feel soft: his brain felt like a hot water bottle, his insides all heavy and curdled. He continued gazing into the mirage, seeking his fate.

There were no answers. Only a smudge of gore from the roadkill.

If I really did see someone, then there's gotta be a town nearby…

He prayed that there was, otherwise that great demon Summer would definitely eat Jerry Smith alive.

The sign came into sight a mile past where his car had turned to dust:

GILA WAY
One Mile

Secured to a rusted metal post, the rotting wood sign stood in solitude like a scarecrow left years behind to guard an abandoned field. Judging from its sad condition, Jerry feared the town of Gila Way would be similarly forsaken, a ghost town.

He grasped his temples, tried to suppress an approaching headache. His very survival was on the table now, a fifty-fifty shot in hand. If Gila Way no longer existed, then Jerry would lose the game of his life.

Tony and Vito raced along I-15 in Tony's bright red Corvette at a cool ninety miles an hour. Red and yellow lights from the dash lit up Tony's seething expression. The big Italian was sickened, his rage blooming like a dozen red roses. He wanted nothing more than to strangle the dirtbag Jerry from Steamboat who had him driving around the desert like some lost tourist. Who'd have thought the putz would have the balls to lam it on his way to the john? He glanced over at Vito, who was busy digging for gold in his nose.

"Hey Tony, ya really think dis guy was stoopid enough to take dis road?" Vito asked, examining a booger parked on the end of his finger. "There ain't nothin' out here."

Like the inside of your skull... Tony reached into his blazer pocket, pulled out a grainy black and white video surveillance shot of Jerry at the poker table. Kid had a big smile on his face. It was probably taken before he lost all his money. He tossed the photo on the dashboard. "Only one way back to Steamboat."

"Oh..." said Vito, flicking the booger to the floor.

Tony shook his head with disgust, put an Alice In Chains CD in, good and loud so he wouldn't be able to hear Vito talking. When the Creator made Vito, he no doubt omitted his brains and directed all efforts towards the manufacture of his muscles.

Tony figured that when they eventually got a hold of Jerry from Steamboat, Vito would get to use them.

Like a sickened Clint Eastwood in *The Unforgiven*, Jerry stood at the edge of the town, all hunched over, his shadow stretched long and crooked by the setting sun.

It wasn't much, but it *was here*, and he couldn't be more thankful. It sat at the end of a dirt and gravel road that tapered a quarter mile off the highway. A battered sign, like the first, welcomed him: "Gila Way".

The town appeared to be only one street that extended on for about a half mile, buildings running along each side like those in an Old West community, maybe two dozen in all. A few people gathered out in front of a saloon.

Jerry staggered to the first building on the right, a small weathered structure with a wrap-around porch and wooden steps that led to a rusty screened door, slightly ajar. Wooden posts that at one time must have supported guardrails encircled the porch, standing at various angles like the remaining teeth in the mouth of an old dying man. Like the door, the two front windows were also screened, allowing the arid desert air to flow freely through.

Alongside the steps a six-foot painted statue of a lizard stood on its hind legs, arms outstretched, rows of teeth smiling wide. A sign hanging from its neck read: *Gila Way Souvenir Shop. Come In, Were Open!* Another smaller sign chained around the statue's belly bragged: *Gila drinks, Gila snacks!*

He stepped up the creaky stairs, pulled open the screen door. It screeched like a *lizard* and Jerry was eerily reminded of his roadkill incident two miles back down the highway.

Inside, the shop could have passed for a lizard museum. If you could fit a picture of a lizard on it, then it was here. Key chains, mugs, pictures, postcards, tee-shirts, cluttered on tables and shelves. Pictures hung from the walls, mobiles from the ceiling. There was barely enough room for Jerry to walk to the counter where a man glanced up to greet him.

The man looked as though he had spent his whole life baking in the desert sun, stringy, bony, leather-skinned, thousands of lines adorning his face. His head was unnaturally wider at the top and thinner at the chin, and to Jerry he kind of looked like a lizard. He cradled a small gray lizard in his arms—about a foot long, nose to tail—and stroked it gently with his free hand. The lizard responded with a yawn.

"Looks like you could use something cold to drink." His words were as dry and as gritty as the windblown sand scraping the rusted screens in the windows of the shop.

"More than ever." The words practically stuck in his throat.

The man stopped petting the lizard, reached behind and opened a cooler. He pulled a bottle of Cola. Jerry drank half the bottle in one breath; it was good and cold, and it made him feel better. Looking around, he asked, "What's the scoop with all the lizards?" He picked up a plastic replica, gave it a once-over and placed it back.

"Oh…not lizards. *Gila monsters*. This must be your first visit." The man smiled wide and every aspect of his misshapened head and wrinkled face seemed to change, as though it were constructed of jelly.

Now why in God's name would anyone want to come back? "Yes," he said politely. "First time."

"Well then welcome to Gila Way."

Jerry smiled, walked around. "Aren't Gila monsters poisonous?"

"Only if they bite'cha!" The man let out a laugh that was almost a hiss, then held his pet up and kissed it on the lips. "You wouldn't bite me now, would ya'?"

Jerry chugged the rest of his soda, placed the bottle on the counter. The whole scenario seemed dreamlike, the merchant, his pet, all the lizard faces peering down at him from the plethora of trinkets. It made him feel...paranoid, panicky. He suddenly wanted to hightail it out of there but immediately told himself not to overreact. He simply needed some rest. "Is there a hotel?"

"Just down the road." The man stopped stroking his lizard and pointed out the window behind the counter.

Jerry bought another cola and turned to leave.

"Ya might want to pick yisself up a souvenir...while you're here that is," the man added.

Jerry stopped, scanned the shop again. All the lizard faces spooked him. "I think I'll get you on the way out."

The man smiled. "Well, alrighty then. See you on the way out."

Jerry forced a wave goodbye and went to find the hotel.

"Look at that," Vito said, pointing a fat finger.

An abandoned car. Tony eased the Corvette to a stop and the two of them got out. Sweat dotted their foreheads as the desert rudely welcomed them from the car's cool interior.

Tony knelt down at the Nova's front bumper. Footprints headed forward alongside the highway.

"Looks like someone walked away," Vito offered.

Brilliant, Einstein. Standing, Tony said, "There's no way he could survive in this heat for too long." He squinted, looked around. Lots of nothing. "Let's drive."

"Bring his thumbs back as souvenirs!" Vito yelled, giving Tony two thumbs up and a dumb, open-mouthed smile. He looked like a cross between Al Capone and the *Fonz.*

Tony closed his eyes, shook his head as they returned to the Corvette.

"Hey…" Vito said, pointing. "Look…" Tony turned. Squatting on top of Jerry's abandoned Nova was a Gila, about three feet long, its tail draped down over the open driver's side window. Tony grinned, plucked the .44 neatly hidden away in his pants.

One shot and the Gila was soup.

He blew on the barrel of the gun, tucked it away. "C'mon, it's getting dark. Let's go get him."

They sped off, leaving the setting sun behind.

Night had assumed its identity over the desert. Darkness congealed into clouds that pressed in from the west and settled beneath the moon and stars like a blanket of cold stone, hiding Jerry's elongated shadow as he walked down the sandy street.

When Jerry Smith was young, he would sit at the window of his room in his parent's home, gazing at the night sky. The stars and moon, shining brightly in the night, would remind him that there was indeed another world beyond Caplowe, Colorado, a world where the possibilities were infinite and where a young man from a small mountain home might be anything he wished to be, especially if he had the commitment to pursue his dreams.

When he left home ten years ago for Los Angeles, he pursued his dream to be an actor, paid his way through all the auditions by working nights and weekends as a cashier in a supermarket. It was there he met Louise Parker, and fell in love. She was one of the prettiest girls he had ever seen, upbeat, sincere, had a natural gift for friendliness. Jerry's pursuit in the acting field evaporated as his passionate quest for her grew, and by the time they started dating, it was a notion of the past.

They moved in together, stayed in a tired old flat for three years. The times were memorable, but were also demanding, and they quickly grew tired of the hustle and bustle lifestyle of Los Angeles. They both agreed that they were better suited for a quieter life in the mountains. They picked up and moved to Colorado, the dream to build a home and family as diamond-bright on their minds as the stars in the sky.

But their visions of a happy life together fell far short of standard. Louise started drinking, and Jerry's unerring knack for failure followed him around from job to job. They had agreed to save what they could, at least enough to help them escape the trashy trailer park they ended up living in for six years, but Jerry was impatient, couldn't wait, and woke up feeling lucky three days ago.

He found the motel, called The Desert Inn, a seedy dive with a front office at one end anchoring a strip of twelve cookie-box rooms with tattered doors. Each door had its own patch of dirt out front that served as a parking spot, two occupied with run-down pick-ups, the other a mini-van with Arizona plates. The entire establishment was painted a pale sickly green with three cartoon lizards smiling and waving on a sign alongside the office door, the word *Vacancy!* floating in neon next to their mouths. Jerry entered the office.

Inside, behind a small counter, a man sat alone at a fold-up table playing cards. All wrinkled up, he looked a lot like the merchant in the souvenir shop, and Jerry figured that a lot of the people in this God-forsaken town must be related in one form or another. He wore dirty trousers and a yellow woven shirt with brown sweat-stains at the armpits. He stood to greet Jerry. "Howdy. Help you?" His voice was sharp, his lips so thin they disappeared into his mouth when he smiled.

"I need a room."

"Sure looks like ya do." The man raised an eyebrow. "Been walkin' around the desert?"

Jerry forced an impatient smile. "How much for the night?"

"Oh...ten bucks'll do it. Keys are in the back." The man walked into a curtained-off room.

Jerry rubbed his tired eyes. Inky blotches on the insides of his eyelids formed the shapes of lizards, each one dancing about on its hind legs, taunting him with sharp, reaching claws and gaping mouths.

He heard a hissing sound.

He tore his hands away from his face. The paranoia that had tempted him back at the souvenir shop flirted with his mind again. This time he could not ignore it, regardless if it was simply exhaustion deceiving him.

He heard it again, coming from the back room.

Clenching his fists, he circled behind the desk and pulled the curtain aside.

Jerry gasped at the sight.

Two old wooden ladders had been arranged in the center of the room about five feet apart. A plank of wood ran from ladder to ladder, tied to the top steps. Three Gilas, each about three feet long from nose to tail hung upside down from the plank, their rear legs and tail bound to it with a length of rope. The lizards on the ends had one front claw tied to the second step on the ladder next to it, the other bound to the adjacent leg of the Gila in the middle. A small metal rod had been inserted into their jaws, prying them open, and a yellow, pus-like discharge dripped into large tin cans below.

"Venom."

Jerry leaped at the voice. He clutched his chest, as though to keep his expanding heart from escaping his throat. "I...I didn't mean to sneak back. I heard the hissing..."

The proprietor grinned, shrugged his shoulders. "I store it and sell it. Quite valuable, you know." The man handed Jerry a room key, smiled. His teeth were mottled with dark stains, and Jerry thought he saw a drop of that vile venom trickle from his top lip.

You're hallucinating again...

Jerry eyed the key. Room 11. Lucky number. He handed the man two fives and quickly escaped outside.

Bright moonbeams leaked through the clouds and entered his wake like a flashlight's flicker searching a musty cellar. The neon from the smiling Gila sign illuminated the arid surroundings in a sickly, phosphorescent glow.

He allowed his eyes to wander about the dry, decrepit environment. He wondered if Tony and Vito were lurking just beyond the periphery of his eyesight, waiting for the perfect moment to pounce...

He heard a scream.

It came from behind the motel, not the playful wail of a girlfriend being tickled, or a child in a game of chase, but a scream of fear, of sheer and mortal terror that might shred one's lungs into bloody strips.

Jerry raced around the motel to a small courtyard of grass that tapered into the dark expanse of the desert. Deep in the distance he saw a bonfire raging, flames jutting high into the night sky, their dancing spires in prayer to the semi-blanketed moon. Gathered around the site were a crowd of bustling people, maybe forty or fifty, hands raised high, excited. They cheered in unison.

Jerry moved towards the gathering, crouched, trying not to draw any attention to himself as there was no cover in the open field of sand and tumbleweed. An escaping shaft of fire-light illuminated the congregation as he approached, and he had trouble understanding what he saw. It looked like a bizarre Halloween party, all of them wearing masks and head-dresses, clad in green rags like the roadkill man. Men, women and children alike—all dressed like Gila monsters.

The crowd suddenly quieted. Jerry stood rigid. At first he thought that maybe he'd been spotted, but none of the masked faces were pointed in his direction.

Something was about to happen.

He half expected to hear another scream, but from amidst the hushed whispers of the looming horde, tired labored moans leaked through like the ghostly cries of a soul trapped in the woodwork of a haunted house. They sounded helpless, drained, the voices of individuals all but prepared to surrender to whatever horrific fate awaited them.

Jerry inched closer, fifteen feet away. He leaned to his right, peered through a break in the circle.

He felt suddenly ill and clutched at the air until his fists turned pale-knuckled. Stupefied, he couldn't move—he could only feel the muscle-tearing beat of his heart as watched the terror unfold.

A middle-aged man and woman, both decked in tourist garb—cotton shorts, floral tops—had been taken prisoner, their ankles and wrists bound to wooden poles as if they were to be burned as witches in a Salem witchcraft trial. The woman's head gyrated wildly around on her neck, and even in the firelight Jerry could see the pallid, eye-bulging contortion of her face, mouth twisted in an impossible shape. The man, whose tire-roll of fat was escaping his belt, thumped and hissed in a fit, trying to twist his way free of the binds.

The Gila people began to chant a syncopated rhythm. The couple screamed again, and then again and again, high blood-maddened wails that were quickly swallowed by the desert night.

Jerry cast a wary eye to the ground at the woman's feet and had to choke back his own scream. The woman's left foot was gone—into the mouth of a large Gila monster. Her sneaker, nestled in the sand, was soaked with blood.

The crowd chanted louder, their echoes whirling about like maniacal phantoms. Two more Gilas appeared, just as large as their predecessor. They perched up on their hind quarters and leaned against the man's naked legs, their black beady eyes aglow in the fire light, their mouths gaping, spitting forth the most evil of sounds. Their claws swiftly ripped into the exposed flesh of the man's thighs, releasing a stream of blood that was urgently lapped up by their thick slithering tongues. The man let out another huge whooping scream that quickly tapered down into a bubbly moan, and he slumped, unconscious and blue.

More Gilas gathered, hissing and squealing in a frenzied state, tumbling over one another. The woman, her leg now consumed to the knee, started convulsing, gnashing and contorting at the sight of the additional monsters. They attacked, their razor-sharp claws slicing into her body. Blood, thick and red, gushed down, swamping the Gilas, and soon her legs were strips of gore dangling at the knees like blood-drenched ticker tape.

In death, only their faces were untouched, but their final, lasting expressions were frozen in a rictus of terror.

Still more Gilas gathered. As many as fifteen reptiles were now clinging to the tourists like giant parasites, and even more were still trying to clamber up, to get their share. Soon the poles, burdened from the weight, uprooted from the soft sand and gave way, and what was left of the tourists toppled to the desert floor.

The Gilas ate, devil-red mouths sopped with gummy venom and blood, gnawing through muscle, sinew, and bone. Jerry, utterly sickened, finally broke his inaction, bent over at an odd angle, closed his eyes and vomited cola and bile.

When he opened his eyes, a pair of bare feet were there, edging his vomit. He looked up, head pounding so hard it felt it would split in two. A lizard mask peered down at him. "I believe this is yours," the muffled voice behind the mask said.

A tire-mauled Gila dropped to the sand.

An unmasked moon cast beams down that reflected off the hood of the Corvette as Tony and Vito crawled into the town of Gila Way.

A celestial bonfire raged in the distance. Tony hit the brakes and switched off the lights in the same motion. The windshield appeared to be alive with firelight. They were both silent at first, mesmerized by the dancing flames. "It's so...*spooky*," Vito finally said.

For once Tony agreed with him. It didn't seem to fit. Something strange was going down in the town of Gila Way. The street was deserted, yet a fire burned bright on the outskirts. In his mind, Tony felt as if the fire was alive, an entity beckoning him forward with spectral strength. He swallowed. "Let's go check it out. He's gotta be around here somewhere."

Tightly bound ropes dug into Jerry's wrists and ankles. He tried to wriggle free from the pole, but could only manage to twitch.

By this time, the Gilas had completely ripped the two tourists to shreds and dragged every piece away into the dark of the desert. Jerry could hear the reptiles squealing in the distance, fighting over the last juicy morsels. Only smears of blood and shreds of clothing remained of the couple.

A horde of lizard faces surrounded him. They began to chant.

Jerry screamed, quietly at first, then at the top of his lungs, his voice filling the desert. He trembled violently. The locals chanted louder. A creeping, tomblike cold raced through his blood.

He heard a demonic hiss, not too far away. The Gilas. They were coming for him.

The locals crowded in. Jerry tried to cry above their rising incantation.

A gunshot tore into the night.

At once the locals scattered like fish avoiding a rock dropped in a pond, leaving Jerry to fend for himself on the pole. He couldn't believe his eyes when he saw Tony and Vito making their grand entrance through the parting crowd. They looked awfully ridiculous walking through the desert, wearing suits and gold chains, guns raised high. Tony yelled "Yah!" or something like that then fired off another shot in the air. The locals scurried further—some all the way back into town— allowing the goons total access to a helpless Jerry.

Tony faced Jerry, smiling. "I can't wait to hear this one."

Jerry was shaking wildly, his nerves jangling like fire alarms. His spent mind tried real hard to figure out whether he was happy to see the two goons or not. "H-help me, please..." he pleaded though cracked, stuttering lips.

Tony grinned, so wide his teeth looked like Christmas lights. "I should let these nuts have their way with you. God only knows what you did to piss 'em off." He glanced about the scene. Vito was holding the crowd at bay, swinging his .44 in a wild arc. "Looks like they were gettin' ready to shish-ke-bob your ass." He laughed, then grabbed Jerry's face, gave it a hard squeeze. "Don't you worry though...I wouldn't let anything happen to you before I got my money."

Tony summoned Vito, who at this point had successfully scared off the locals. All of them had retreated, but still kept a watchful eye on the goings-on from the safe distance. Vito jogged over, whacked Jerry on the cheek with the butt of the .44. White-hot pain ripped through his skull. The goon then leaned down and untied the ropes, and Jerry fell helplessly numb into the desert sand.

Vito grabbed him by the shirt. In the distance Jerry could hear the locals starting their strange chant again. He tried to crawl away, fingers digging into the sand. He was terrified. *The chants...*

"C'mon!" Tony yelled. "Let's get outta here." He sounded panicky. He must've seen something...

Then Vito screamed. Jerry smelled copper. Blood.

Vito's grasp on Jerry suddenly came free and Jerry spun around in a rambling circle to see what had happened.

A Gila had found Vito's leg and was digging its claws into his calf muscle. The goon was trying to kick it away, with no success, and then there was an indescribable ripping noise as the lizard dug its jaws into Vito's muscle-bound thigh and bit a hunk of fleshy meat away. Vito stumbled down, helpless, blood squirting from the gaping hole in his leg, slashing haphazardly at the reptile with the gun. He caught it good in the neck a few times and green blood squirted from its wounds. Wicked squeals blurted from its mouth as it spit away pieces of pant fabric and scraps of flesh. Then suddenly from behind them there were countless hisses and squeals, and they appeared like magic, twelve, maybe fifteen Gilas, mouths saturated with sticky venom and blood-red residue from their earlier meal. They pounced on Vito like lions on a Zebra in the jungle, ripping though his suit as if it were made of paper-mâché.

On his back, Vito dropped his gun and stared up in silent terror, in perfect position as the ultimate sacrifice.

Tony stood petrified, witness to the grotesque horror, and when he could take no more he finally found the inner strength to turn away, put a convulsive arm around his gut and throw up.

It wasn't nearly enough to spare him. Two squealing Gilas pounced him as he vomited, attaching their razored hooks to the sides of his head and tackling him to the sand. The goon screamed at the top of his lungs, arms and legs flailing in seizure-like fashion. Another lizard trotted over and swiped at his chest. He grabbed the lizard around the abdomen, tried to pull it away but was unable to, and it savagely closed its bloodied mouth around his lower jaw and ripped it from his face in a single effortless jerk, leaving behind a stringy mess of tongue, blood, and vomit.

Through it all, Jerry managed to wobble to his feet and take a few steps back.

But he did not flee the carnage. Instead he kept his eyes pinned to the fray, staying close by, waiting, just in case...

Slowly, one by one, just as before, the Gilas dragged their share into the desert. One ran by Jerry with an arm in its mouth, another with a dress shoe, the foot still in it. And just as before, when the Gilas were gone, all that remained was spatterings of blood, shreds of clothing, and the wild squeals of distant pleasure.

Jerry took a few wary steps forward, heart pounding crazily. Stepping through blood and sand, he sifted through Tony and Vito's bloodied clothes until he found what he was looking for.

Then he ran as fast as he could out of the desert, back into the town of Gila Way.

Jerry knocked on the door of the trailer.

He heard slow, tired footsteps. A banging noise inside. The door creaked open and Louise was there, eyes mid-drift, hair disheveled. It had been four days since Jerry left with her money. She had never expected to see him again.

She let out a hateful scream and tried to slam the door but Jerry was too quick. He forced his way in, tackled her to the couch, held his hand over her mouth as he pinned her down. Two gold chains dangled from his neck.

Louise grabbed the chains. "You bastard! Where'd you get these?" Her brow furrowed into an angry triangle.

Jerry smiled. "Never mind that. I brought *you* something from Vegas."

Her words froze and her tantrum ceased as he dropped a thick wad of hundreds in her lap. Her anger immediately turned to astonishment. She grabbed the money, sloppily fanned it. "Where did you...? H-how much is it?" A devilish smile appeared on her face.

Jerry tucked Vito's wallet further into his pant pocket. He returned the grin. "A little more than fifteen thousand." He stood up. "C'mon, I got another present for ya". He pulled her up and led her out to the side of the trailer.

Her jaw dropped.

A red 1998 Corvette. He held up a set of keys, a gold "Tony" dangling from the key chain. "We're getting outta here."

"How did...gold chains, a car, money?" She was bedazzled and dumbfounded.

He pressed his lips against her cheek and whispered in her ear: "Let's just say I got lucky."

The morning sun peeked over the mountains. The Corvette's shadow stretched out long and thin behind them. Jerry reached over and held Louise's hand.

He hoped that going east this time would be the start of a better life together.

He pressed on the gas, pushed ninety. They drove in silence, into the mountains.

They slowed when the roads curved.

They passed a sign:

Eagle's Nest
One Mile.

Somewhere above them, a screech. Jerry shuddered.

He pressed harder on the gas. It could take the curves. Besides, he knew he wouldn't have to worry about *this* car breaking down.

He peered at the dashboard.

The needle read "E".

Jerry coughed. So did the car.

Upside Down

SATURDAY MORNING

It's hard to believe, but my life has really turned upside down since yesterday.

Really.

You'll have to excuse me if my writing seems a little messy. A great deal has happened, this pencil isn't very sharp and...well, you'll understand after you read this.

As usual, when Friday five o'clock rolled around, I felt the need to simplify my mind. I took the customary trek with Mac and Steve over to Praline's for a couple of beers. My wife Julie doesn't mind me taking happy hour with the boys because she has bowling on Friday nights, and besides, we could both use a little "away time" from one another every now and then. I think she would agree with me that it has helped our marriage over the past twelve years.

Now, I have to think back, so please bear with me. My mind is a bit cloudy, with all that's been going on. Okay. This particular Friday night, me and Mac and Steve talked—admitted more like it—that we would all consider a little extracurricular activity in our lives if the chance presented itself. Now don't get me wrong, I love my wife, but there has been a little something missing of late, a *spark* maybe, or just...something. Well, things just haven't been the same. And all those cute girls at Praline's just walking on by. Temptation abounds.

Our conversation was typical. "Look at her!" Mac would say.

"I'd like to get my hands on that!" Steve would say, and I would just sit there and smile like an idiot and agree with everything they said. So what? I mean, I wasn't *doing* anything, I was just looking and talking, and...I didn't *plan* on causing any problems, they just...*happened.*

But that's not where the *real* problem exists.

Sometime during the course of the evening, I went to the bar to buy a round.

"Three taps," I ordered.

The bartender, a guy in his mid-twenties with glassy eyes and a goatee poured two beers from the tap, brought them over, placed them on the bar.

"I ordered three," I had said.

"Sorry," and he picked up another glass. I watched him as he pulled the tap and allowed the beer to flow all over the *bottom* of the glass. He pushed the tap back into the place and brought the wet glass over, placing it on the bar, just as he held it under the tap.

Upside down.

I turned and expected to find Mac and Steve laughing and slapping their knees and just having a grand old time at my expense, but they had their eyes glued on the backside of a cute redhead playing a game of pool.

I turned back to face the bartender.

"That'll be nine," he said, holding two hands up, one digit curled down, as if I didn't understand English.

"Is that for two beers, or three?"

He stopped, looked at the two filled glasses, then at the upside down one. His brow arched into a perplexed triangle. "Three."

"I changed my mind," I said. "I'll take mine in a bottle."

The bartender made a small grimace, removed the inverted glass, and brought me a tall-neck. I gave him a ten and rejoined my friends.

"You guys set that up?" I was a bit annoyed, and wasn't in the mood to be the brunt of anyone's joke.

They didn't hear me. They were too busy watching the girl at the pool table.

Two beers later, with the incident long forgotten—the bartender had chosen to bring me my drafts right-side up—I decided to leave Mac and Steve and their prayers to themselves. I was getting a bit tired, and hungry, and wanted to go home.

I had one foot out the door when she called to me.

"Hey," a soft female voice cooed from behind.

I turned and saw an astounding lady, twenty-four, maybe twenty-five, long, silken blonde hair flowing down to the upper arch of her perfectly round breasts. Her eyes were as blue as an azure sky, her lips as full and as red as a crimson rose in bloom, and her pinpoint nose graced the center of her face like a monument erected to honor her exquisite beauty.

My heart almost skipped a beat. Stammering, I said, "Hey…what?"

"You leaving so soon?"

At this point I realized that I had been still walking, and was along the sidewalk, about five or six feet from Praline's entrance. I stopped. "Four beers is my limit." I didn't even hear myself speak; I was so caught up in her good looks.

"Then how about a bite to eat?" she asked.

It was at this point that I noticed her necklace. Dangling from it was a cross…upside down. I ignored it and looked at my watch. Julie was probably starting her second game. Plenty of time. "Sure."

I was sitting at a table at La Rotunda—a fine Italian restaurant on Vine Street—opposite one of the most beautiful, and for some reason I couldn't figure, frighteningly familiar women I had ever laid eyes on.

But I had trouble simply concentrating on her. Things around me were getting out of hand.

First the waiter poured my water just as the bartender did at Praline's, saturating my half of the tablecloth. Both the waiter and Lisa—that was her name—pretended that nothing out of the ordinary had happened. I started to make a scene, but when I noticed those dining at other tables were served their drinks in the same manner— and were actually "drinking" from their glasses that way, I stopped my complaining and started to pay more attention to everything around me.

Dinners and salads were being served on the bottom half of plates, and when my chicken parmesan came, the cheese and sauce was sandwiched between the plate and the meat. Lisa buttered her bread and ate it butter side down. Soon, it seemed that everything being served and eaten at La Rotunda was being done so, upside down.

By the time our dessert came, I had trouble believing that all that was happening was for real and not dreamed. Gravity seemed not to exist anymore. The cake we ordered was brought to us on the normal side of the plate, but was served *completely* upside down, plate and all, as if glued together, and placed on the table cake-down.

Even liquids—our coffee—seemed to defy gravity and were poured up into cups and placed inverted on the table. Nothing spilled out this time. Lisa had no problem drinking her coffee from an upside-down cup, but me—I was getting nauseous.

I had to leave.

"C'mon. Let's go." I had said.

"Where to?" she asked, smiling slyly.

Gazing at that smile—that familiar smile—helped me forget for a moment all the craziness that was happening, until we stood to leave and I saw that half the tables and chairs in the restaurant were now upside down, legs in the air.

Walking down Vine Street was an adventure. Every third or fourth car at the curb was parked with its wheels facing the night sky (don't ask me how they're driven this way, I haven't seen it), next to inverted parking meters and flipped fire hydrants. Every store window, whether it be clothing or antiques or jewelry, was decorated completely, well…you know…

At this point I got real confused and things went blurry and out of focus. The last thing I remembered was getting real nervous and dizzy, and then everything went black.

I woke up with sharp designs of sunlight warming my body, the covers of my bed pulled up to my chin. I was in a cold sweat, and thought I had been dreaming.

Julie *and* Lisa were standing over me.

I darted up, eyes wide. Julie sat next to me on the bed. "Rough night last night, huh."

I looked at her, then at Lisa and her excellence, then back to Julie. "I…I…" was all I could get out.

"Lisa said you were a perfect gentleman, treated her to dinner," Julie said, a mocking smile on her face.

I didn't know what the hell was going on. I nodded. It was a weak nod. I thought I was a dead man.

"It's a good thing she got my note. She said she caught you on the way out of Praline's."

Got my note? I looked at Lisa again, at her *familiar* face, and the moment she winked at me realized who she was. Oh God, how could I have forgotten? Lisa was Julie's cousin. I had forgotten she was coming up from Florida to visit for the weekend. It was amazing she recognized me; she was only thirteen when I last saw her. Must have assumed that I knew it was her all along.

Or had she? Could she have been that dumb? Or was she playing a game?

What a mess.

"Why don't you get yourself together," Julie said. "We'll be downstairs."

My heart racing, I spent a moment to gather my wits. I closed my eyes, rubbed them, and when I opened them, I was back in hell.

Everything in my bedroom was flipped over. Every picture, every piece of furniture (I was now lying quite uncomfortably on the bottom of my bed), even the carpet was turned around, foam-rubber padding facing up.

Every. God. Damned. Thing.

Upside down.

I closed my eyes, rubbed them again, opened them, repeat, repeat, repeat.

Everything, upside down.

Panicking, I got up, looked out the window. My legs felt as if they were constructed of wet leaves as I witnessed the unbelievably fantastic sight that was once my all-American neighborhood. Every car—including mine—on its roof, wheels skyward. A bird flew by upside down, looking like a sick fish in an aquarium. The trees lining the sidewalk reached their roots in the air like giant Rastafarian haircuts. And I watched, I actually watched my front lawn ripple from a glorious green to an earthworm-laden brown in a manner of seconds.

And then I blinked my eyes, and my neighbor's house across the street was on its roof, the chimney lost beneath the earth forever.

I freaked. Badly.

I ran downstairs, tripping along steps that seemed to want me to climb them instead.

I reached bottom and found things as I feared they would be.

My entire living room looked just like my bedroom, and my kitchen—where Julie and Lisa were making breakfast like nothing was amiss—was just like my living room, and so on through all the rooms in my house. The television, refrigerator, carpets…

I must have appeared a bit crazed because Julie raised an eyebrow and gave me a strange, questioning look. "You okay?" She took a drink from the bottom of a milk carton.

I stood my ground, and as I was about to speak, both Julie and the flirtatious Lisa flickered a bit, like old light bulbs, then kind of...spun, head over heels, as if they had been attached to the end of pinwheels, and floated feet first up to the ceiling.

I ran.

I didn't know where to go, so I locked myself into the basement—which is now the attic, mind you—where I am now, writing all this down. As for Julie and Lisa, I hear them walking around upstairs, downstairs, wherever, and it appears they've forgotten about me. Maybe it's because I'm the only thing on the face of the earth that's right-side up.

And I'm too afraid to go up *there*. Down there. I'm confused.

I'm feeling suddenly tired and the pencil point is quite dull now and...

Something feels funny...I feel the blood rushing to my head.

And I have the uncontrollable urge to write with the eras

Sleep Tight, My Love

A iry beams of harvest moonlight sifted through the floor-to-ceiling windows, gently illuminating the master suite, Sia asleep in her canopy bed, the baby in its lace-shrouded bassinet.

Her nameless and still sexless baby produced a gentle gurgle, then a tempered cry. Sia flinched awake, trembling hands habitual in their struggle to pacify her anxiety, her exploding heartbeat, tight chest...eyes wide open, pupils adjusting to the gloom so to examine her only environment, her place of comfort and pain and happiness and terror, her shelter from...*it*.

Slowly, she turned her head and looked at the bassinet, but only through the corners of her eyes. She did not possess the strength, nor the power to face it head on, just yet.

The lace veil moved, ever so gently as though caught in a gentle breeze, but Sia knew better, even in her slumbrous state. The room produced no drafts, her direct suspicion confirmed by one of the infant's beetle-like pincers rising and falling, rising and falling, gently grazing the shroud's intricate weave. The dreamlike ambiguousness of the moment shrouded her ability to discern whether this ghastly vision was steeped in reality, or rather some stressed-induced delirium.

The dreadful headache that never went away beat against the muscles of her eyes, terror-induced tears bursting from rheumy ducts, drowning her sight, obscuring away perspective, distorting reality. The veins in her forearms swelled, hot rushing cells passing through her entire body, her *essence*, a sudden but reasonable reaction to the horror resting in the cradle alongside her—the moon's cool blue beams spotlighting it as her only reason for remaining here, always and forever, away from her abusive husband. *Him.*

The lesser of two evils...or not?

A swarm of spasms assaulted her from neck to toes, body trembling uncontrollably as if exposed to a winter gale, hips raised, feet cramping into impossible crescents, fists clenching the sateen sheets in damp bunches, pulling, twisting, writhing, hot sticky perspiration sheathing her face and body, dampening the coverlet, muscles tightening into cords, tendons contracting, jaws clenching, taut with distress, silk nightgown gathered uncomfortably around her waist, exposing her bruised femininity to the unseen element in the room.

She bolted upright, not of her own choosing, and remained in the position until gently released back down upon the mattress. There she stayed, staring at the canopy's intricate floral pattern, lungs heaving in cool air, exhaling hot-bitter breath, the white moonbeams strengthening as they passed through the floor-to-ceiling windows, wavering on the air as though alive, their reach growing brighter the further in they traveled, laced with veiny black streaks reaching into and winding throughout the cradle's lace shroud, onyx orbs materializing within, staring out at her from multiple points, multiple *perspectives*, below them serpentine fangs glistening with venom, jutting upright from translucent maws, these crystallizing serpents now positively *aware*, slithering bodies converging into an intentional tangle, invisible rattles delivering dreadful resonance to the moment. Sweat escaped her downcast brow and trickled into her eyes, her mouth, *salty*, the twitching skin on her arms and neck and back again rippling with dread as the floating thing coalesced to form a single solid entity: a great face twice the size of her own, pink maw scowling into an impossible shape upon a mask enigmatically arising from a squirming orgy of vile reptiles, converging to create new features: scales, horns, teeth.

Him...

Sia pulled the damp covers up to her neck, legs still exposed, the otherworldly thing swirling now inches from her face, putrid breath torturing her nostrils, tempting her gorge, burning her eyes, threatening her very existence.

She squeezed her eyes shut. The stench, the noise, her perception of the creature's presence, all ceased to exist. When she opened her eyes, a minute or an hour later, it was gone.

She looked up and down and side to side, then inched the covers toward her jawline, biting the edge of the soft fabric as the reptile-insect-demon reappeared, hovering vaporously over the infant's bassinet, its ungodly countenance *smiling* at her before bearing down upon her first born.

Sia tore away the safety of her covers and rolled her body back and forth, adjusting the smooth silky fabric of her nightgown back down over her contusions. Rolling onto her stomach, closer to her offspring and the ghostly creature nursing it, she rose up onto her elbows and knees and edged across the mattress to the foot of the bed. The floating entity aimed its wicked eyes at her, *all of them*, onyx, bulbous spheres.

She rose onto her knees and clasped her hands together, feeling somehow protected beneath the bed's canopy. She prayed tearfully that this monstrosity in her sanctuary would leave her baby untouched…that and for the strength and power and means to scare it off before it did more than just nurse her child.

An abrupt voice inside her head: *The drawer, Sia! Remember? In the drawer!*

Her subconscious, calling out to her, a fleeting memory from a previous night when a similar peril had distressed her. Lord, *yes*! She remembered her plan for *next time*! The drawer—something in it could protect her!

She wriggled backward across the bed, away from the bassinet, eyes still pinned to the demon now encompassing the gauzy veil shrouding Sia's child.

Reaching the end table, she ever so quietly pulled the drawer open.

Inside, six inches of razor-sharp steel winked at her. A formidable weapon, the handle black serrated rubber, blade twinkling eagerly.

She grabbed the knife and turned to face the demon.

It was gone! The features, the movement, the stench, everything! No longer in existence! Vanished! In its place, cool white moonbeams filtering into the suite, just like earlier, untainted and seemingly purifying everything in its wake with fresh delicate light.

Confused, she climbed out of bed and stood in place for long, drawn-out seconds, wavering on her feet before taking slow, tentative steps toward the bassinet.

She lifted the lace veil and peeked inside…

…and all blackness returned, encapsulating her like a great rushing tide swallowing a castle made of sand on the beach. All of her relief, now washed away in a second's time, replaced by a fear greater than the horror of the terrifying insect-reptile-demon itself.

At first contemplation it appeared that her infant child had vanished, the soft gentle image she nursed by day now gone, only to be replaced by something wholly dreadful. Despite her damaged ability to see things clearly, she was still able to absorb the occupant within the bassinet, and that the baby, *her baby*, had *not* been switched. It had *become something else*, cherub features still faintly recognizable beneath the hideous, malformed likeness staring up at her.

Again. Just like every night, for as long as she could remember…

Tearing through its newborn creeper, the baby's exposed flesh had grown a coating of scales, a gross overlaying of hardened leaflets with white-encrusted edges culminating into sharp points. Like an armadillo, its face was similarly masked, black orbs for eyes (not unlike those of the monstrosity nursing it moments earlier) pondering the looming figure upon it—what it could only assume to be a threat to its existence. It opened its mouth and a forked tongue rolled out, at once chased by a procession of guttural grunts and viscous matter.

It reached its insect pincers up toward Sia. To its mother? Or…*in defense?*

Fear robbed Sia of her of her voice, weakened gasps emerging from her throat as she tightened her grip on the knife. She pressed the cool steel blade against her cheek in vain effort to test the reality of the moment, its stabbing threat issuing shudders along her spine.

She managed a deep labored breath, a forced entry burning her lungs. Then, eyes closed, she raised the knife and plunged it into the baby beast.

First, a cry, soft but heard. Very real and very *human*, it seemed to surround her, as if her baby were someplace else, perhaps in the walls, or in the attic above. Then it hissed at her, hot spittle spraying her face.

She opened her eyes, blinking, her mind unable to maintain its feeble grip on sanity. God help her should another glimpse of the creature enter her sights.

But the thing was gone, her *human* baby back in its place in the cradle, knife buried to the hilt in its pink gut. Her beautiful infant, boy or girl she did not know, once again soft and sweet-smelling as it should be, now dead by her hand, *but there was no blood*. Where the eyes should have been bright, the smile buoyant and happy to see its mother, existed nothing but death.

Sia threw the knife to the bed. Crying, she picked up her baby and held it close, singing a panicked lullaby, the sensation of its scaly skin still with her, the acrid stench too, despite the *change* she witnessed. She rocked the infant to sleep, feeling the knife's hilt against her bosom, praying for the hideous evil tormenting her to abandon its hold, so that she may finally escape this room—away from it, away from *him*—and return to living a normal, peaceful life.

Ever so gently, Emily the housekeeper opened the door to Sia's suite, one arm against the paneled door, the other holding sleeping baby Amelia. Behind her, Sia's husband Michael looked over her shoulder into the room.

"Anything?" he asked.

Things looked somewhat amiss in the room. The sheets on Sia's bed were strewn about, Sia herself asleep in an awkward position, arms and legs twisted, head pressed against the mattress, muffling her snores.

Emily and Michael tiptoed forward, careful not to rouse the sleeping woman.

Emily noticed the knife first, gleaming blade peeking out from within a soft crease in the sheet. She paused and observed the scene—the sleeping Sia, the silent bassinet—then looked at Michael, slowly nodded, and said, "She's getting close."

Slowly, Michael walked to the cradle and placed a gentle hand on the edge...then lifted the lace shroud and smiled.

"It's still here," he said, reaching into the bassinet. "And look at this..."

A welling of emotions beset Emily, reckless thoughts ruminating first of baby Amelia...how her silent repose would meet Emily's loving gaze every night upon falling asleep in her arms, tender skin unblemished from harm, thank God, miniature eyes fluttering like baby moths. Emily would always and forever wish that *she* were the mother that gave birth to Amelia, though she knew that could never happen, not in this lifetime, her insides damaged from years of miscarriages, what the doctors called an "incompetent cervix".

So, she would have to settle for second best. Sia's daughter, Amelia.

As if displaying a trophy, Michael raised the hideous silicone doll he put in Amelia's cradle long after Sia fell asleep, and looked over every inch of it. "It's got a big hole in the middle of it. You're right. She *is* getting close. Even though you said she'd kill herself, before killing her own flesh and blood."

Emily scowled, then turned away and grabbed the knife from the bed. She placed it back into the drawer, right on top where it could be easily grasped by Sia.

Sia. Emily stared at her with contempt, fists clenched in frustration, almost a year's worth of effort still fully unrewarded. *I've got the husband,* she thought, wondering how many times she'd have to sleep with him before Sia finally put the knife into herself. *Small price to pay when his money and her baby become mine.*

Michael shook the latex monster-baby at Emily and said, "Boo!" before putting it back into the cradle.

Tonight, she thought, *everything would change.*

She would increase the dosage.

A full tab of LSD in Sia's evening tea, instead of half.

That should do the trick.

She grinned at the sleeping Sia, eyebrows raised in anticipation.

Sia's eyes rolled gently beneath her lids.

Now awake and fidgeting in Emily's arms, Amelia began to cry.

"Sleep tight, my love," Emily whispered, tapping the baby on the back. She then took Michael's hand, and without looking back, quietly closed the door behind them.

One Last Breath

…kill her…

Will Cast was scared. Even more than that, he felt as if the muscles that held his sanity in place were under a great strain, creating a tension he had never felt in his forty-two years of age. And as he pulled up in front of Tanis Petter's home on Stanley Avenue, he knew that if he didn't show someone the pictures, he would go crazy.

There was really no one to confide in other than Tanis. He was a close friend that had been there for Will through all his grief in life, including the mess of a divorce that Leslie had put him through. To this day Will was still dealing with her harassment, her antagonism. He would rather take a shower in Ajax and wipe down with sandpaper than deal with her now. Even though Will had been well-familiarized with her caustic personality before he married her, her beauty beguiled him and ultimately dragged him along for the bumpy ride. Marrying Leslie had been the biggest mistake of his life.

That is, until three days ago, when he tried to save a man's life.

…did you hear me? I said kill her…

He staggered across the lawn to Tanis' doorstep, tripping a bit along the way, nearly dropping the large yellow clasp envelope in his right hand. He arrived at the doorstep and rang the bell. The door opened and Tanis was there.

"Will…" Tanis said, surprised to see his friend. "What brings you here?" He pushed open the screen door to let him in.

…who's the jerk…?

Will nudged past him. "Is Diane here?"

"No…she isn't," he said slowly, stroking his gray hair, seemingly confused at Will's impetuous entrance. "She left about ten minutes ago. I was just fixing myself a drink, and by the looks of you, you should have one too. You look terrible." Will noticed a grimace on Tanis's face, telling him that his friend got a nice strong whiff of his terrible breath.

Tanis shut the door and turned up the lights as they walked through the short hall to the living room. The pallid glimmer no doubt lit up the worst of Will's worn-out features: the deep wrinkles, the unkempt beard, the reddened eyes, perhaps the small abrasions on his face. Will was forty-two. Tonight he looked sixty-two.

"I think I will. A big one, if you don't mind."

…yeah, I'm thirsty too…

"No bother." Tanis wandered into the kitchen to fix the drinks.

Without delay, Will spoke out, pacing across the wood floor. "I'm a dead man Tanis. I can feel it." There. He finally said it. Those muscles straining to hold his sanity together relaxed a touch. God bless Tanis. He really needed to talk.

Tanis returned with two Dewars and sodas, handed one to Will who hadn't realized he was shaking so much until he grabbed the glass and spilled some whiskey over the lip. Leslie always gave him the business every time he felt like a drink. *Have another, Willy, why don't you!* she would screech, stalking around the house like the madwoman she was, ranting and raving about how "Willy" (he hated it when she called him that) never took her out, then would stay out herself until the wee hours at those nightclubs on the strip where all the kids would hang out with their fast cars and loud music.

Tanis stood steadfast in front of him. "Dead? Will, what the hell's going on?"

Will emptied half his glass in two gulps, thinking back to about a year ago when Leslie hit him in the face with a wooden clothes hanger and knocked two teeth out. The pain was excruciating. And then the dentist's bills that followed. He paid for that night for the next six months. But that whole event—the pain, the bills—was a mere tickle in comparison to the dread he felt now.

...thinking about the bitch again, Willy...?

"Sit down, Tanis. You're going to have a hard time believing this."

Tanis sat on a chair across from Will, placed the toes of his slippered feet upon the coffee table between them.

Will fingered the rim of his glass for a few seconds. He hoped that Tanis, the picture of rationality, would be willing to sit through it all. Actually, he probably would. Getting him to believe everything would be the difficult part. Well, he did have the pictures...

"I...just got back from the library, Tanis. Before that I was in the hospital. Came right here after I was done."

"Done with what? Why were you at the hospital?"

Will was silent at first then took a deep breath. "Something...something is very wrong." He held up the yellow envelope he brought. "It's these..."

...oh it's much more than those pictures. Tell him Willy...

Tanis held out his hand, reaching for the envelope.

Will drew it back. "You need to hear what's happened to me during the past three days. It'll help you understand everything a little better."

"All right, start at the beginning."

"Okay. But first, make me another drink..."

Will Cast awakened with the unremitting nausea he'd experienced almost every morning since all the anguish with Leslie's bullshit started.

He rose unsteadily, shuffled to the bathroom and perched himself in front of the sink. He squinted at the face staring back at him from the mirrored medicine chest. The grief of Leslie's tumult had wrought on him features that transformed his face into an unfamiliar one. He tried to blame the wrinkles, the gray hair, the receding hairline on his ripening age, but knew the stress and anxiety brought on from the divorce played a larger part in his physical decay.

It was Saturday, a good thing because there was no work. Will planned to spend the day by the pool and do nothing, gather some peace of mind, whatever was left of it.

He shrugged into a pair of swim trunks, then breakfasted on a cup of instant coffee and the ends of a stale loaf of bread. As he ate, he closed his eyes and wished away the roller coaster in his stomach. A day relaxing in the sun would definitely do some good.

He retrieved a towel from the hallway closet then roamed to the backyard via the sliding doors in the living room. Like a cat nuzzling the leg of its owner, he snuggled into the lounge chair on the patio, drew a deep breath and realized as he looked ahead to the tranquil waters of the pool that today, regrettably, would not be the day of rest and relaxation he looked so forward to.

A body was floating face down in the pool.

"Was the body clothed?" Tanis asked.

A full moon had risen in the sky by this time and Will couldn't help but be spooked at the pale light silhouetting his friend from the window behind. "Yeah. They were puffed out and kinda looked as though they were keeping him afloat." Will downed his second drink and remained silent until Tanis returned with two more full glasses.

…another drink, Willy? My, aren't we exciting tonight…

Tanis sat back down, pushed his spectacles up and twirled his thick graying moustache. "Well, what did you do?"

"I checked to see if he was alive…"

Will, pool skimmer in both hands, thrust the netted end into the water. He gave the body a nudge, almost as if he were trying to wake the man from a nap. The body floated to the opposite side of the pool.

He dropped the skimmer in the pool and ran to where the body came ashore by the patio. With all the strength he could muster, he hauled the body up onto the concrete and turned it, face up.

The body was that of a man, probably in his early forties—*close to my age*, Will thought—with blond hair and about a week's worth of growth on his face. The features were soaked and starting to bloat. Will thought that maybe he didn't have it so bad after all. The wrath of Leslie was a more acceptable purgatory than death by drowning.

Then Will froze. *Death by drowning.*

Maybe the guy isn't dead…?

"Will, was he alive?"

…now tell the jerk the good part…!

"Tanis...I can't possibly put into words exactly what happened next. It was so strange, it felt as if...well let me try to explain...

On his knees, Will gripped the man's wrist, felt for a pulse. The skin was frigid, and he wasn't sure if he actually felt anything. He dropped the wrist; the hand *thunked* to the concrete. He then crawled to the side of the head, placed his right hand beneath the neck and arched it up. With his left hand he pinched the nose and pulled back, forcing the mouth into a wide-open position. Will's nausea—previously forgotten—returned as he readied himself for action.

"Say AH," he said aloud and placed his mouth over the gaping mouth. He blew hard. He had no idea what he was doing, but felt as if it was the right course of action. What if the man was alive?

He arched back, then blew again. Four times, five, six, seven. No response, no signs of life. He put his fists together, raised them high, then brought them down into the midsection of the body. He repeated this action, three times, then four. He returned back and blew another gust of air into the lungs of the man.

With no warning, the body came to life, sucking back with a force stronger than a vacuum. Will, blowing, was forced to release more air from his lungs than prepared to. His lungs emptied and he found himself with nothing left to exhale. With amazing strength, the man continued to inhale, staking a claim to every last precious drop of breath that Will had left. Will gripped the man's hair and pulled, tried to break away. He was stuck. His head began to feel as if it would float away. He tightened his grip on the sides of the man's head and pulled with all the remaining strength his faltering body would allow. His hands came away with clumps of wet blond hair. Blotches of black light began to blanket Will's vision. Just when he heard his inner self say, "this is it, it's all over," he heard a noise.

The man began to growl.

It was a chattering growl, like the syncopated sound a stomach makes when it's fed something it doesn't like. On the verge of passing out, Will started to spasm. His legs and arms flailed in all directions as if he were performing a grotesque tap dance.

The growling from within grew louder…and with the mouth-grip still intact, the man took one last breath and exhaled a mighty surge of air and water into Will. Helpless, Will inhaled and fell away, gasping and coughing.

Will—on his third drink—sat back and allowed the alcohol to create a welcome lethargy in his body. He looked at Tanis, who was silent, probably trying to convince himself to believe everything.

"Well," Tanis finally said, breaking the silence. "What did you do then?"

"I got up, walked around, in shock I suppose. Went back to the house and paced, looked out every window, at the body, just lying there by the pool. I guess I was just trying to catch my breath, you know? After a few minutes, when I regained my wits, I called the police."

"And the body?"

"Dead. It took one last breath and died."

…but not really now, Willy, right…?

"At your expense."

Will looked at his drink, then said, "More than you know, Tanis. More than you know…"

Will sat in his living room sipping instant coffee with two policemen and a balding middle-aged man who'd identified himself as Detective Ballaro. A group of detectives and police were outside by the pool scouring the scene. Crime scene tape barricaded out a few curious onlookers congregating in front of his home.

"It really is quite amazing that this guy just showed up floating face down in your pool," Detective Ballaro remarked.

Will said defensively, "I did. I tried to give him mouth to mouth, but really didn't know what I was doing."

Ballaro tried unsuccessfully to hold back a smirk. "Mr. Cast, I hope you'll forgive me but I find this situation a bit humorous, of course not putting aside the trauma of you finding a dead man in your pool. But we've been looking for this guy for a long time. He's eluded us for two years. Last night a couple of my men finally got a beat on him, but he got away. We brought out a search team—dogs, helicopters—but we couldn't track him down. It appears that while fleeing he must have fallen and drowned in your pool."

Will looked up at the detective. "So you know this guy?"

Ballaro nodded. "Mr. Cast, that man whose life you tried to save is the Cedar Crest Mangler."

Tanis sat agape. His voice was a rusty shrill by the time he found it. "Will, that guy raped and murdered about a dozen women."

"Fourteen," he corrected, toying with his empty glass.

"How come I didn't hear about this? I mean, I knew they got him, but I didn't know it was in your backyard!"

...hey Willy, I can't stomach this jerk much longer...

"They protected me in case he has any friends, you know? They might try to come after me thinking that *I* had something to do with his death."

"Did you tell them what happened when you tried to..."

"No. They did their work, which took most of the day, and then left..."

That night, Will peered out his bedroom window into the dark of the night. The pool, so tranquil now, reflected the light of the moon off the soft vapor rising eerily from the surface of the water. Under ordinary circumstances, this scene would've relaxed him. But circumstances were far from ordinary.

He crawled into bed, covers at his feet. All day a foul taste invaded his mouth. It was a bitter taste, like rotten eggs, and he could smell it on his breath. He tried brushing his teeth and rinsing with mouthwash but the odor overcame all attempts to scrub it away. It was as if something crawled into his mouth and died.

He fell asleep...

...and awoke the following morning with beautiful summer sunshine making warm, sharp designs on his body. *It was all a dream,* he thought with inconceivable relief. *Just a nutty dream.*

He swallowed and almost puked. His mouth was putrid. He sat up and a missile of pain burst through his head. It wasn't from drinking—he knew that feeling well. This was different, his *entire* head hurt, face and neck included, as if he had been beaten in the middle of the night. Soon his stomach took part in the physical melee, brought a knotting, twisting agony that felt as though it ripped his insides apart. He tried to rise from bed but the cramps wouldn't allow it. He gripped the sides of the bed and lunged to the floor. Crawling, he found his way to his desk and pulled the handset from the phone. It felt as if a thousand lit cigarettes were burning unbearable holes in his stomach. He dialed 9-1-1, got an operator.

All he could manage was his name and address before his mouth dropped open and then snapped shut. His eyes rolled uncontrollably and his groping nails scraped bits of flesh away from his cheeks. His stomach began to undulate, blood dripping from his navel. The pale skin covering his entire stomach darkened into a hideous shade of yellow, as if those lit cigarettes smeared ghostly nicotine stains there. Portions of the skin turned a deeper shade of yellow, the outer fringes showing traces of brown. Welts swelled up and twisted around his waist and abdomen as if hideous worms were crawling beneath his skin. Bold blue veins gorged with blood surged forth. When he was able to finally bring his eyes around from inside his skull and hone in on the blight savaging his midsection, the stains, the lines, the welts, the veins—they all came together to form what appeared to be a face looking back at him.

Show him my picture, Willy...

Tanis glanced at his watch. They had been in conversation now for over an hour now, and Will could tell that deep inside Tanis wanted to pass judgment on his story. *C'mon Tanis,* Will thought, *why would I make up such a tale?*

"Well," Tanis said, "I did notice when you walked in that your breath was, well, pretty bad. And there are a few small cuts on your face."

Will nodded, thankful. Tanis believed him, or was at least trying to. "Next thing I remembered was waking up in the hospital…"

"Mr. Cast…how are you feeling?"

Will looked at the doctor, who after walking in grabbed a clipboard attached to the end of the bed and jotted something down.

"Honestly," Will answered, "I can't remember anything. Was I in an accident?"

"I was hoping you could answer that for me." The doctor dragged a stool over and sat next to Will. "A 9-1-1 call was received yesterday, presumably from you. When you came in you were in a lot of pain, something with your stomach…"

…remember the body in the pool, Willy…?

"…your complaints led us to believe you had appendicitis…"

…well, the body was alive…

"…but the lack of fever puzzled us…"

…it's me Willy, the Cedar Crest Mangler…

"…so we did a series of sonograms on your stomach…"

…and I showed myself on your tummy last night, remember…?

"…and they came out negative. Mr. Cast, you're fine. You may have the beginnings of an ulcer, however I see nothing at the moment that should be a cause for alarm. Unless there's something you're not telling me."

Will stared up at the doctor. He had visions of being sent off to a loony bin. "No…there's nothing."

"Good. I'll see your release at once."

"That was this afternoon."

"You mentioned you were at the library?"

...show him my lovely face...

Will unclasped the envelope he was holding. "Take a look at this," he said, handing a photocopied newspaper article to Tanis. The headline read, "CEDAR CREST MANGLER FOUND DEAD".

Tanis eyed the article, then nodded. "This is from Sunday's paper. I saw this."

"Take another look at his picture." Tanis looked at the familiar shot, a driver's license photo of an expressionless man in his early forties. Beneath, the caption read, "JEFF GOLDSTEIN, a.k.a. THE CEDAR CREST MANGLER".

"Okay. What are you getting at?"

"Now, don't ask me how the hell the doctor missed this. Actually, I think he saw it and didn't want any part of it." Will paused, took a deep breath.

"What? What is it?" Tanis was sitting at the edge of his chair.

"As I was leaving, a nurse came and handed me this envelope. She said that they were my sonograms. I didn't think anything of it at the time. My stomach felt better. I didn't look at them until I got home."

He handed the printouts to Tanis. "This is what I found."

Tanis took the sonograms from Will. After looking at them for a few seconds, he quietly turned them face down on the table and poured himself another whiskey, this time straight up. There was no mistaking what he saw those images.

Amidst the grainy black and white twists and blots, a face looked out.

The face of the Cedar Crest Mangler.

"He's in me Tanis," Will said. "I can feel him. I can hear him. He's been talking to me constantly. It's only been a day and I can't take it much more. He's pure evil Petter, and it's in me."

Tanis was about to speak when the phone jolted him. "Hold that thought," he said standing. He moved to answer it, said hello, then scowled. "Hold on. Will, it's Leslie." He put his hand over the mouthpiece. "She doesn't sound too happy."

...it's the bitch. Let's add her to my list, Willy...

Will shook his head from side to side. It couldn't get any worse now. He stood up and Tanis handed him the phone, giving him a flat, apologetic grin.

"Hello?" That was all he got in. He pulled the phone away from his ear to lessen the volume of Leslie's yapping. Will hung up the phone after twenty seconds.

"Well?" Tanis asked.

"She told me she has a gun and will use it if I don't pay the alimony I owe her."

"You owe her money?"

"About four months' worth."

Tanis blew out a nervous *whoosh*. "You seem to have more than one problem here."

The phone rang again. "Let me get it," Tanis said. He picked it up, said hello. Listened. Nodded. "Okay Leslie, he'll be right over."

Will's mouth fell open. "What are you nuts?"

Tanis hung up the phone and gazed at a disbelieving Will. "This may sound crazy, but I have an idea. Get in the car and I'll explain on the way over."

...this is getting good...

"Good luck, Will."

"Thanks. I could use it." Will got out of Tanis' car. He clutched his stomach which was starting to pain him again.

...what are we gonna do Willy? I can't hear you too well, the alcohol is clouding your pathetic little thoughts...

Will arrived at Leslie's door. "Work with me on this one…"

…are we gonna kill the bitch…?

"You'll see."

He rang the bell. Leslie was there in a heartbeat. She reached out and pulled him in by the shirt, spun him around and threw him against the wall. Weakened from his ordeal, Will had no energy, nor time really, to fight back. His back slammed against the hard sheetrock. He fell like a drunk losing all sense of balance, meeting the floor with an ungraceful *thud*. Through blurred eyesight, he saw his ex-wife—blond hair disheveled, red knit top stained with sweat—towering over him.

"Get the hell up, dirtbag!"

Such a lady, Will thought through the garbled mumblings of the Mangler. Then, on his clammy forehead, Will felt the pressure of a cold circle of metal.

"Now," Leslie said with authority, holding the gun to his head. "Where's my God-damned money?"

Will held his hands up, still cowering on the floor against the wall like a child fending off the blows of an angry father. "P-please, don't shoot me…" A dribble of saliva ran down his chin.

Still holding the gun to his head with her right hand, Leslie gripped him by the collar with her left and pulled. He followed her lead by helping himself to rise. In the process, Will's sweat-soaked t-shirt split down the back and peeled away in Leslie's hand.

First Will saw her take a step back and lower the gun, his shirt dangling in her hand. Then he saw her face, a frozen combination of fear and fascination: her mouth agape, eyes wide like coins. She stood remarkably still like an ancient tree.

"Leslie…? What's wrong?" He took a step closer.

She struggled to get the words out. "S-stay away from me you…you…" Will followed her line of vision to his bare torso where the sweat-coated face of the Cedar Crest Mangler loomed from his stomach, the cheeks turgid, the nose disfigured by bursting veins and capillaries. The eyes were terrible, glaring like black lights, glittering but empty. The mouth and lips in his skin were stretched wide, and from within a slab of flesh stretched forward, wriggling like a larvae trying to break free from the confines of its milky shell.

A tongue. The soul of the Mangler was sticking its tongue out at Leslie.

Leslie screamed.

Will's reaction was one more of surprise than of shock. Looking back up, he took a calculated step forward.

...what are doing, Willy...?

Leslie raised the gun back up in his direction. "Stay away from me..." she bellowed, but that was all she got out. Will put Tanis' plan into action. He leapt forward and grabbed the sides of her head, feeling the coarse waves of her unkempt hair beneath his palms. He squeezed, then took his open mouth and attached it to hers. Out of the corner of his eye he saw the gun rise up. He squinted, expecting a blow, but it never came; her arm froze in shock along with the rest of her body, and then the madness unfolded.

It was a repeat performance from three days earlier only now Will was dishing out the goods. All his insides went into turmoil, like a violent bile storm twisting and buckling in his body. His lungs began to pump—so hard that he felt her tongue slide deep in his mouth. He saw Leslie's eyes bulge, and she tried to yell but all that came out were muffled wines. Then Will heard a familiar low grumble rising in volume, sliding up to a wholly savage sound as if an animal were in the room with them. With a surge that seemed to burn away his esophagus, something strong, something *alive*, rushed up and out of him and into Leslie like a powerful drain being emptied.

At once Will's lungs stopped pumping and his mouth-grip on Leslie came loose. She stumbled backwards into the armoire behind. The gun dropped from her hand to the carpeted floor and she quickly followed with a dead weight *thud*, gasping and wheezing.

Will fell back, too. He tasted blood and realized he had bitten his tongue. His heart pounded. He wiped his face with his hands, then cast a wary eye at Leslie, who was now lying on her side trying to catch her breath with labored gasps and coughs.

Will shifted his gaze down to his stomach. It was red, a few abrasions, but the face, that horrible face was gone.

He again forced a glance in Leslie's direction—she was all but passed out. He crawled, bobbing a bit from a dizzied head, to where she lay. Ever so gently, he pulled up her shirt.

No face. Not even a sign of swelling.

"Crap..." he said, releasing the shirt and turning to face to the window. He stared at his sorry reflection.

And saw her rise up behind him.

He turned and she was on her knees, shaking wildly, gun pointed at him. "I don't know what the hell you are, but bet your ass you're a dead one..."

The stench hit him. Her breath. "Leslie, you don't understand..."

"Stay away you freak!"

Will stood helpless, arms raised and at a loss. Then, like lightning—like someone possessed—Leslie violently slammed backwards to the floor. All the windows in the room rattled, the lights flickered. She howled and rolled around uncontrollably as if she were on fire and was trying to put it out. Will stood and quickly stepped back, watching Leslie twist like a worm out of earth. She gripped her midsection and started to gag. He caught a glimpse of her face, her bulging eyes, and knew what was happening. She pulled her shirt up, presumably to survey her pain, and saw a vile yellow discoloration on the skin of her stomach. She turned to Will, her eyes pleading for an answer.

But he just smiled. He then pulled a dollar from his pocket and dropped it on the floor. "Here's your alimony." He then walked out the door, leaving her screams behind.

Will opened the door and crawled into the seat next to Tanis.

"What's happening Will?"

"Shh...listen...." They heard Leslie's prolonged screams, howls of pure terror. To the ears of Will Cast though, it was sweet music. "I don't think he likes her."

Through the apartment window they saw a body storm by, a body with a red shirt and scraggly blond hair waving a gun. Lights were going on in neighboring homes.

"Will, we better get out of here," Tanis said.

Will put his hand on Tanis' arm. "Wait, one more second."

Actually, they had to wait about ten seconds. A gunshot sounded, and then her screams stopped.

Tanis looked at him, an incredulous grin spreading over his face. "It worked. I don't believe it. It worked."

Will shrugged. "Quite well. Tanis, you're a genius. Only *you* could have thought of it. The ultimate woman hater in a woman's body."

Tanis, head shaking, pulled the car away. "I just wonder which one of them pulled the trigger?"

After a minute of uncomfortable silence, Will turned to his friend. "Tanis?"

"Yeah?"

"With all the crap I've been through with Leslie, our friendship was one thing she could not break up. Thanks for always being there."

Tanis smiled slowly. "In a way, I'm now your partner in crime."

Will smiled back. "I'm feeling much better. Just rid myself of a homicidal maniac, you know."

"Actually, you just rid yourself of two of them."

They laughed. The tension eased. "Buy you a drink? I do owe you a few."

"Actually, it's kinda hot. How about a swim in your pool?"

"Okay. Good idea." They laughed all the way to Will's house.

1-800-S-U-I-C-I-D-E

1-800-S-U-I-C-I-D-E.

That's the number they call. The Suicide Assistance Hotline. It's the city's only official hotline for those down on their luck. For those who haven't led lives worth telling about. The utterly depressed.

You know the type very well. You should. You've been working for the state-funded organization for three years now. Yeah, the pay isn't that great, but the rewards are splendid, and the action is unrivaled. You never know what you're gonna get when that phone rings and you pick it up and there's someone holding on for dear life at the other end struggling to find the right words to explain how shitty they're feeling. You know the scenario, it's quite familiar. They're usually laboring for breaths, and you can almost hear the sweat dripping from their pores, the blood racing through their veins. And then those strange tappings you sometimes hear on their end of the line—they just might be the barrel of a gun or a bottle of pills trying to find the inside of their trembling mouths as they speak their woes, their miserable existences an overdose of Quaaludes or a single pull of the trigger away from putting an ungodly end to it all.

Many ask why you've chosen such a disturbing profession. The answer is quite simple: the thrill of rescuing these people from a future filled with dismay, to successfully make them see even the faintest drop of light at the end of the dark dreary tunnel they've traveled is unequaled by any thrill or reward that life has to offer. That pretty much sums up your job: to answer the phone, to provide suicide assistance.

The office holds its usual banal atmosphere when you arrive Saturday evening at six. The phones sit as dead as statues on the twelve messy desks, their occupants ceremoniously gathered around the coffee machine to vulture in on the pizzas delivered a few minutes earlier. Free food is another benefit working for a city-run public assistance operation. But you have to get your eats in quick, because in no time the food will be devoured and the calls will start pouring in — just after the bars and taverns have been open long enough to serve the right amount of drinks qualifying for a binge.

After two slices of extra cheese and pepperoni, you take a can of cola to your desk and begin your duties for the night. Since your phone hasn't started tolling yet, you gather your paperwork from the previous night and enter each incident in the appropriate database. You took six calls, two of which were "false alarms". False alarms are calls from those lost souls who really don't prove to be a true threat of suicide, who in actuality aren't even capable of any form of violence. They are folks who make up the insecure and the lonely, cheerless individuals in search of a willing ear to absorb their mostly miniscule problems. They don't drink, smoke or do drugs — anything self-abusive for that matter. They are simple human beings in a temporary funk who, through a volatile stretch, find themselves with the impulsive need to chatter their nonsensities until their wits automatically fall back into place.

The other four calls you took had a more serious tone to them. These people, although a bit more distressed and somewhat stupored, still hadn't exhibited that entirely convincing expectation of self-affliction. Three of them were males suffering from the all-too-familiar classic sickness commonly known as "broken heart syndrome". They'd been spurned, the women whom they emphatically trusted and presumably knew to love them had secretly shared their affections with someone else. The men only realized this after discovering their wives or girlfriends in uncompromising situations with other men — some of whom they knew — and had felt a quick and painless death would be a fate much easier dealt with than the humiliation sure to arise in the days to follow. These "crackers" as you call them are weak, spineless individuals, a sorry representation for the male populace whose backbones were better off preserved in jelly jars. And you tell them that too, nice and slowly so that they hear every disparaging word. These insults sober them up real quick, and show you that their threats of suicide are nothing more than feeble attempts to garner pity.

The other call you took had been from a woman. She'd been depressed for months, or so she said, despondent over her weight and lack of self-worth. You realize the alarming potential for a suicide here, but after a good half-hour of prying into her current situation, you find that she really hasn't adequately planned out her means for ending it all, that she's much too chicken-shit to slit her wrists or throat, and that all she has are thirteen generic aspirins she dug out from the bathroom's medicine cabinet. You tell her that if she chows down these aspirins, she'll only end up vomiting for a day and a half, wishing herself well the whole time, and that the physical discomfort she'll experience will only make her feel even more miserable and averse to ending it all. In the end, she thanks you for your advice and moves on with her sorry life.

One of your co-workers walks in and begins to tout a tale of success. He'd been on the afternoon shift. A call had come in from a woman who'd threatened to blow her own brains out, proving her possession by firing into her living room wall while on the phone with him. Your co-worker then goes on to brag about how he got her to reveal her location, and when he felt sure enough that her harmful temptations had been temporarily quelled, he made a "housecall" as they are aptly referred, taking himself to her place of location in an attempt to provide assistance. Although not ostracized, this diversion is not a recommended course of action, as many ill-effects could potentially arise. You, on the other hand, not unlike your co-worker, revel in these rare opportunities to "play the field". Why? Because this is where the action lies, where you get to experience what it feels like to teeter on the edge of life and death. Where, if things go as planned, you really get to shine.

As your co-worker is now. He saved the woman's life.

Your phone rings. You answer it. "Suicide assistance."

You hear heavy breathing at the other end of the phone. The intimate click of a gun's barrel against aching teeth. The silence that dominates is heart-pounding. Finally, a voice. Male. "I-I need help."

You are somewhat alarmed, yet still raring to go. This individual, you realize, could very well be in need of a housecall. "Where are you?" you ask.

The signal breaks up. A cell phone perhaps? "I-I'm in an alley. 34th and 11th Avenue. Next to a shuttered bar."

"What is your first name?"

"John." It escapes his lips as a harsh whisper. , you realize, .

He just may kill himself.

"John," you say, "I will be there in ten minutes. Can you wait until I arrive?"

John says yes. You inform your co-workers that you will be making a housecall. They wish you luck and you enter into the night.

You find the alley John spoke of, near the corner of 34th and 11th Avenue. The establishment forming one wall—what used to be a tavern—is boarded up, a tapestry of graffiti masking its surface. You peek into the alley. Dark. Dismal. Cold. Empty.

Like John's life perhaps.

You enter the alley, sneakers slicing through grime. You announce your approach. There is a reeking dumpster hugging the right corner, mottled with rust and grime.

Against one side leans John. He is no older than you are, thirty, if that. He shivers, shirtless, his sinewy torso swathed in foul perspiration. His head hangs heavy, dead-like. You approach him. You see his cell-phone in the dirt at his side.

He looks up, eyes cold and empty, devoid of the will to live. Yet still, filled with the fear of dying. A gun hangs loosely in his left hand.

All you have to do is grab the gun…

You hold out your hand.

John's eyes fill with tears of indignation. He hates himself for not having the balls to accomplish the only thing that will make him happy: suicide. This, along with everything else in his life, proves only one thing. That he is a complete, utter failure.

That's where you come in. You're here to help, to make a difference in John's life.

So you quickly snatch the gun from John's hand. His eyes widen, then bulge as you place the barrel of the gun against his head. He freezes, tries to speak, but you just smile.

Then you pull the trigger, ending his sorry, pitiful life.

You smile to yourself as you place the gun back into his hand. You then leave the alley, your personal task fulfilled, the job well done.

You go back to the office and reveal to your co-workers that you arrived too late. A depressing silence fills the office. Everyone is hurting inside.

Except you. You silently savor the thrill of your recent experience as you sit at your desk and wait for the phone to ring again, obsessively tapping out the number on the keypad over and over.

1-800-S-U-I-C-I-D-E.

That's the number they call.

The Suicide Assistance Hotline.

Becoming One with the Great Old Ones

The day of my father's death, I fell in love with a woman on TV.

With hope and fate embracing as lovers, my life's poor fortune has reached an unavoidable cliff, one which I've clearly and decidedly leaped from, straight into the arms of something wholly unfamiliar...and yet, strangely welcoming. The pinning of *love* upon me has all my life been riddled with something akin to a dreadful rash, never expected, unwanted, and unasked for, willingly fought with agents to force its disappearance.

But that has all changed now.

I found my father dead in the same place he lies now, in his bed, his soul surrendered during the time I willfully accepted the ambiguous roles of my own dreaming mind, the positive reinforcement of one educated in medicine not needed to verify my immediate diagnosis, for my father's wrinkled mouth gaped dryly, devoid of the rancid breaths habitually occupying that space; his eyes, coated in a creamy film, slightly sunken into their sockets, mimicking the beginnings of rot in the pumpkins that grow at Whitmire's farm; his skin, gathering the pallor of something drowned.

Then and now: he's dead.

The television remains on in his room, and it becomes directly noticeable that his sudden passing occurred between the moments of locating his programming of choice and falling asleep...unless, of course, he met his death in some uniquely disconcerting dream where some unexplainable demon prodded his terrified heart until it no longer pumped. His fingers, withered and bone-like in life, here and now protrude like twigs, emaciated in death, the once-swollen blue veins atop his hands compressed into narrowed ribbons, one palm still clutching the remote, a sole fingertip perched weakly upon channel four.

Only now do I realize it's long before the dawn hours, night's cold encirclement around our home gathering firmly, womblike. On the television screen, my sudden love's countenance peers into my father's room, a once-dainty face wrought with suppressed terror, tears glossing azure eyes, red lips quivering as she reports a series of unforeseen happenings taking place in multiple cities miles away. I wonder how it's possible I've never noticed her before: not the atypical talking head delivering the evils we humans have not been able over the millennia to secure a foothold upon; where one would find some square-jawed banterer delivering yet another universal wrongdoing, now...*now* existed perfection. Her beauty, her sadness, her utter faultlessness rescuing me at this decisive moment from the soon-to-be ruined world.

I kneel before the television, eager mind only momentarily questioning my decision to do so instead of enacting this same performance before my father's lifeless body. The woman—my *love*—speaks of a series of events leading to this very moment in time, a small inset picture displaying a video of blackened skies overcome with a shower of brightness, not one purposefully induced through some July 4th merriment, but consequently overflowing with unforeseen chaos and fire—of the promise of death and destruction to millions.

An animated marquee of the words *December 21st, 2012: Wormwood Comet* scrolls below the video. Below that, in smaller letters: *Why were we not warned?*

The woman speaks of a football game in the city, the stadium packed hours earlier for a night game, now afire, those in attendance doing nothing to escape the burning terror, but instead falling to their knees (much like I am now) in prayer to the lights seen streaking across the night sky. I pay them no attention, for all that matters now is this newfound emotion that prevails over everything I've ever felt...all that I should be afraid of now. This woman, with pink lips and glossy eyes, delivers unto me a power I have no choice but to embrace, despite my father's death and the deaths of millions she laments.

For the slightest moment, as my new eyes divert themselves away from her image on the television toward the window, where amid the darkness snow falls, she speaks to me, calls my name and bids me to abide her command: *Under the bed.*

My head jerks back to the television, her unanticipated words drawing my undivided attention as if marionette strings were tethered between us. Her prominent eyes do not look past me into the world which she cannot see, but directly into me—into my own startled gaze. I raise a hand and touch her glass lips, still moving as a bearer of bad news, but at the same time sending forth to me my very own personal message—a twin voice overriding that which still emerges from the tinny speakers in the television. *Look under the bed.*

I pull my gaze from the television, my internal stream of thoughts and sensations abruptly accelerated. Though my sudden willingness to profess *love* for this woman has supplanted all I've come to know of life, it has not blocked my ability to see the tangible realities before me, so my efforts to understand her better—to know her better—will not be squandered.

She has asked of me a simple task, and I see no other option but to comply.

The home I reside in, (*my* home, now inherited I suppose), is old and rural, loaded with picturesque refurbishments amassed in years past by my deceased mother. The bed is no exception, four-posted and wood-worn, the floral-quilted mattress beneath my father's dead weight sagging. I crawl away from the television, my newscaster lover droning on, the story of the moment being imparted upon the still-living world a tale of the earth's oceans being saturated with Wormwood's dust, which she claims in a voice that now sounds bland and dissonant from my new position alongside the bed—alongside my father's corpse—still falls from the skies. I peer out the window and observe the snow I noticed earlier...but *not* snow. It's the dust she speaks of, raining from blackened skies caused not from the earth's rotation, but of the comet's aftermath, now forever preventing day from making an appearance in the foreseeable future, if indeed there is one. I am reminded at this moment of a story once viewed on television of explorers visiting a white-barren expanse of some glacial land, and I wonder with no concern or regret if this is what will become of the land outside my home. I peer back at my love and as she continues her report, staring at me with an urging sense painted upon her furrowed features, the words emerging from the speakers in my television not matching her twittering lips: *Under the bed…*

I take a deep breath, tasting the flowering stench of my father's death upon my parched tongue, then lean down and peer beneath the bed.

Despite the near-palpable darkness filling the slight space, the glistening of something wet catches my gaze. Beyond the window behind me, where the beams of the porch light out back reflect off Wormwood's heavily falling debris, I begin to discern the truth of what lies beneath my father's bed. I can tell now that it's not any one thing, but a series of what my knowledge can only presuppose as a gathering of tentacles, not unlike those belonging to an octopus. They're unmistakably sentient, squirming and writhing, twisting and knotting together into a singular embrace—a joining entity formed into something altogether stronger, smarter. The clutch reminds me of an old knotted vine, like those in the woods behind my home, although one doused copiously in sap; if it weren't moving I might consider it as such.

The manner in which it entered my father's bedroom, through the flooring—of which multiple splinters lay askew, jutting every which way—confirms its sentience, its purposeful intent, its *strength*. A vine this is not.

Pressing my face directly upon the warm floor, I roll my eyes upward and behold the true manner of my father's demise; if indeed some dream demon had been chasing down his heart, it is quite clear to me now that it did not succeed in its quest, and cannot be held accountable. No. The squirming, entwined shaft of tentacles are to blame, having burrowed through the box spring, through the mattress, and as it appears, into my father's back, as evidenced by the droplets of blood and gristle trickling through the ragged hole and down the surface of the entwined entity.

Beyond the drone of the announcer's voice, the part of her that loves *me* says:

"Behold, the people are now fed with Wormwood."

With no fear, only exasperation, I scamper back across the gritty flooring, pain registering on the skin of my knee through the flannel pajama pants I'm wearing, my wide-eyed gaze redirected back toward the television like a gunshot where she of brunette hair, made-up eyes, and trembling red lips stacks upon the world the evils occurring beyond the walls of my home. I cannot help but wonder if my home can be considered a safe haven, given destruction's clearly-made path beneath my father's bed; is it practical to speculate that many more writhing tentacles are gathered below the house, awaiting me to assume a prone position before carrying me to my death?

The inset box on the television beside my lover's face now shows an immense stretch of ocean waves where the debris of a once-burning city now floats upon its murky surface as far as the eye can see. The expansive view, shown from either a helicopter or airplane, pans across the covered water toward the coastline of an American beach, it too amassed with mountains of wood, cement, and steel. Farther back, flames burn on and on, the charred remains of hundreds if not thousands of people littering the land amidst crushed buildings and hollowed-out vehicles.

I crawl back toward the images of devastation on the television and again place my fingers against my lover's lips. As she tearfully drones on and on, words meant for me and only me spill out over those heart-wrenching, tear-jerking, gooseflesh-provoking utterances the rest of the world hears. *"Seek out the Great Old Ones."* It occurs to me that in my little landlocked section of the United States, where Wormwood's ruinous path has not hit directly, but tangentially in a second-hand wave of destruction, that the very nature of its detriment would prove much different than that of what I see on TV. The woman who I unexplainably love knows this too, and has sent me a unique message, because she *loves me*, and I will abide by her and do what is told of me.

My father's body begins to writhe, not of his own life, but that of the life inflowing into it. I perch up on my knees and gaze curiously at his corpse, now twisting back and forth amid the tangled sheets, bare abdomen distending, stretch marks forming about his cherry-red and ulcerated navel. For a fleeting moment I feel fear, and my mind tells me in this momentary time of release I damn well should be paralyzed with terror...and then my body does freeze up the very instant my father's stomach tears open, blood bursting out, spattering the walls, the octopus tentacles writhing and twisting free, yanking up loops of intestines and knotting them unto themselves as they gather into a singular entity: one massive embrace of suctioning appendages, rising up...up...up to the ceiling, squirming, thrashing, squelching, burping, adhering to the stucco my father never got around to sanding...and during this time, my father's body becomes less recognizable as a human corpse than some populated mass of carrion, one with a human head, doused in blood and the opaque, gelatinous, globular secretions that plop down off the now massive tentacled organism.

"The Great Old Ones. Go!"

The fear and terror that had for an instant seeped through the dampened walls surrounding my subconscious has now been cloaked, as though treated with some anxiety-quelling pharmaceutical, something I regret to admit I am considerably familiar with; amazingly and quite suddenly, I seem to no longer be capable of fear or dread. All I know is the promise of *love* the woman on television offers, and like that devoted prince willing to face a dragon for the love of a princess, I obey the command of my talking lover, climb to my feet and stagger out of the bedroom, away from all that matters to me, away from the embracing tentacles and the supporting carrion previously known as my father.

There are six windows in the living room from which the porch light filters through dimly, more brightly than that of the bedroom. The snow (or whatever it may be—ashes, detritus?) continues to whip at everything in its boundless wake, and it's only now that I peer through the dusty film on one window and regard the grand scope of Wormwood's aftermath. It is said that the dinosaurs died out due to similar circumstances, perhaps to give way to the birth of mankind: a more intelligent life form. Can it be assumed that God has ultimately found Himself unhappy with mankind's development, and has elected to steer their path toward one similar the dinosaurs were forced to take? Has mankind been deemed expendable, taken off the face of the planet with one great blow to pave the way for a more suitable race of beings fit for Earth?

The television in the living room, dark when I first entered, springs to bright life, my lover's face suddenly there, addressing the dying world sadly, forlornly, dreadfully, staring directly at me, her lips once again discharging a personal message over her tearful monologue: *"Locate The Great Old Ones. Bring them to me."*

I stare at her, feeling waves of emotion, a level of ecstasy never fathomed imaginable. Something akin to orgasm speeds through my body, and I reach for her...her staring eyes, her moving lips...

"You will learn to live free and wild, beyond all that is good and evil. Push all that was considered law aside. It no longer exists. Liberate the Great Old Ones. Bring them to me."

I ask my lover, "Where do I find them?" but receive no answer, for she returns to her dedication of the conquered world, the inset screen now displaying a painting of the Chernobyl Nuclear Power Plant, the words *NUCLEAR EXPLOSION* below. The announcer—my god, she allures me in a way words could never correctly explain—talks of massive destruction and a death count in the tens of millions. Part of my inner self screams at me to look away, to shun what I find so magically appealing and move on with my life...but the sudden power of *love* (and the word love is the only way I can explain this feeling, only it is indeed much more than that) drives me to press forward with what is asked of me.

One might assume a person of right mind to seek out the comfort of their loved ones under such circumstances—to witness together the unfolding horrors, court their final breathing moments. But I am somehow convinced that my mind is not *right*, that my only loved one is on television, her one true purpose to assure my survival. Hence, a plethora of questions roll through my head, all of them unanswerable at the moment. Who are the Great Old Ones? Where do I find them? What should I ask of them once I locate them?

As though reading my mind, my lover whispers, "*They will guide you...*" I look at the television, but she is gone now, replaced by amateur footage of what appears to be a group of twelve white-robed men—their faces unseen from the high distance the video had been taken—walking briskly down a demolished city street, the unbreathable air seemingly unaffecting them as they enter a burning building, flames leaping from the windows, edges black with soot. The street they leave behind is littered with the smoldering shells of cars and the charred remains of humans. The handheld camera zooms in on one body, burned to a crisp, forever trapped in a position of final prayer. Then, a quick jump in the video, the camera shaking, jerking back to the robed men emerging from the building, only now there are thirteen of them, their robes (and presumably their bodies) unaffected by the inferno they've just faced. The video disappears and my lover returns, the promise of tears welling in her eyes.

"Are these the Old Great Ones I am to find?"

Over her tearful discourse, she utters dreamily, "*Yes...*"

I do not recognize the city-like environs, and am again about to ask where I might locate these robed men when my lover declares to me, and only me: "*There are many more...find them.*"

Staggering into the kitchen which leads outside, I open the refrigerator, aiming to quench my thirst, and discover by the warm stench that all the food and milk is spoiled, the tiny light inside dark. I step back to test the overhead fixture in the kitchen, but the wall switch provides no power.

I move back in the living room, try the light switch there. Nothing. And yet the porch light still blares and the television continues on and on with my lover still there like a shoulder to cry on. Beneath the television is the electrical cord, the smooth black rubber snaking away like a tail, the connectors lying on the floor, dead to the world. Confounded, I go to the television.

My lover peers into me, silently demanding me to go outside.

A tiny window opens in my conscious mind, allowing a sliver of terror to leach in. Here I am compelled to move away from the television, toward the front door of the house. Wearing no jacket or shoes, I find myself twisting frantically at the doorknob, sensing something akin to a knife-wielding killer at the back of my head, the point of his weapon pressing against my skull...

I open the door, and leap outside into Wormwood's path.

Torrential winds grab and jostle me roughly, the white gristle and dust coating me instantly, sticking to my skin, my tee-shirt, my flannel pants. I stagger a few feet into the back yard toward the expanse of white-coated woodland fifteen yards back. The rotted log that's been sitting on the lawn for years meets my struggling feet, entangling them further. With no delay, the hard, frigid ground races up to meet my face with a painful knockout punch.

Sometime later, seconds or minutes but not much longer I surmise, I find myself once again faced with harsh reality, spitting white ash and struggling first into a crawling position. In the time of my courting darkness, the storm and wind has wrapped the back yard and encompassing woodland with drifts of white ash, transforming the world into a sickly winter wonderland. My beleaguered mind attempts for no good reason to imagine Santa Claus riding through this stuff in his sleigh, but instead envisions a host of dead reindeer, the once fat jolly man at the helm half-eaten by the woodland creatures, gauzy beard flapping up and down in the wind.

Ahead, from the encompassing veil of white, three men in white robes appear. They seem to materialize out of nothing, the windswept dust not only parting as they make their approach, but providing an impression of ushering them toward my location. At first the three men seem old, ancient, but it's only as they come within a few feet of me do I gaze up into the white world and realize that not only are they covered in the white ash-like substance descending from the sky, but by some means have been infused with the wispy material, the white robe not a robe at all, but a formation produced onto them, *into* them, lending the appearance of a cloak and hood. Their beards are fashioned in the same respect, a billowing two-foot mesh of unearthly material seemingly grafted onto their faces, scarce spots of visible skin beneath swollen from the substance rooting itself there. It's here I am reminded of my father and how the tentacles beneath the bed had used his body in a similarly parasitical fashion.

Through the dust on my lashes, I can see their eyes, red and glaring, unblinking as they contemplate me.

I think to myself: *The Great Old Ones.*

The three men encircle me, arms raised toward the blanketed heavens in what I can only assume is some form of alien prayer, their barely visible faces guised by the storm, the wind, the ash. It's here I observe small fragments of the storm accumulating on them like snow collecting on a statue, tiny grains forming webs that draw together as though sentient, enmeshing with the material already there like cotton candy on a paper cone. In a scenario where I should be terrified, I find myself strangely allured instead, drawn to the progression now transforming me, revolutionizing me, my arms and legs lost beneath a quickly thickening veil of the white matter that right before my disbelieving eyes alters into the cloak of the Great Old Ones, somehow, incredibly, painlessly sewn into my skin, becoming one with me, a part of who I am, who I am becoming.

From the house behind me I hear my lover's voice call out: "*Come to me, Great Old Ones.*"

I've found them as she asked and see now in my mind's transformed eye her true being, not the woman previously beheld on TV, fallen in love with, but instead the tentacled creature that has roosted itself into my father's corpse. It has taken my father, yes...but has also seemingly rewarded me with a position amongst The Great Old Ones. I have become the one with them. For that, I feel grateful.

The trio of brothers, once humans I can only presuppose, now members of the tentacled creature's dominion, guide me forward toward the house, and in the twenty steps it takes me to get there, my robe is nearly formed and my beard is long enough to flutter in the wind. One of the men takes me by the arm and glares at me with his red eyes. His lips do not move but in my mind I can hear his words to me: *We have come with Wormwood to rule the world. We no longer live, but will never die, as we are preserved by the spells of mighty Cthulhu, for resurrection when the stars and the earth are right.*

The man who sends his message into my head nods once, then unblinkingly (and it's now I realize they possess no eyelids) turns from me and walks into the house, his brethren close behind. Despite retaining a sense of who I once was, I am vulnerable to their charms and pursue my new family.

The first thing I do upon re-entering the house is look at the television in the living room. The plug remains uncoupled, the screen rightly dark. My lover's face, a fleeting memory fading quickly into nothingness, becomes a memory no more once I enter my father's bedroom.

The thing coined as Cthulhu is here, rooted into my father, who aside from random smatterings of blood, is gone. In his place, in the place of the entire bed and half the bedroom, is a creature of unimaginable comparisons, a massive, pulpy thing possessing numerous tentacles that wriggle and writhe, slurping and slapping aimlessly above and about a pair of prodigious claws. Its head can only be described as octopus-like, the face a throng of feelers, the body below massive and rubbery-looking, swathed in glutinous scales. As *we* four Great Old Ones form a semi-circle before the unspeakable Cthulhu (it occurs to my evolved mind that we are not currently creating our own decisions, but are being directed entirely by the creature's will), it spreads out a pair of previously unseen wings from its back, narrow and diaphanous, dripping in slime and blood. I watch as globules form on its wings, growing larger as they trickle along the filmy surface and fall to the ground. It's here that something equally amazing and horrifying as Cthulhu itself evolves. Cthulhu speaks to me from inside my head, uttering **"Protect the Star Spawn, Great Old Ones"**, and in this instant and the moments soon to follow, the droplets of slime on the wood floor form into tiny versions of the beast before me, no larger than hermit crabs but far more uncanny as they scurry to and fro like frightened mice.

I peer about the room, catching a glimpse of myself in the mirror and see, despite still being aware of my former self, a stranger glaring back at me with red eyes, translucent skin, and a flowing beardlike growth of dust of webs dangling from chin to veiled sternum. My familiar consciousness fades into something newfound, *collective*. I wonder: Why me, why here?

And Cthulhu replies in a familiar female voice: *When the stars were right, I plunged with Wormwood through the cosmic framework. It has led me here, and here is where my kingdom will flourish.*

I recall my thoughts earlier and realize now that my supposition was correct, that God, *Cthulhu*, has come to replace man with a more suitable life for earth, and I have been chosen to become one with the lifeforms He has created. The Great Old Ones, here to protect the Star Spawn of Cthulhu.

As the very final vestiges of my prior life's memories slip away, I become in totality one of the chosen few.

I have become one with the Great Old Ones.

Meet the Author

Michael Laimo is the author of eight novels and over 100 short stories. Twice nominated for the Bram Stoker Award, his novels *Deep in the Darkness* and *Dead Souls* have been made into feature films. He currently resides on Long Island with three women, two cats, and a parrot fish.

Curious about other Crossroad Press books? Stop by our website:
http://crossroadpress.com
We offer quality writing
in digital, audio, and print formats.

Subscribe to our newsletter on the website homepage and receive a
free eBook.

Made in United States
Orlando, FL
23 March 2025

59739187R00141